TIDEMAGIC

TIDEMAGIC

THE MANY FACES OF ISTA FLIT

CLARE HARLOW

ALFRED A. KNOPF
NEW YORK

THIS IS A BORZOI BOOK PUBLISHED BY ALFRED A. KNOPF

All rights reserved. Published in the United States by Alfred A. Knopf,
an imprint of Random House Children's Books,
a division of Penguin Random House LLC, New York.

Knopf, Borzoi Books, and the colophon are registered trademarks
of Penguin Random House LLC.

Visit us on the Web! rhcbooks.com

Educators and librarians, for a variety of teaching tools,
visit us at RHTeachersLibrarians.com

Library of Congress Cataloging-in-Publication Data
Names: Harlow, Clare, author.
Title: Tidemagic : the many faces of Ista Flit / Clare Harlow.
Description: First American edition. | New York : Alfred A. Knopf, 2024. |
Series: Tidemagic | Audience: Ages 8–12. | Audience: Grades 4–6. |
Summary: In the mystical town of Shelwich, where magic waxes and wanes
with the tide, Ista Flit joins forces with Nat and Ruby in their quest to find
missing loved ones and unravel the mysterious connections among thieves,
monsters, and the missing townspeople.
Identifiers: LCCN 2023027437 (print) | LCCN 2023027438 (ebook) |
ISBN 978-0-593-80674-6 (hardcover) | ISBN 978-0-593-80675-3 (library binding) |
ISBN 978-0-593-80676-0 (ebook)
Subjects: CYAC: Ability—Fiction | Magic—Fiction. | Missing persons—Fiction. |
Friendship—Fiction. | LCGFT: Novels.
Classification: LCC PZ7.1.H37134 Ti 2024 (print) | LCC PZ7.1.H37134 (ebook) |
DDC [Fic]—dc23

The text of this book is set in 12-point Bookmania.
Interior design by Ken Crossland

Printed in the United States of America
10 9 8 7 6 5 4 3 2 1
First American Edition

For Mum, who told me stories before I was even born.
And for Ed, who brought me snacks while I wrote this one.

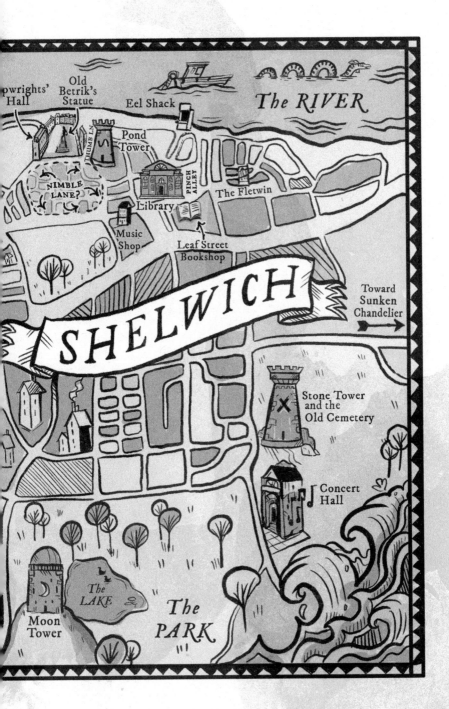

1

THE STREET
THAT MOVED

It was called Nimble Lane because nobody ever knew exactly where it was going to be. Some people claimed they'd been led to its entrance by a strange drift of music. Others said the trick to finding it was to stand at the corner of Bell Street and Bread Street and wait for the wind to change.

It was clear to Ista Flit that none of those people had ever been there.

Lucky them, she thought, turning away from the river that unfurled in the afternoon light like a wide gray tongue. Nothing good came of a visit to Nimble Lane at the best of times, and the timing of this particular summons was far from ideal. The Tide was coming in, sending tingles down Ista's arms and sighing in her ears. Mist was drifting in too.

She gave a shiver that had nothing to do with the chill.

1

Magic, mist, and darkness—that was what the monsters liked.

At least High Tide was over half an hour away, and dusk further off still. Nevertheless, if it had been up to her, Ista would have hurried indoors before the magic climbed any higher. But a blue handkerchief had been pinned to the awning of the eel shack, and that was the signal, so instead she set out through the honeycomb of streets to the south of Shipwrights' Square, pausing every few paces to take a deep sniff of air so cold it made her shudder, despite the thickness of her oversized black coat.

The lane was a sneaky thing, but it was around here somewhere. She could smell it—smoky and brackish all at once, as if someone had blown out birthday candles beside a silty tide pool. *A sharp nose,* her aunt had once said, not so very long ago, when Ista's life had still included such uncomplicated things as aunts and birthdays. *You've a sharp nose for trouble, girl, and your sharp tongue will do little to get you out of it.* Which was probably true. Yet, funnily enough, it was Ista's actual nose, a slightly longer-than-average one that conspired with her raggedy limbs to make her look like a startled heron, that led her into trouble these days.

Well, that and the talents the Tide brought her.

She took another step. Another sniff. *There.* At the very edge of her peripheral vision—where a split second earlier there had been nothing but an unremarkable row of merchants' houses—an impossible pathway came into view, like a dark throat opening. The mouth of it dripped with shadows, and a voice at the back of Ista's skull whispered, as it always did when she found Nimble Lane, that this was all a very, very bad idea.

Another, more practical part of her, however, knew that she didn't have any choice. There were not many things left that she cared about, but one of them was down there, and so was the person who was holding it hostage.

Ista squared her shoulders and walked into the gloom. The path widened; cobbles sprang up under her feet, and dark-beamed buildings crowded in on either side. A door creaked open as she passed, closing again with a snick when she turned to see who was there.

At the end of the lane stood the Shrieking Eel Inn. Tide-lanterns lit the way to it, their blue glow strengthening by the second with the rising magic, casting a watery sheen over the wonky timber frames and limewashed walls. Over the porch, the rusty sign squeaked on its pole, as if rocked by an invisible hand. The front door was completely bare: no handle, no bell, no knocker, no letter box. No hidden latch or pull cord or even a keyhole. Anyone who didn't know better would have assumed it only opened from the inside.

Ista did know better, though. She placed her palm on the wood. Above her fingertips, a faint line appeared, like the scratch of a well-sharpened claw. The line lengthened, curving to form a jagged circle around Ista's hand. When the circle was complete, the door swung inward, a low voice rumbling in greeting.

"Welcome, wanderer. Enter and make your choice."

Inside the stone-floored entrance hall, two elevator cars waited, their safety grilles formed of ornately patterned metalwork shaped into snakelike river weeds and curling tentacles. Next to each door was a brass plaque: one engraved with an arrow pointing down and the word BUSINESS, the other with an upward arrow and the word PLEASURE.

The only other object in the room was a hooded leather porter's chair. A large white cat dozed on the seat. He opened his green eye—he only had the one—to squint at Ista as she bent to offer him a stroke.

"Hello, Terrible," she said, because Terrible was the cat's name and she always had the sense that he liked to be spoken to. "No prizes for guessing which option I'll choose."

Terrible raised his chin, granting her access to the thick fluff at his throat. Ista allowed herself a few seconds of his purring and warmth, then straightened and turned to the elevators. She had never set foot in the car on the right, which supposedly led upward to food and music and rooms for weary revelers who needed a place to lay their heads.

In the car on the left there were no buttons to press.

The grille and doors swished closed, sealing her in. You had to be desperate or dangerous to come to the Shrieking Eel on business—everyone in Shelwich agreed on that.

I am dangerous, Ista thought fiercely as the car rattled downward. *I am dangerous. I am dangerous.*

She emerged into a hallway lit by a single shivering Tide-lantern that swayed from a chain. Ahead was a door. *I am dangerous,* she told herself again. But deep down she knew it was desperation that had brought her here.

Before she could knock, a breeze swept up, blowing the door open and carrying her across the threshold as easily as a wave carries a piece of kelp to shore. The room in which she landed could have been labeled a study, a library, or even a workshop, depending on who was doing the labeling. Under different circumstances Ista might have said it was cozy. The space was crammed with ancient-looking books and mismatched furniture and shelf after shelf of what she thought of as Curiosities—all kinds of trinkets and gadgets, from chutney spoons to microscopes to a whole menagerie of mechanical animals.

Ista edged through the clutter, careful not to knock anything. "You summoned me."

At times like this, it was as though someone else were controlling her mouth. Someone older and much, much braver. They must have had control of her hands, too, because she didn't wipe her clammy palms on her coat or flatten the tuft of her short brown hair that was sticking out at an angle—no matter how much she wanted to.

The reply came from the shadows on the far side of the room. "Hello, little thief. I have an errand for you."

There was nothing cozy about Alexo Rokis. He was fox-faced and wolf-eyed, sharp all over, particularly at the chin and elbows. Everything else, from his age to how long he'd lived in the city, was slippery, but it was generally agreed that he had a finger in every black-market pie in Shelwich and a knack for letting silences stretch uncomfortably long, just as he did now.

Ista felt his smirk like a burn. She kept her own face blank—or at least she hoped she did—and after a few slow ticks of the clock, his voice curled out to her again.

"I want you to steal me a telescope. Only a small one. It's on display at the Moon Tower. In the Hall of Maps." He peeled away from the wall, the smirk widening into a hard slice of smile. "Governor Hettle's making a speech tomorrow night. In the Great Hall, just a few corridors away. You're going to be one of the guests."

Ista did not smile back. She trusted him least of all when he was in this kind of mood, handing out orders as if they were tickets to adventures.

"Who?" she asked. She hoped the guest was someone around her own age this time. It was tricky acting like a grown-up. They hardly ever said what they meant.

Alexo just grinned as he stood before her. He held out his hand, palm to the ceiling.

Magic scuttled down Ista's spine.

An inch above his fingers, a marble-sized bubble blinked into being. It hung in the air like a tiny moon. Then it began to grow, its surface misting over, swelling bigger and bigger until it was as large as the globe that balanced precariously on a nearby stack of books. Through the mist, leaflike shapes swirled, then snapped together, lengthening into the outline of a figure.

Alexo clenched his hand into a fist. The bubble cleared. The figure was a boy, captured perfectly, as if they were looking at him through a window.

"Oh," Ista said. For a moment, it was all she could say. "But that's Jarmak Hettle!" Disbelief lifted her voice embarrassingly close to a squeak.

Alexo nodded. "The governor's son. What better cover?"

No. The word sparked in Ista's throat. As if he'd heard it, Alexo raised an eyebrow, then threw a glance at a glass-fronted cabinet near the hearth.

Ista tried not to follow his gaze but failed. Behind the glass, locked away with a key that Alexo wore strung on his belt, was a clarinet case. Her pa's clarinet case—with her pa's clarinet inside it. The only piece of Pa that she had left.

She swallowed. "If I get caught . . ."

"They'll chain you up in Shipwrights' Square and leave

you for the grilks? Yes, probably." Alexo's smirk was back. "But you won't get caught."

Ista fought a shudder. As a rule, she didn't let herself think about the time she had seen a grilk up close, but the memory crashed over her now. Wings like torn sails, sword-sharp teeth, and the wide black void of the creature's mouth opening behind them. Worst of all, the awful feeling of her magic draining away.

That had been her first night in the city—and were it not for Alexo, she would never have escaped. The rescue was such a blur in Ista's mind that she couldn't say what had happened exactly, but somehow his arrival had scared off the grilk, and in the process he had taken her pa's clarinet. *Run a few errands for me,* he'd said when she'd realized and demanded that he return it to her, *and you can earn it back.*

He'd saved her and then stolen from her, almost within the same breath. And Ista, frayed with exhaustion and fear, had seen little choice but to shake his hand. Only afterward did she think to ask what he'd meant by "a few." *Let's say twenty,* he'd said, shrugging. He was most likely planning to sell the clarinet if she didn't prove useful. He hadn't known then what she could do.

"Well?" he said now.

Ista returned her attention to the boy in the bubble. She'd seen Jarmak Hettle from a distance before and knew that he was about her height, although a fair measure broader, but this was the first time she'd observed him up close. His features were soft, his hair a little longer than Ista's short crop, slicked back from his face, and his skin was a rosy pinkish white with a small birthmark on his right cheek.

Not that the details mattered. Magic pulsed in her fingertips and whispered in her blood. The Tide was racing toward its peak. It would do the work for her.

She closed her eyes—and *changed*.

As it always did, it started with a prickle at the nape of her neck and ended with a twitch of her toes. When she finished, her head felt too heavy and her feet felt too flat, and she knew that if she glanced into the gilt-edged mirror on the wall, she'd see an exact copy of Jarmak Hettle staring back at her.

"That'll do." Alexo waved his hand.

He could sound a pinch more impressed, Ista thought, scowling at him as she changed back.

A Tide-blessing, people called it—called any gift that came in with the Tide.

And hers turned him a handsome profit in stolen valuables.

She examined her nails. "I'll need smart clothes."

"I'll send them." Alexo turned away.

The bubble shrank in on itself and vanished, leaving behind nothing but a faint whiff of snuffed candles and salt.

That's me dismissed, then, Ista thought, meeting her own brown eyes in the mirror. She let her gaze stray to the clarinet case once more, just for a heartbeat, before she left.

Twenty errands. That was the bargain they had made. Tomorrow would be nineteen.

She only hoped he would keep his word.

2

ONE GOOD DEED

The difficulty with pretending to be someone else was that you had to keep track of where the real someone was. Fortunately, Governor Betrika Hettle was a stickler for punctuality. As the sundown chimes rang out across the city, a black sol-car cruised up the wide central avenue of the park, its roof panels gleaming in the dwindling winter sun.

Ista, snug in the crook of a chestnut tree, wriggled forward to get a better view. Long ago, so she'd heard, in the time before the Tide, vehicles like that used to queue all the way from Shipwrights' Square to the Great East Bridge. Now, spare parts were so scarce that only the wealthiest could afford tech like that, let alone the enhancements needed to keep such engines running when the magic rose. So it was carts, bicycles, and pedal-cabs for everyone else—or the trundle-track, if you had enough coins in your pockets, which Ista never did.

She was better off walking in this case, though. The park was on a steep slope, with the Moon Tower at its crest, marooned like a shipwrecked galleon against the sky. There were countless routes up, but the quickest was a narrow set of steps. Ista dropped lightly from her tree and loped across the grass toward them, the sack she carried bumping her hip with each stride.

By the time she reached the top, the first guests were trickling in—some in carriages, others from the nearby trundle stop. The sol-car whooshed past and pulled up inside the main gate. Ista watched through the bars of the tall wrought-iron fence as the governor climbed out, her high-collared evening robes billowing behind her as she strode toward the building.

Jarmak Hettle trailed after his mother, looking thoroughly bored. Ista supposed he must have to attend a lot of events like this—especially lately, with the election coming up. She wondered what his Tide-blessing was. The governor's, as everyone knew, was that her eyes could change color, from pale gray to bright blue, but Ista had never heard anyone mention Jarmak's magic.

Not that it mattered. What did matter was that his robes were made of the exact same purple cloth as the robes in her sack. (Alexo had contacts with every tailor on Pin Row.)

Still, she liked to guess at the blessing when she borrowed a face. Pa had taught her to be respectful, to not be nosy about people's minds or bodies when she copied them, but it was fun to wonder about their magic. The Tide brought almost everyone something. The ability to sing an exceptionally high note, or to levitate ever so slightly off the ground. People said the Tide's magic was growing stronger every year, giving the younger generation far more powerful blessings than their parents and grandparents possessed, although Ista had never met anyone with a gift like hers.

Alexo didn't count. His influence stretched all over the city, but his magic was tethered to Nimble Lane. That was why he needed Ista. Her magic was everywhere. In the sky and in her bones. A hum and a drumbeat and a high-pitched whine. Sometimes she thought it would snap her in two.

Turning away from the Moon Tower, she looked out over the city. *It's beautiful here,* Pa had said in his last letter. And it was, especially on evenings like this when the sinking sun blazed orange and pink through the mist, and the high-rise ruins of Glass Island loomed across the estuary like ancient giants. Beautiful, but cold. Ista's breath plumed in the air, and she was grateful for her layers of thermals. Pa hadn't warned her about how much colder Shelwich winters were compared to winters at home.

He hadn't warned her about the monsters, either. She guessed he hadn't wanted to scare her.

"Just over half an hour to High Tide."

A voice drew her attention back toward the tower. Guests streamed through the main gate. Most of them made a beeline for the columned portico, but several people had paused to consult a noticeboard that had the week's Tide forecast pinned to it. The magic rose and fell twice every twenty-four hours, its highs and lows shifting a little later each day, so there were charts like this all over the city to help everyone keep track of what to expect.

She never needed Tide-tables. She could follow the rise and fall of the magic almost as easily as reading the time on a clock. Right now, power fizzed in her veins.

"And it's Moon Tide tonight," someone else muttered, frowning. "I don't know what the governor's thinking. We'd all be better off home in our beds."

Ista was inclined to agree. The Tide climbed to an extra high peak every new moon and full moon—hence the name Moon Tide. It was particularly risky, being out on a night like this, not because magic flooded the city just as the river rose so high it sloshed up onto the harbor walkways, but because . . . well, everyone in Shelwich knew the rhyme.

When the magic sparks upon your skin,
And the mist is high, and the night creeps in,

Stay inside, lock the door,
Or you'll be lost forevermore.

Her mind flew back to her first night in the city, to the feeling of her magic unraveling like a cotton reel as the monstrous creature loomed over her. No one knew anything about the grilks, except that they came in darkness and in mist, and always when the magic was high, and that once they'd got you, you were never seen again. She was the only person she knew who had managed to escape them.

As for Pa . . .

But she mustn't think about that. Mustn't dawdle, out at Moon Tide with the light fading fast. Soon all that was missing would be the mist, and that often swept in without warning.

Ista stayed on the park side of the fence, hurrying to the next gate along. This was the staff entrance. A short, stern-looking woman checked names off a list. She peered enquiringly at Ista over the top of her half-moon glasses.

"I'm from the Grebe and Gimlet Laundry." Ista's voice was calm, but her heart was in her mouth. Alexo's schemes were intricate webs of detail. She feared that one day she'd fall through a gap and go plummeting into trouble.

The woman frowned at the sack, then at the list, then at the sack again. Her fingernails kept changing color, from purple to red to gold to green, as if they were being painted and repainted by an invisible brush. "You're very late. Table linens, is it?"

Ista nodded. If it came to it, there was one tablecloth on top of the robes.

The woman's eyes narrowed, but she stepped aside. "On you go."

Beyond the gate was another courtyard, less grand than the one at the front, overrun with moss and ivy. The flagstones had been salted, and Ista's boots crunched as she walked. The Moon Tower, as well as being the city's observatory and archive, contained many grand rooms that were used for all kinds of concerts, exhibitions, and ceremonial events. Pa had mentioned playing here. This was the way he would have come. She could almost see him, his clarinet case in one hand, his hair (which, like hers, had a tendency toward rebellious tufts) slicked down with pomade.

It won't be much longer, he'd promised. *I only need to save a little more; then I'll find us a place of our own, and you can leave Aunt Abgill in peace and join me here.*

A new life. That had been the plan. Instead, Pa's letters had stopped. And then the clarinet had arrived, along with a very different letter—from Mikkela, Pa's trumpet-player friend, saying Pa had vanished. *Vanished,* as if he were a recalcitrant cat or a misplaced sock. And Ista's aunt had just accepted it, saying Pa had often wandered off from time to time when they were younger and that he'd turn up again soon enough. Ista still burned with fury at the memory of that—as if Pa would leave *her.* She'd begged Aunt Abgill, *begged* her, to bring her to Shelwich so they could search for Pa together.

When her aunt had refused, Ista had taken matters into her own hands. But Pa *had* vanished, as surely as if he had been plucked from the pavement and flung off into the ether. After one hundred and four days of searching, memories were all Ista had left of him—and the clarinet, if she got it back.

Not *if. When. Soon.*

Ista focused. The smell of well-spiced stew wafted toward her. *Go in past the kitchens,* Alexo's instructions—delivered with the robes—had read.

Two girls blocked the porch, struggling with a stubborn-wheeled cart. Sisters, judging from their matching grimaces and identically styled braids.

". . . going to be so late," the older one, who looked about Ista's age, was saying. "Push properly, Saf."

The younger girl—Saf, Ista supposed—glared. "I *am* pushing. *You* aren't pulling hard enough. This is sinking silly, Ruby. The magic's up. I don't see why you won't let me use my b—"

Blessing, she must have been going to say, but before she could, Ruby's voice lashed out. "Do you want *them* to get you? As if your stunt the other day wasn't bad enough."

"That was at lunchtime!" Saf shot back. "There's never been a single attack in daylight."

"It's almost dusk now, though, isn't it?" Ruby said with practiced patience. "The governor must have decided she cares more about votes than about people's safety now that the election's only four days away." She noticed Ista loitering and snapped on a smile of standoffish politeness. "Yes?"

Ista shrugged at the cart. "Want a hand? Easier with three." If she didn't help, they might be stuck out here all night.

"Yes," Saf said quickly. "Yes, please."

A protest budded and died on Ruby's mouth. "Fine," she said, glancing back at the woman at the gate. "But we should shift. Tide's teeth, it's freezing out here."

The cart had other ideas.

"What have you got in here?" Ista's breath huffed with effort. *Something made of glass,* she thought; it tinkled under the waxed cloth cover.

"Pickles," said the sisters, straining in unison.

"And preserves," added Saf as one corner of the cloth fell back to reveal rows of jars with a duck logo stamped on the lids. "You name it, we bottle or jar it. Gran's recipes, passed down from her grandma's grandma. Our pepper sauce is the best in Shelwich. You should come to the shop and try it sometime."

"She doesn't need the pitch." Ruby rolled her eyes

fondly, reaching round to open the door. "We had a last-minute order for the event tonight," she explained to Ista as warmth flowed out to greet them. "More trouble than it's worth, if you ask me."

Party noise filtered down a stone-floored passage, while kitchen smells and clatter drifted through a doorway to the right. A line of tunicked servers glided out, bearing jugs of greengage wine and platters loaded with tiny, fiddly skewers of fish and miniature cheese-topped tarts. Ista left the sisters without a word, slipping into the procession and staying with it until the passage joined a more elegant hallway that marked the boundary between the part of the building that was for staff and the part that was for show.

Opposite was a door, papered in the same cream-on-mint spiral pattern as the walls, making it practically invisible to anyone who wasn't looking for it. A disused storeroom, according to Alexo.

She ducked inside, not bothering with the light switch. No generator worked at Moon Tide. Even oil lamps sometimes faltered, which was why Tide-lanterns were dotted throughout the tower this evening. In the dark, magic scuttled over her, thrumming behind her knees and under her arms as she pulled the robes over her own clothes. It was almost too strong. Normally her power was like a bowstring, taut and ready to release when she chose. Tonight, the full moon seemed to make her control slip slightly, and the transformation began a fraction sooner than she intended, like a musician coming in a beat too early. She ended up in a tangle, a straggle of hair caught in the embroidered collar.

Thankfully, being Jarmak's hair, it fell neatly into place when she wrenched it free, and his feet just about fitted in her boots. Still, Ista's heart hopped wildly as she inched the door open. The next part of the scheme was all *should* and *supposed to*. A single misstep would crack it in two. The guests, including Jarmak, should be congregating in the Great Hall for the governor's speech. She was supposed to go the other way—and this she did, taking careful strides as she adjusted to Jarmak's extra bulk.

So far, so straightforward. Nobody barred her path. The main staircase curled off to one side, just as it should, dancing round and round up toward the tower's central dome. *It's the south wing you want,* Alexo's note had said. *The one with the sky in the walls.*

Sure enough, the wallpaper of the next corridor dimmed to a deep-night blue, sugared with paler blue flecks of Tide-pearl that shone like tiny stars. *Keep going, all the way to the end.* She could almost hear Alexo's voice in her mind.

But there were other voices ahead. Real ones, coming from round the corner: the first defiant but streaked with indignation, the other two dripping with malicious laughter.

"That's mine! Give it back."

"Ooh, *give it back,* he says."

"Give what back? This? Aren't you a bit old for toys?"

Kids from the fancy houses up near the heath, Ista guessed, based on their smoothed-out vowels. They must have been invited with their parents, which meant they were supposed to be—she felt the word *supposed* splinter beneath her—on the other side of the building. Yet here they were. In her way.

She could backtrack. There was a second, more roundabout route to the Hall of Maps (there was always a second route where Alexo was concerned), and the whole point of her being disguised as Jarmak was so that she could move around freely without anyone challenging her.

"Give it back," the first voice said again as she turned to go. *"Please."*

Ista stopped. She shouldn't interfere. It certainly wouldn't do for "Jarmak" to make a scene. But something in the *please* strummed deep inside her, like a minor chord on a vespalin. She knew all too well what it was like to have something precious taken from her, with no certainty that it would be returned.

"Oh, *please,* is it?" snickered one of the thieves. The other thief laughed too, low and long, as if they had all the time in the universe for games like this.

Sink it, Ista thought. *I am dangerous. Dangerous.*

Thinking it twice didn't make it any truer, but it was too late for doubts; she was already propelling Jarmak's legs round the corner.

3

A BOY WITH NO BLESSING

"Well, well, well." Ista spoke and Jarmak's voice rolled out with the same pebble-polished accent as the three robed figures who leapt apart at her interruption.

This section of corridor was wide but windowless, the dark blue wallpaper studded with more fragments of Tide-pearl. The three figures made an eerie tableau against it. Two of them were tall and broad, hulks of shadow in the half-light. The third was a short, twig-limbed boy, who shrank back from the other two even as he glowered up at them.

Two rooks and an injured wren, Ista thought. Pa had taught her the names of all the garden and woodland birds. He used to get cross with the rooks for swooping in and chasing the wrens from the nuts and seeds he left out for them. In the end, he'd fashioned a special feeder with holes that were too small for the rooks' beaks—and scattered more food a little way off on the grass so that the rooks wouldn't go hungry either.

She wished Pa were with her now. He'd have found a way to defuse this situation too. As it was, she was on her own.

"Oh, hello, Hettle," drawled the taller rook. He smiled, but something nervous scuttled, crablike, behind his eyes. Not friends, him and Jarmak, Ista could tell. Not quite, anyway. Rivals, perhaps.

"What's going on here?" She tried a smile too, although Jarmak's mouth didn't seem to like it.

The second rook shrugged. "Nothing, really. We found Shah sneaking around."

"I wasn't sneaking," the smaller boy snapped.

"Yes, you were, you dropless runt." The ringleader added a sneer to his drawl. "Just like you're always sneaking around at school, watching people and scribbling in your little notebook." The book was in his possession now, of course. He held it up, strumming the pages with his thumb. "You want to watch him, Hettle. Your name's in here."

The short boy darted a glance at Ista. He'd clearly been up to something, but she needed to unpick this knot, and questions would only tie it tighter.

"How interesting," she said with an indifferent shrug. "But we should all get back or we'll be missed."

The short boy set his jaw. "Not without my things."

The other rook, Ista noticed, had one hand hidden. At her sigh, he brought it out, displaying an extremely sorry-looking toy mouse, one button eye missing and one cloth ear coming loose at the seam. He sent it arcing through the air with a flick of his wrist.

The short boy scrambled to catch it, but someone's magic spiked—Ista felt it crackling over her skin—and the mouse stopped dead just beyond his reach. He made a grab for it. It moved again, leaving him clutching at air.

"Say *please* again," said the boy holding the notebook. He didn't even look up, just leafed idly through the pages, although he clearly wasn't reading them.

It was his magic, though. That was plain from his smug little smile. Ista clenched her fists. To have such a clever blessing and use it to pick on someone. She could feel the sting of the short boy's humiliation.

"No." She leveled a stare at the tall boy. "That's enough. Give him back his stuff."

He snapped the book shut, his eyes sharpening. Unease trickled down Ista's spine. There was suddenly danger in the air, a static fizz under the magic. Jarmak might lead a soft life, but strength coiled in his muscles like a fuse waiting to be lit. It centered between his shoulder blades, throbbing with a strange cold tingle as the Tide lapped nearer.

"Whatever, Hettle." The tall boy rolled his eyes, and all the tension evaporated. "No need to be so dramatic," he added, earning a snicker from his friend. "It was just a bit of fun."

Not to the short boy, Ista thought.

He flinched as the cloth mouse hit the parquet floor. The notebook sailed across to meet it, landing with a slap.

The rooks strolled away, wearing coordinating smirks.

"Thank you," the short boy murmured once their footsteps had faded.

Dropless, they'd called him. Untouched by magic. Ista had never met anyone without a blessing before—and the boy was old enough that the Tide would have spoken to him if it was going to. He looked perfectly unremarkable, more marsh owl than wren, now that she observed him closely, with his brown skin, wide-set dark brown eyes, and thick, grumpily slanted eyebrows. How must it feel to have that emptiness inside him?

She could hardly ask. He was already staring at her as if the shred of kindness she'd displayed had been completely out of character for Jarmak. Her heart gave a squeeze. The ringleader rook had implied they all went to the same school. She hoped there were some other, friendlier students there too.

But she had to press on. She swept an arm in the direction the others had gone. "You're welcome. Now get lost."

The boy nodded, as if this dismissal was far more in line with what he expected from Jarmak, and hurried away.

Ista hurried too, in the opposite direction. The corridor widened like the river running into the estuary, and the Tide-pearls multiplied, studding the ceiling and floor as well as the walls, so that she seemed to be moving through a tunnel of stars. Ahead, a doorless archway beckoned.

The Hall of Maps is impossible to miss, Alexo had promised.

He hadn't lied. A vast space swelled before her, a great glass dome soaring up to greet the sky, so that the false stars on the walls dripped into the real ones. The effect made Ista's stomach lurch. She paused, breathing in the smell of polish, anchoring herself to the details of the room. At the center, an enormous telescope, much too large to be her target, stood on a plinth, its eye gazing vacantly skyward. Beyond it was a fleet of brass-handled cabinets, which must be where the maps were housed. A long table, presumably for people to view the maps on, stretched toward a narrow doorway that was the only other entrance.

Near that doorway, on a pedestal and protected by a glass dome of its own, was another, far smaller telescope.

You'll know it when you see it, Alexo had written. *It's about as long as your arm.*

Perfect, in other words, to hide up the loose sleeve of an evening robe.

Ista had been clumsy when she'd arrived in Shelwich more than three moons ago. Now she walked as if she had paws. The only sound as she crossed the floor was the groan of the Tide at the back of her skull.

Alexo usually wanted Curiosities he could take apart and reassemble, as if he was trying to understand how they worked before he sold them on. *Human ingenuity is a puzzle matched only by the inner workings of the human heart,* he'd explained once when Ista had found him surrounded by the bolts and springs of a typewriter he was in the process of deconstructing. However, she didn't think this telescope would occupy him for long. It was a shabby, underwhelming object: three wooden tubes of increasing size that looked as though they would slot into each other. Still, it merited being covered by the dome, so there must be value to it.

The glass was secured to the pedestal by a hook. Ista reached for it . . . and froze. Half-hidden by the twist of metal was a Tide-pearl. This one had a thin black stripe through the middle, winking at her like a tiny feline eye. Ista stared at it, trying not to let her panic take flight.

It was just a Tide-pearl, after all. Just a tiny fragment of magic-touched pebble or grit washed up by the river and left behind when the Tide went out again. The pearls gave off a blue glow whenever the magic rose, and people used them for all sorts of things. Pearl-combers gathered them by the bucketful at Low Tide and sold them to the lampers, to be fashioned into Tide-lanterns or decorations like the fake starlight in the walls of the corridor. People wore them as jewelry, too. Some folk even claimed that having the pearls next to your skin would enhance your blessing, although Ista thought there was as much chance of that as of increasing your magic by drinking the river water—and enough fools had learned the hard way that *that* only made you sick.

A Tide-pearl with a streak of black through it, though . . . Alexo had warned her to stay away from those, especially if she found one concealed under a handle or fastening. *That's an old magic, little thief. It's called a Tide-lock. Only the maker can undo it.*

Was this *it*? Nineteen errands in, was there a flaw in one of Alexo's flawless plans?

At Low Tide, he'd told her, breaking a Tide-lock would "merely" burn your fingers or set off a loud noise to summon a guard. When she'd asked what happened if the magic was up—and oh, it was up now, ringing and stinging between her ears—he'd given her a dark look and said, *If the Tide's high, make sure you get well clear of the pearl before it lands. If someone else is nearer to it, so much the better. It'll go for them instead.*

And what then? Ista had asked.

Trust me, little thief, you don't want to know.

But if she left without the telescope . . . She thought of Pa's clarinet. Just this errand and the next. She was so close. There had to be a way. Perhaps she could move the dome without breaking the lock.

Behind her, something creaked.

Ista started, whipping round. It was the boy from earlier. The no-blessing boy. Her, or rather Jarmak's, out-of-character kindness must've made him suspicious enough to follow her. She'd been careless, so lost in thought that he'd managed to sneak up close beside the map cabinets. He was pointing a trembling finger at her like a guard about to capture a suspect.

No, not at her. At the pedestal. Her arm had caught the edge of it. It wobbled, and time seemed to wobble too, pulling at its stitches. She saw her reflection—*Jarmak's* reflection, his mouth opening wide in horror—in the glass dome as it slid sideways, taking the telescope and the Tide-lock with it.

The floor was stone. The glass shattered as it landed, and all the clockwork precision of Alexo's scheme shattered with it.

Ista flinched, but there was no burning. No alarm. Nothing sprang up to snare her.

Perhaps she could salvage this. She couldn't see the pearl, but the telescope was in one piece. She plucked it from the debris, shaking it free of glass.

"Jarmak? Wh-what's that?"

The trip in the boy's voice made her turn. He was looking at the pearl. It had rolled between them—there must have been a slight slope in the floor—and come to a stop, its light extinguished. A shadow stirred beneath it, spreading outward like spilled ink.

"I broke a Tide-lock," Ista said. "We need to go. Now."

"I . . . I don't think I can." The boy sounded almost apologetic.

"You . . ." Time slowed to a drip again as she took it all in. The strain in the boy's neck, as if he was trying to move but was rooted in place. The shadow oozing, thick and oily. *Traveling,* with purpose, not toward her but toward him.

The pearl must have ended up closer to the boy when it rolled. Anger flared under her fear. If he'd gone after the others like she'd told him to, he'd be safe in the Great Hall—puzzled at how Jarmak had beaten him back there, maybe, but safe. But no. He'd had to follow her, hadn't he, the nosy little prawn. And now . . . the shadow reached for him, five long greasy tendrils extending across the floor, like the fingers and thumb of a huge gloved hand.

"Jarmak?" he said again.

Every cell in Ista's body urged her to flee, but she couldn't just leave him. She thought frantically. The boy didn't have magic, so the shadow must have locked on to something else. Something in his skin or his blood or his bones. Whatever it was, if she borrowed him, she'd have it too.

An idea unrolled in her mind as cleanly as a sail. She forced her feet forward, setting the telescope on a table as she passed and making sure to leave the boy a clear path to the door.

"What's your name?" Shah, the others had called him, but the way they'd said it had made it sound like that was his family name.

"My name?" The boy's eyes had turned dreamy. "I'm Nat." His eyelids drooped.

"Nat," Ista said, and his eyes fluttered open. "Hey, Nat. I need your help with something. Do you think you can help me?"

A sleepy nod. "Mm-hmm."

"Good." *I am dangerous, I am dangerous.* Ista's heart galloped, but her voice held steady as she crept forward. "See the door in front of you, Nat? I'm going to count down from three, and then you're going to run to that door as fast as you can. Can you do that, Nat?"

He made a sound that could have meant yes or no or anything in between. It would have to do.

"Three . . . ," Ista said. The Tide sang in her blood. "Two . . ."

The shadow looked almost exactly like a hand now. Its fingers stroked the hem of Nat's robes. She took another step closer, right up to the edge of it.

"One . . ."

She changed, holding Nat's face tight in her mind. A

strange hush swept through her, the Tide's voice suddenly muffled as if calling to her from the other side of a thick wall. But her own magic was still there, a tiny bright flame.

"Run."

She leapt forward—and landed right in the middle of the shadowy palm.

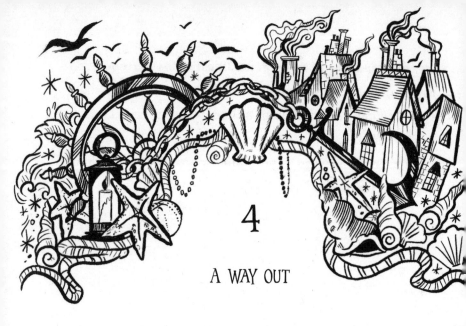

4

A WAY OUT

Breathe, Ista.

It was Pa's voice Ista heard as the shadow swarmed over her. *Just breathe.* His first remedy for all her fears and frustrations, from nightmares to math problems to not being able to reach the next branch of the tree she was climbing.

Breathing wasn't easy, though. The shadow had been a slow, seeping thing before. Now it was a surge. The tendrils that had been reaching for Nat bent back on themselves to coil around her instead, clamping her in place and sweeping an icy prickling sensation all over her body.

That's it, Ista thought—somewhat foggily, for her head felt as if it had been stuffed with wet wool. *It's me you want.*

It was working! Her ridiculous, reckless gamble had paid off, and Nat, free from his trance, began staggering toward the door. Ista willed him to move faster. The prickles reached her throat, and she changed back into herself, not daring to let them climb higher.

The shadow released her, dropping to the floor. It lurched round hungrily, streaking toward Nat. He stumbled, as if caught on an invisible hook. Ista borrowed him a second time, setting off at a run as the shadow lunged for her again. She led it on a dance across the room, changing over and over, never quite letting it catch her, until Nat was in one doorway and she was his double in the other.

Surely that was enough. Ista's heart kicked with panic. The shadow couldn't keep going forever . . . could it? It made another grasping surge toward her—then slowed to a halt beside the central telescope. If it could have worn an expression, she would have said it looked confused. It seemed to hesitate, inching a short way toward her, then shriveled and shrank, fading to a greasy smudge that dissolved into the stone.

She'd done it. Relief crashed over Ista in waves.

"Who *are* you?" Nat gaped at her from the doorway.

"I'm no one." Borrowing Jarmak again, she swiped the little telescope from where she'd left it and tucked it up her sleeve.

"I'm not going to tell. You saved me. I owe you."

But Ista didn't want anyone owing her anything. She strode toward Nat with a scowl that gave him no choice but to move out of the way.

It was time to get back on track and get out.

The stealing aside—there was, unfortunately, always stealing—she didn't understand why Alexo *always* insisted she borrow someone when she carried out her errands, and why he *always* insisted she be seen. Some errands were so simple that anyone could have done them, like eating a particular dish in a particular café before swiping the salt and pepper pots on her way out, or occupying a prominent seat at a concert and being sure she stayed until the end, when she would slip away with the opera glasses that were supposed to be returned to the ushers.

Other errands, though, were as precise and delicate as the innards of a wristwatch. Tonight, for example, she was to follow the next corridor past the Hall of Clocks and the Hall of Souls and round the back of the Great Hall (nerve-janglingly close to where the real Jarmak would be). There, a member of staff would be guarding the door to the governor's private cloakroom.

Ista was to make certain that the guard saw her enter the cloakroom as Jarmak, then to immediately climb out of the window, which would lead to a walled garden with a convenient gate that would open easily and lock again behind her.

Change back as soon as you're clear, sooner if you need to. That, or something like it, was always the last instruction. Not to stay a moment too long in the face she'd borrowed. Never to get caught, even if it meant abandoning an errand before it was complete. Her blessing made her too useful to risk losing.

Unfortunately, as Ista hustled into the corridor, the stern-faced woman from the entrance came gliding round the corner.

"Jarmak?" The woman was all politeness now, her half-moon glasses gleaming keenly. "Shouldn't you be in the Great Hall? Your mother's speech is about to begin." Her fingernails were still changing color, like kaleidoscope segments—mauve, teal, ocher, puce.

"I . . ." Ista clamped the telescope tighter as it threatened to slip from her grasp. "I feel unwell. I think I need some fresh air."

The woman's brow furrowed. "Already?" she said, which struck Ista as a very strange reply—perhaps Jarmak disliked crowds and often needed a break after a certain amount of mingling. "And you require company?"

Company? Ista glanced round. Nat was loitering. She should have known she wouldn't shake him so easily. His face revealed nothing, but perhaps it would be better to keep him with her than risk him breaking his promise and giving her up the moment her back was turned.

"Yes," she said. "Yes, my . . . um, my friend should come."

The woman opened her mouth as if she wanted to object.

"Mother says it's fine," Ista added.

"Oh." The woman still sounded unsure. "Very well, then. I'll escort you."

She led them off in the exact direction Alexo had instructed Ista to go, past the Hall of Clocks and the Hall of Souls. This errand had been far from perfect, but it was also far from the disaster it could have been, Ista thought, running a finger over the end of the telescope. She just needed to lose her escort and find the governor's cloakroom.

But instead of turning left to go round the back of the Great Hall, the woman took a right turn down a smaller hallway, ushering them toward a glass-paneled door, which she proceeded to unlock. Frigid air streamed in. Outside was a courtyard: a long, thin, green-smelling space, laid out in a herringbone pattern of brick and partially veiled in mist. Dead center was a fountain, burbling contentedly to itself.

"Here we are," the woman said brightly. "I'll make sure you aren't disturbed." With a nod, she disappeared back inside.

For a moment Ista half hoped she might have somehow ended up in the very walled garden through which she was meant to escape. No such luck. There was no convenient gate here. Three of the courtyard's sides were formed from other walls of the building. The fourth ended in a viciously spiked fence, pots of tall shrubs standing sentry in front of it. The magic was almost at its peak, shooting glitter through her blood and jumbling her thoughts. She had an urge to vault for the sky, as if the fat golden moon would reach out and pull her into its arms.

What she needed to do was go back into the building, but she could see through the door that the woman had planted herself just on the other side of it, her back to the courtyard, clearly meaning to stop anyone from disturbing Jarmak.

So Ista strode in the opposite direction, past the fountain and toward the fence.

"Where are you going?" Nat trotted after her. "You can't get out that way."

"Watch me." She'd climb if she had to, although she might need to change again; the peculiar burn between Jarmak's shoulder blades was back, sharper than before, as if he'd pulled a muscle.

Whatever she did, she'd better do it fast. A *lot* of windows overlooked the courtyard, including some large, grand-looking ones that she had a horrible suspicion must belong to the Great Hall. Twice already she was sure she'd glimpsed a curtain twitching. There wasn't a crab's nostril of a chance she was sticking around to be seen by the governor and all the guests. The mist was thickening, rising in woolly drifts, but it wouldn't be enough to conceal her completely.

The mist! Ista's throat went dry. Magic and mist and only a drop of light left in the sky.

". . . wondered if you'd help me." Nat was talking again,

puffing breath into his hands to ward off the cold, words tumbling out of him as if he knew she'd be gone soon. "Well, help *us,* actually. Me and my mum. She's Priya Shah." The name was clearly supposed to mean something. "From the *Daily Conch.*"

"The newspaper?" That was all Ista needed. She could only imagine what Alexo would say about her talking to a journalist.

"I help her out after school." Pride warmed Nat's voice. "That's why we're here. Mum's reporting on the speech, and I'm . . ." He shot a glance into the shadows, as if someone might be lurking there. "I'm helping her investigate, and we could really use your magic. She's got a theory, you see, about the grilks. She thinks someone's controlling—"

Ista rounded on him. "Be *quiet.*"

Don't talk about them. That was her own unspoken rule. Not out in the mist on a night like this, when the Tide was so high that the skin of the world seemed thin.

"You're not superstitious, are you?" Nat just wouldn't shut up. "Mum says—"

"I don't care what your ma says." *Ma.* Some of Ista's own voice snuck through Jarmak's teeth. *Drown it all,* she thought, making her body her own again, the soreness between her shoulders melting away.

Nat was sensible enough not to reply. The quicker she was gone from here—from him—the better. She turned to the nearest shrub, testing its sturdiness, trying to cool her temper with gulps of misty air. There was a peculiar flavor to it tonight, a thicker aftertaste lingering beneath the pure salt cleanness. It was like . . .

Limestone and leaf mold.

Ista went still. She knew that smell. She remembered the sourness it had left in her mouth and how much soap it had taken to scrub it from her skin.

It was the smell of her first night in Shelwich.

"See? You summoned them." Her words were more breath than voice. The memory had swooped down and closed its hand around her throat. She'd been so tired, so desperate. An alcove in Shipwrights' Square had seemed a safe enough place to rest her eyes. But she'd rested too long, lost herself to sleep, and when she'd woken there'd been a noise. The same noise she heard now from the nearest corner of the courtyard. A scraping, papery, dragging sound, like someone hauling a bag of sand.

It was the wings. They were so heavy they trailed on the ground.

Nat's fingers circled her wrist. His mouth was making shapes, but Ista couldn't hear him properly, couldn't hear anything but wings and Tide-song and the white roar of terror in her skull. He pointed to the door, then took off toward it, towing her after him. Somehow Ista's legs got the message and moved. Fear broke everything into jagged fragments. The door. The handle. Nat's hand on it, turning.

The door didn't budge. The latch must have caught, and the woman was nowhere to be seen—and the scraping drag of wings was coming closer. Ista reeled round. The mist had climbed over her ribs. Beside the fountain, a crooked shape jerked up through the whiteness, its long snout lifting as if scenting the air.

"What do we do?" Nat's voice cut through to her. "You knew what to do before. What do we do?"

Ista just shook her head. There was no plan from Alexo or good advice from Pa. The grilk sank into the mist again. She could hear it moving toward them, slowly, as if it knew it could take as much time as it liked.

Nat started. "Wings. That's it!" He must have only just realized what the sound was. "Jarmak. I've seen him. He has wings."

Ista couldn't process what he was saying. All she could think of was that night. The huge jaw unhinging, the teeth flashing like black knives. The terrible emptiness of her magic slipping away.

"Wait," she said. "What?"

Hope flickered behind the fright in Nat's eyes. "When you copy people, do you get their Tide-blessings?"

"I've never tried." Pa had said she definitely mustn't, that someone's Tide-blessing was almost a sacred thing, theirs and theirs alone. "Are you saying Jarmak can fly?"

A fluttery thrill went through her. The burn she'd felt between her shoulder blades—could that really mean . . . ?

The hope in Nat's eyes sparked brighter. "Yes. I saw him. I don't think he wants people to know, because he isn't very good at it yet, but he was practicing in secret after school, and I . . . well, I get curious whenever I notice anyone acting strangely, so I followed him one day and . . . the point is, I saw him. And if he can fly, that should mean you—"

Ista changed before he'd finished speaking. The burn was there again immediately, as if wanting it made it flare brighter. She opened her mouth to ask if Nat knew how the next part should work, but the intention was enough. A pins-and-needles prickle raced up her body, and she heard her robes rip open as a vast soft weight bloomed from her upper back like huge petals uncurling from a bud.

She had wings.

Well, Jarmak Hettle did, but they were hers for now, dark feathers shining in her peripheral vision.

The dragging sound was even closer now, the limestone-and-leaf-mold stench clogging her nostrils and sticking in her throat, but the grilk wasn't near enough to affect her magic yet. The pull of the Tide was so fierce it made her teeth tingle.

And above was only open sky.

5

UP

"Come on," Ista said in Jarmak's voice, reaching out to Nat with Jarmak's hands. "Hold on to me and don't let go."

From behind Nat came a ragged moan. The grilk was on the move, a dark blur through the murk, the swaying motion of its progress almost like dance. Ista rolled her shoulders, focusing on the strange new muscles between them. This had to work. Had to. If she could walk Jarmak's legs, she could fly Jarmak's wings.

Nat looped his arms around her, and she wrapped hers around him in return, still clutching the telescope in the fabric of one sleeve. The grilk moaned again, closer. Ista's power dimmed slightly, diluted by the creature's proximity. There was no time to lose. She bent her knees and jumped.

The wings did the first bit for her, lifting and pushing. Magic glittered in Ista's blood, and Nat gave a whoop as the ground dropped away. But the second stroke was harder than the first. Nat, small as he was, was still a whole extra person to carry. His feet had barely cleared the mist, and already her back muscles were groaning with the strain.

"The grilk!" he yelped. "Higher, higher!"

"I'm trying!" Ista gritted her teeth, but tiredness swept over her, as if borrowing Jarmak's blessing was burning through her reserves of energy. The grilk was directly beneath them, a fishlike shadow turning slow circles in the whiteness. Clever creature. All it had to do was wait. Even if the woman returned, she wouldn't be able to save them, and they'd never make it to the roof. There was no way out.

Unless . . . The fence. It was right across the courtyard but much lower than the walls. Ista kicked like a swimmer, angling her body toward it, and Nat yelped again, clamping her tighter as his legs swung downward. Five floundering wingbeats took them as far as the fountain. Another five should take them the rest of the way, but Ista's strength was fraying like old rope, each flap more effort than the one before.

"Tuck your legs up," she called as Nat's toes dipped into the mist.

"I'm doing my best!" His answer came in a terrified snarl. The grilk bided its time, keeping pace with them, staying low. The prongs of the fence posts jutted like fangs.

Ista struggled toward them, straining skyward. Her muscles were screaming, and although Tide-song chimed in her bones, there was something off-key about it, as if the magic didn't like her using Jarmak's blessing.

She could do this. She was dangerous. If she could only get a little higher . . .

Nat's grip loosened. He slipped with a cry, and Ista flailed frantically, catching a fistful of his robes with one hand while keeping hold of the telescope with the other. What had been difficult before was almost impossible in this new position. Nat's weight dragged them down no matter how hard she flapped. The last tatters of her strength were fading, the burn between her shoulders so fierce it was almost unbearable.

Below, the grilk waited, its snout protruding from the mist, like a crocodile pretending to be a log.

No, Ista thought. *Not tonight.* She reached for the magic, sinking everything she had into three clean strokes that took her and Nat sailing over the fence. She was certain that the grilk would launch itself after them— even though the creatures weren't known to fly high—that any second now she'd feel breath at her neck and an icy weight behind her.

But there was nothing. They were free.

Nat gave a squawk of triumph. "We made it!"

"We have to land," Ista rasped. The Tide pulled sharply away from her, as if it had decided she'd used too much of Jarmak's blessing. "I can't . . ."

The magic drained from her entirely, yanking her back

into her proper form. For a split second, they seemed to hang in the air. Then, with a sickening swoop, they dropped. The Tide returned in a rush, too late to be of any help, even if she had dared test its limits again. The ground glinted like a mirror, flecked with white as if they were falling into the sky.

Not ground, Ista realized, with a stab of relief. *Not sky, either.* There was a lake on this side of the Moon Tower.

She'd barely had time to hope it was deep enough to cushion their landing before the water closed over her in a rush of cold. Fortunately, it *was* deep enough. Almost too deep. Her robes dragged her down, and she resurfaced spluttering. Nat popped up beside her as neatly as a cork, and they swam to the shallows, Ista gripping the telescope tightly in her sleeve as they hauled themselves through the rushes and onto the muddy bank. Back across the water, the grilk was still in the courtyard, pressed against the fence. It splayed its ragged wings, then sank away, disappearing into the mist.

Ista shuddered. That was twice now. Twice a grilk had come for her. Twice she'd escaped.

"I need to go back and warn people," Nat said. "In case anyone else goes out into that courtyard. And . . . I suppose you'd better get going too."

His voice was full of unspoken questions—and something softer. He felt sorry for her. How dare he? She was the one who'd saved him—from the Tide-lock *and* the grilk.

At least the water had washed off the worst of the grilk stink—although she didn't know what Alexo would say about her giving the telescope a bath. He could be awfully precious about the things she brought him. She snuck a quick glance at it, wanting to inspect it properly but not willing to do so with Nat gawping at her.

"Worth a lot of money, is it?" he asked.

Tide's teeth, he was nosy. Ista squelched away from him onto more solid ground, water sluicing from her robes. "Don't know. It isn't for me. It's for someone else."

"Oh." There it was again. Pity. She had half a mind to shove him back into the lake.

But in the distance, across the water and the courtyard, a light in one of the Moon Tower's windows caught her eye, a figure silhouetted against it.

Someone was watching them. Ista couldn't say how she knew; she just felt it, as sure as a touch. She thought of the twitching curtains she'd noticed in the courtyard.

"Nat," she said, a shiver fluttering through her. "What were you saying before? About me helping your mum and her investigation."

"*Our* investigation." The pride in Nat's voice was slightly undermined by the fact that he had a piece of frogweed in his hair. "Mum gets these hunches, you see."

"And she has one about the . . . about *them*? About someone controlling them?"

Nat nodded. "That's right."

"But you don't know who?"

"Well, no, but . . ."

A rusty laugh broke from Ista's throat, rattling up to the sky. "And how exactly does your mum think this someone's doing it? Wandering around with a stash of monster treats in their pocket?"

Nat's tone became thorny. "No, obviously not. We haven't figured out the *how* yet. Like I said, my mum just gets hunches, and then we pull on any loose threads until we find one that leads to the answers. You behaving oddly earlier, that was a loose thread—so I followed you. And now here we are." He gestured to his wet robes. "But there's definitely something fishy going on. Hang on—I've got it all written down."

He reached into his robes, presumably for the notebook, although the toy mouse emerged first, looking even more sorry for itself after its dunking. The notebook followed, in equally bad shape.

Nat looked from one to the other, then back at Ista. "Don't smirk. It isn't funny."

Ista hastily rearranged her expression. "It's not your things getting wet that's funny," she said—gently, because she suddenly had a feeling that he might be about to cry, and she was too tired and cold and cross to know how to comfort him after all the trouble he'd caused her. "It's . . ."

"You don't believe me." Nat sighed. "I probably wouldn't either. Look, I really should go and warn people about the grilk. But come to the *Conch* offices tomorrow and I'll tell you everything. We really could use you—and your Tide-blessing."

"All right," Ista said.

His gaze narrowed. "You're lying. You aren't going to."

She shrugged. "I might."

That was a lie too. It was ridiculous, everything he'd said. You couldn't control the grilks. You might as well try to bottle the Tide or catch a netful of stars.

All she wanted was to go home and put on some dry clothes. Fear had made her forget the cold for a while, but it pressed in on her now, making her teeth chatter. She cast a final glance at the Moon Tower. The figure in the window had vanished. Perhaps she'd imagined them in the first place.

"Wait," Nat said as she turned away. "You still haven't told me your name."

Ista pretended she hadn't heard. There was no point in him knowing her name when they'd probably never see each other again. The trees jutted up against the inky blue-black sky. She squelched toward them, clutching the telescope tightly. The evening might have veered off course, but it had all worked out in the end.

An errand was an errand, no matter how messily she'd completed it.

6

THE FABULOUS FLETWIN

It *was* home, in a way. Certainly, Ista's heart lifted as she rounded the corner of the ramshackle terrace where the Fabulous Fletwin stood. *Leaned* would be a more appropriate word, she supposed, because the building's three black-beamed stories slanted at an almost impossible angle as if frozen mid-stumble.

"Go to the Fletwin," Alexo had said the night they met.

"What's a fletwin?" Ista was watching the clarinet case, which was tucked neatly under his arm.

"A wading bird, normally, with a long red beak. But this one's a restaurant. That way." He'd pointed. "They need a pot washer. Tell them I sent you."

How could something be a bird and a restaurant? Ista had wanted to know, but when she'd turned back to ask, Alexo had been doubled over as if a cramp had taken him.

She knew now that this was because he couldn't stray from the Shrieking Eel for too long, but then she'd been so muddled with tiredness and fear, so grateful to him for saving her and so angry about what he'd stolen, that she'd simply done as she was told.

She hadn't asked how she should contact him about their deal. She'd known he would find her. And whenever she was feeling charitable toward him, she told herself he must also have known that Giddon and Padley would take her in.

At less charitable moments, she felt that Alexo's saving her had been an impulsive mistake and that he had merely deposited her in the first place he could. Either way, she was grateful. The Fletwin had proved to be a port in a storm.

Magic crackled and buzzed over her skin as she eased open the back door. It was only just after seventh bell, although it felt much later. The Fletwin always closed at Moon Tide, when most people preferred to stay home, where they knew they'd be safe. A Tide-lantern painted one corner of the kitchen an underwater blue. Padley dozed in its glow, his rocking chair pulled close to the fire, his soft snores rumbling like a cat's purr. The floor had been swept and mopped. Ista unlaced her boots and peeled off her soggy socks for good measure before crossing the flagstones in long tiptoe strides.

"Padley, I'm back."

Padley shook himself awake, the blanket slipping from his belly. "Hello there, young'un." His eyes were, in his own words, not as sharp as they used to be, and he reached for his glasses so he could peer at her properly. "Good gracious, dear Ista, what happened? You look as if you've fought a puddle and lost."

"I got rained on." Ista ducked his gaze. "Am I the last in?"

Padley nodded, his silvery hair gleaming. "Aye—slide the bolt, would you? Giddon just beat you. He'll be down in a hop. Wants your help with a new recipe, I gather. You must change those clothes first, though, before you catch a cold."

"Is she back?" The voice came from the stairs. It was an old man's voice, threadbare and wheezy, and it was an even older man than Padley who shuffled into view. A long, thin string of a man, immaculately bald, elaborately wrinkled, and wearing pajamas, a dressing gown, and slippers. Ista had never seen Giddon smile, but his brown eyes were warm as he blinked at her.

"Poor young Ista got rained on," Padley said.

"Did she now?" Giddon gave a pointed sniff. He and Padley bent over backward to avoid discussing her errands (Ista suspected they felt that the less they knew, the better, where Alexo was concerned), but she knew they both worried. "Clean clothes and hot brew," he said decisively. "And perhaps a sandwich and a large slice of gingercrumb tart?" He sniffed again. "And a quick wash before we start."

There was enough hot water in the tank for two turns

of the little sand timer that sat by the shower pail, and a scrub with a lovely fresh bar of homemade sage-and-lemon soap. Ista felt much better by the time she went back downstairs, and better still when Giddon set the promised sandwich, tea, and tart down for her at the gap-beamed table. Padley snoozed by the hearth again, his own portion of tart dispatched.

Ista swung her legs as she scoffed and slurped. She was almost always hungry, but especially so after changing, and tonight her stomach was howling like a dog left out in a storm. Once she'd chased the last crumbs around her plate, Giddon beckoned her to join him at the stove, where he was supervising a large cast-iron saucepan that burbled merrily as it simmered.

"My latest experiment." He gestured with his old wooden spoon. Fragrant steam wafted from the pan, the liquid a deep reddish brown like the best autumn leaves. "Unless you're too tired."

"I'm fine." Ista was never too tired to help Giddon. She'd worked her way up from washing pots to stirring them and, lately, to tasting all the Fletwin's soups and sauces. She poured a glass of water, rinsed her mouth in preparation, then took a clean metal spoon from the jar on the counter.

"Well?" Giddon said.

She sampled. Swilled. Swallowed. "There's parsroot, inkle, and . . . light-spice?"

"Very good."

"You need more inkle."

His mouth twitched. "Do I now? How much?"

Ista thought. "Another salt-spoon . . . and half a salt-spoon of ground fennet leaf."

"Certain?"

"Certain."

Giddon fetched the jars, and Ista watched him measure and stir. She wondered where he'd been while she'd been running from monsters. Padley almost never left the Fletwin after sunset if the magic was up, but Giddon said that he wasn't giving up his card games and music nights at his age. If it had been cards tonight, she suspected he'd lost. There was an extra grumpiness under his usual gruffness, as if something hadn't gone his way.

"With a clean spoon, if you please," he scolded when she reached toward the pan again. "Haven't I taught you properly?"

"Sorry." Ista hastily deposited the used one by the sink. "Yes," she said, tasting. "Much better."

"We'll make a chef of you yet." Giddon nodded with approval. "Bed now. You and Padley have an early start."

Ista sagged a little. Most of the Fletwin's suppliers delivered to them, but Padley was particular about vegetables and liked to choose them in person, and on market days it was her job to rise early and pilot the long-handled cart that he would load with his selections.

"Perhaps I should go instead of you tomorrow," said Giddon when she couldn't quite stifle a yawn.

But Ista wasn't having that. The Tide played havoc with Giddon's dreams, making them so vivid that he often woke as exhausted as if he hadn't slept at all. He did claim to have once successfully predicted the future, when he'd dreamed that someone had eaten the freshly baked plum cake he'd left on the counter, then discovered the next morning that Padley, feeling "snackish" in the night, had indeed polished off three large slices. But, that supposed premonition aside, Ista knew he found the gift the Tide had given him to be more of a curse than a blessing—especially around Moon Tide, when the magic never completely left him in peace.

"No," she told him firmly. "I really don't mind."

"Thank you, young'un." Giddon gave her a grateful nod. He moved to Padley's side, speaking gently. "Padley, old man, it's bedtime." A chuckle escaped him. "Ah, he's at it again."

Ista turned to the rocker where Padley slept. His cake fork hovered in the air, level with the pale tip of his nose, and was pirouetting like a weather vane, each of his gentle snores sending it off on another spin.

"Your Tide-blessing's showing, my love," Giddon murmured, placing a hand on Padley's shoulder.

Padley started with a snort. "Oh, bless me, did I drift off again?" He wiped his chin, blinking up at them both.

"Hmm, bedtime, I think. First light tomorrow, Ista, don't forget. I hope you sleep well, after your busy evening."

Ista yawned again. She was drooping like a flower, half asleep already.

"On you go, then. Tide keep you," Giddon said.

Taking a candle from the dresser, Ista headed for the stairs.

Her bedroom was formed from a wedge of the attic and contained a driftwood bed frame, a bookcase, and a velveteen chair that was struggling to hold on to its stuffing. The bottom shelf of the bookcase was for books (most from the library, although two she'd bartered for at the secondhand bookshop on Leaf Street), the top for clothes, and the middle for keepsakes, miscellaneous items, and the cloth pouch where she kept her wages and tips. In the middle of the middle shelf, between a stack of letters and a large jar of shells, was her photograph of Pa. Ista tapped him hello as she passed.

Her night's work was almost, but not quite, complete. The robes and the telescope were in the corner where she'd left them when she'd come upstairs to wash and change. Now she carried them to the window. Air poured in like black wine as she opened the shutters and sash. Below the narrow sill, a tarnished metal chest squatted on the sloping roof.

Fresh magic nipped Ista's fingers as she flipped back the lid, the smell of brine and candle smoke tickling her nostrils. This was Alexo's chest, and inside was a nest of green pebbles, each polished as smooth as river-glass.

These were not normal stones, though. Glass-bugs, Ista called them. They were very special indeed.

She swaddled the telescope with the robes and laid the bundle in the chest, shut the lid, stepped back, and pulled the shutters closed. From outside came a creak, followed by a scrabbling sound, like an army of tiny pearl-crabs hurrying across the slates.

She waited. The scrabbling moved higher, passing over her head, and vanished into the distance. Ista pictured Alexo in his study, his fingers tapping expectantly. She had never been able to work out how the glass-bugs were connected to his magic, had long since given up trying to count the number of tricks he seemed to have up his sleeve.

Ista retraced her steps to the window and opened the shutters again. The glass-bugs were gone. The chest lay empty—almost. In the bottom was a shell: one of the twisted, pointy kind that the fishers called elf ears. She reached in to retrieve it, cradling it close as she shut every-thing up again, then added it to the jar, where it landed with a soft clack.

Number nineteen.

"Almost there, Pa," she told the photograph. Pa gazed back at her, his eyes certain in the candlelight, as if he didn't doubt her for a heartbeat.

One more errand, and then what? The question hung

over Ista as she climbed into bed. Pa would still be gone. She'd been here practically all winter, and she'd learned almost nothing that hadn't been in the letter Mikkela the trumpet player had sent along with the clarinet. The note was in the pile of Pa's letters now, not that Ista needed to reread it. Every word was singed into her brain: *I am so sorry. There is no trace of him. People do vanish, sometimes, in Shelwich. He made me promise once that if anything ever happened to him, I'd let you know and be sure to send his clarinet to Ista, and so . . .*

Ista's aunt had hidden the clarinet and waited four whole days before she'd even told Ista what had happened. *You'll stay with me, of course,* she'd said.

Of course, Ista had agreed. (She suspected, looking back, that her aunt had needed the extra days to commit to this generosity.) She'd been sure it was a misunderstanding. That Mikkela would write again. That Pa would write himself. She would have felt it, she'd reasoned, if someone had taken the ribbon of her life and snipped it clean in two.

But Pa didn't write. And Aunt Abgill did nothing, so . . .

The memory rolled over Ista like a wave. Padding through the house, boots in hand. Taking the clarinet from the high shelf where her aunt had hidden it—and a pouch of coins for the fare on the midnight coach. Not having enough money for the last part of the journey. Arriving in the city on foot. The grilk. Alexo.

Since that first night, Ista had searched the room Pa

had been renting, visited every place he'd mentioned in his letters, every concert hall and café where he'd played, and spoken to every musician she could find. She'd asked at the hospital, every day at first—she still checked there three times a week.

Nothing. *People do vanish, sometimes, in Shelwich.*

People got taken by grilks, more like. But grilks were drawn to magic, everyone knew that, and the ability to mimic animal noises was all the Tide had given Pa. He could do it so accurately that you found yourself checking whether there really was a lamb bleating under the dinner table or an owl hooting on the hat stand, but it was a very small blessing in the grand scheme of things. A grilk going after anyone with magic as slight as his made as little sense as a shark chasing after a skim-fly.

It was the only possible answer, though. No one had seen anything.

Or so they'd claimed. Fear of the grilks had such a tight hold on the city. Whenever she asked anyone about Pa, they clammed up as soon as they learned he was missing and brought the conversation swiftly to a halt.

She'd even tried Alexo, once she'd realized how well connected he was. *Is there anything you know, anything you can do?* The ghost of the words still burned the back of her throat. She'd hated having to ask him for help.

To her surprise he'd looked almost stricken, as if he hadn't quite understood before how badly a child could miss a parent. But the next instant he was his usual self again. *I know nothing, little thief.* Even if he did, Ista wondered if he'd tell her. Probably not, unless it suited his own needs somehow.

So that had been it. Dead end after dead end after dead end. Nat Shah was the first person she'd met who'd really been willing to talk about the grilks at all.

What if he was right?

Ista sat up, her mind whirling. She had been scared that the grilk might break out of the courtyard after them, but how had it got *in* there? No one had ever seen a grilk take full flight, so it couldn't have flown over the wall. There was no way into that courtyard other than from the main building.

What if someone *was* controlling them? Pa had always been curious, always asking questions, trying to figure out how things worked. What if he'd seen something he shouldn't have? Poked his nose where it wasn't wanted? A kernel of resolve hardened deep in Ista's gut. She couldn't fight monsters, but people were another story. If it was a some*one* rather than a some*thing* that had taken Pa from her, she would find them—and then, perhaps, she would find him.

7

ISTA INVESTIGATES

The Tide dipped right down and rose again overnight. Ista woke at almost dead-on High Tide, sun bleeding through the slats in her shutters, and magic making her teeth tingle.

She needed to talk to Nat, that was the crucial thing, and find out what he knew about the grilks. That would have to wait until his school day was over and she could find him at the *Conch* offices, though. For now she'd have to be content with Padley, but as he'd lived in Shelwich his whole life, perhaps he was just the person to answer some of her questions.

At least *she* didn't have to go to school, Ista thought as they set out along the river path, her pulling the little cart and Padley consulting his shopping list. He and Giddon had put her name down for the school where the traders', makers', and shopkeepers' children went, with classes scheduled around apprenticeships and the work they needed to do for their families. She'd be able to start there in the spring, but meanwhile, Padley had been teaching her himself in whatever scraps of time they could find.

The route to the market took them past a row of fishers' huts and a bench facing out across the estuary toward Glass Island. Padley was in the habit of pausing there to rest his bad knee. Today, despite the chill, was no exception. Ista angled the cart so it wouldn't roll away, then took a seat beside him. The river licked the edge of the walkway, and she was careful to keep her feet well back from any stray sloshes that might come higher. Her boots were damp enough as it was from the lake yesterday.

"Would the combers have been out last night, then?" she asked. When the tide was out, a thin strip of beach revealed itself at this spot, and on other mornings she and Padley often saw the pearl-combers working the sand and pebbles with their rakes.

Padley rubbed his gloved hands to stave off the cold. "Aye, always a fine haul after a Moon Tide. They wouldn't miss it."

Just the idea of that made Ista yawn. Poor pearl-combers. It must be horribly hard, having to work the beaches in the dark, especially when the rest of the city was warm in their beds.

"I don't suppose they like the governor very much," she

said, remembering the fine food and grand rooms she'd seen at the Moon Tower.

Padley turned to her in surprise. "Are you taking an interest in politics, young Ista?"

Ista shrugged. "Well, the election's soon, isn't it?"

And the grilk last night had gone after Jarmak Hettle—the governor's son. If this *was* a plot—and she still felt it was an enormous *if*—could the person behind it be out to make trouble for the governor? *No,* she chided herself. That was clutching at straws. Even if that grilk had been waiting for someone, there was no way of knowing for whom.

Padley was giving her a fondly despairing smile. "Soon? I should say so," he said. "Voting's only three days away. Sink me, why do you think the whole city's covered in posters and the governor's galloping around making silly speeches every other evening?"

Ista hadn't thought anything about it. She'd been too busy with Alexo's errands. Now that she looked, there *were* a lot of posters around, even out here where the damp and salt would get them. VOTE BRINTAN BROOK FOR A PROSPEROUS SHELWICH! proclaimed one plastered to the nearest hut. BETRIKA HETTLE: TRIED, TESTED, TRUSTED! declared another.

"Betrika Hettle." Padley pursed his lips. "For all the speeches she makes, you'd think she'd come up with something different to say every once in a while. We all *know* that we must keep our eyes peeled for grilks and raise the alarm if we see one. It'll be interesting to see if she holds off Brintan Brook, that's for certain. Most folk only gave her a chance in the first place for her grandpa's sake."

"Her grandpa?" Ista was lost.

"Old Betrik Hettle. *The* Betrik Hettle, who governed this city for sixty years. Whose statue stands down there, in the middle of Shipwrights' Square." He pointed to the mouth of the street just beyond the fishers' huts.

Ista got up to look. The street ran in a straight line to the square, and the statue was indeed visible in the distance, standing proudly outside Shipwrights' Hall. She must have walked past it hundreds of times, although she'd never paused to examine it. It was hard to tell from far away, but something in the statue's profile did sort of remind her of the governor and Jarmak.

"You're such a part of our lives now, young'un, I forget sometimes that you've barely been here a season," Padley said as she returned to the bench. "It's an interesting story, though, how Betrik came to power. No one could fathom why he was standing in the first place. The Hettles were always more involved in the arts than in politics. Betrik's father was an eccentric man, and he'd sunk most of their fortune into . . . oh, what was it, now? Anyway, Betrik was a weedy, uninspiring fellow, and his opponent was a clear-thinking sort. Popular, too—she had the support of the shipwrights' *and* the fishers' guilds, and seemed destined to win."

"But she didn't," said Ista. There was no statue of *her.*

"No, she didn't." Mystery glinted in Padley's eyes. "It'd been a hard winter that year. Some folk turned to thieving, and one particular thief caused a stir across the city. Lightning Lucy, she called herself—because not only was she fast, but she was dramatic as lightning, too. She'd advertise in the paper which house or business she meant to target next, and *still* no one could catch her."

Like me, Ista thought. *Well, the not-being-caught part.*

"It got to the eve of the election," Padley went on. "Lightning Lucy announced she would strike that night—and that her target was none other than the Hettle house! And Betrik . . . well, he managed to set a trap and catch her!"

"How?"

"Left out a vase encrusted with Tide-pearls where it couldn't be missed—with a Tide-lock set to catch her when she reached for the bait." Padley shook his head at the wonder of it. "Turned out Lightning Lucy was only a girl about my age—the age I was then, that is. She never did admit how she'd done it all, but the room she was living in was full of the stolen property, so that was that. They sent thieves to Glass Island back then."

His gaze drifted across the water to where the ruined towers loomed like shards of obsidian and diamond in the morning light. Ista shuddered, hunching deeper into her coat. She'd rather face another grilk than spend even one night over there. They said that if you listened closely, you could hear the ghosts of the old world howling in the ruins after dark. The island wasn't even used as a prison anymore. No self-respecting boat folk would make the crossing nowadays.

"As for Betrik," Padley continued, "the next morning, before the vote began, he made a speech in Shipwrights' Square, in the very spot where his statue stands today. I was there in the crowd. Like a man transformed, he was, as if he'd settled into his skin overnight. 'I hope I've proved myself to you now,' he said, 'and that you'll trust me with the future of our city.' People did, of course. He won by a tidal wave—stayed in office his whole life. Ninety-nine he was when he died last summer. He declared on his death-bed that his granddaughter Betrika should take his place till there could be a new election, and he was so well loved that the Council honored his wishes. Right, young'un. We should get on." He hefted himself from the bench.

Ista took hold of the cart again, falling into step beside him. "But last summer was ages ago. Why's the election only happening now?"

Padley's expression soured. "That's an excellent question, young Ista. Grilks is why." He lowered his voice, glancing to either side, as if he'd forgotten there was no chance a grilk would appear in daylight. "There was a third candidate: Wicka Honeyball. If you ask me, she'd have made a fine governor, better than either Betrika Hettle or Brintan

Brook. But grilks took her right on her own doorstep—*that's* why the election got postponed. Only a day or so after you arrived in Shelwich, it was. Awful how people being taken's become such a normal part of life here."

"You mean it wasn't always?" Ista couldn't imagine the city without grilk attacks any more than she could imagine it without Padley and Giddon, or Alexo and Nimble Lane.

"Tide take me, no. There were always stories, mind. People who claimed to know someone whose friend's cousin's neighbor had been taken, or who swore they'd faced one themselves and survived. But it was only a year or so ago the creatures became bold enough to appear in plain sight. It's the magic, I reckon. It's grown so strong they can't resist it."

They had reached the harbor; he broke off, making way for a woman heaving a barrow of glittering fish toward the warehouses that lined the street side of the walkway. The woman's honey-colored hair was draped over her shoulder in a thick plait, the end of which grew another inch as she passed them.

That, Ista thought, *would almost certainly be more of a curse than a blessing.*

"What makes everyone so sure the magic's getting stronger?" she asked as she and Padley moved on again.

"Put it this way, young'un: time was, I never felt it at all until just before High Tide. Whereas these days . . . well, you saw my fork last night. And I definitely feel strong ripples of magic now, and we're . . . well, how many minutes past the peak would you say?"

Padley pulled a paper Tide-table from his pocket, as Ista had known he would. It had become a game they played: her guessing the level of magic and him checking to see how close she was.

She shut her eyes, feeling the rush of power bubble around her. "Almost an hour. Fifty minutes, maybe. No, fifty-five."

Padley looked from the Tide-table to his wristwatch and back to the table again. "Extraordinary. And this just proves my point. As sure as the world's round, the Tide's magic is getting stronger. You young folk have blessings that would've been unthinkable not so long ago. Kip the potter said they were buying jam or some such the other day and they saw a young girl—a real scrap of a thing, no older than you—lift a loaded wagon off the ground using only one hand." Padley smiled. "Makes me wish my mother was alive. She always said this"—he made a vague waving motion—"was part of a cycle."

Ista frowned. "A cycle?"

"Well, most folk think the Tide just *arrived* one day, as suddenly as a meteor crashing into the planet. But my mother believed that just as the magic rises and falls with the river, so the Tide's very presence has ebbed and flowed over the centuries. She used to tell me all sorts of tales—stories she swore had been passed down generation by generation—about magical creatures that supposedly lived in and around the river thousands of years ago."

Ista had a lot more questions about that, but they rounded a corner, the harbor's fish-fresh sharpness giving way to the warm early-morning smells of the bakeries on Bread Street, and Padley reached for his shopping list.

"Keep your eyes peeled for tomatoes and oranges when we reach the market," he instructed. "I heard the greenhousers might be in."

"I'll have my elbows ready too," Ista assured him. Anyone with enough space kept a greenhouse—or at least a green box—of their own, but the professional greenhousers from outside the city came to the market only once or twice a moon. There would be quite a crowd at their stall.

The early edition of the *Daily Conch* was on sale at the newsstand on the corner. Ista scanned the cover, but there was no mention of a grilk sighting at the Moon Tower—perhaps Nat's mum was going to write an article about it for the late edition instead. A whisper of wind brushed past, fluttering the corner of a faded poster tacked to the booth. WICKA HONEYBALL FOR GOVERNOR! A VOTE FOR CHANGE IS A VOTE FOR HOPE!

"Padley," Ista said, her mind darting back to their earlier conversation, "if Wicka Honeyball was still here, might she have won the election, or would it always have been between Brintan Brook and the governor?"

Padley gave a noncommittal shrug. "Honeyball would have had my vote, that's for sure, and I'd say she'd have been the choice of almost all the makers and traders. She was a practical type, you know, someone who'd get things done. The people's champion, folks were calling her. As it is, Brook's gaining popularity every day." A distinct line of disappointment ran through the last sentence.

"But you don't like him?" Ista said.

Padley weighed his answer before he gave it. "Brook's got too much of a ruthless streak for my taste, especially when it comes to business."

He looked as if he might say more, but the market was before them, and he clapped his hands together. "Right. Oranges and tomatoes. And yellow courgettes if you spot any."

8

THE CONCH

It was well past Low Tide when the last lunchtime stragglers drifted out of the Fletwin. The magic was returning and seemed to be filling the world from the ground up. Ista felt it nibbling and sucking at her calves, as if she'd disturbed a shoal of curious fish.

She flipped the sign on the door to CLOSED and helped Cauldi, the waitress, wipe and set the tables for the evening while Giddon and Padley dished up the staff meal in the kitchen. Today's was big bowls of broth and hunks of seeded bread, then shortcakes and marsh honey.

Ista's appetite never vanished for long. She wolfed down two helpings and was considering a third when Giddon asked if anyone would mind taking a parcel to the post office for him.

She scraped back her chair. "I'll do it." The central

post office was only a few doors along from the *Conch,* and it wasn't long until the schools let out and Nat would be on his way to help his mother. She should speak to him as soon as possible, just in case there was any chance that what he knew about the grilks might somehow lead her to Pa. Besides, she was only too happy to help Giddon. He looked gray around the gills with exhaustion. The Moon Tide must have made his dreams especially vivid last night.

"You sure you don't want me to bring over some of my granddad's tangleroot tea, Giddon?" asked Cauldi, helping herself to another shortcake. "It's worked wonders for my nana. She sleeps right through now, even with her sore hip."

"No, no." Giddon was firm. "I've told you, I must keep my head clear. But thank you. And thank *you,*" he said to Ista, rising to fetch the package.

"Yes." Padley smiled across at her. "How did we ever manage without you, young'un?"

Never mind how they used to manage without her, Ista thought as she left them all snug and warm at the table. How would she possibly have managed without them? She wouldn't have had a room or a job or three meals a day, of that she was sure.

Alexo would've given her a room at the Shrieking Eel. The idea floated like a feather and was carried off by the wind. Maybe he would have and maybe he wouldn't.

Thinking about him reminded her to loop along the river path and past the eel shack on her way. The awning, though, was handkerchief-free. Errand number twenty obviously wouldn't be happening today.

The *Daily Conch* was the oldest surviving newspaper in the city. Both it and the post office were on Saltwillow Avenue, a grand tree-lined street to the west of the park. Ista had hoped to be quick at the post office and then find a good position to keep watch for Nat, but the queue for the counter was long and snaking. By the time she was finished, the sky was dimming, the magic crawling steadily higher, pouring a jelly-like fuzziness into the spaces between her ribs. The afternoon's shoppers were departing, one or two in sol-cars, although most clambered into carts and carriages or lugged their purchases toward the trundle stop.

The *Conch* offices occupied the tallest building on the avenue, topped with a gleaming golden shell large enough that she could have climbed inside it. Ista idled on the opposite sidewalk, bouncing on her heels to stop the cold numbing her feet. Nat had to be there already. *Come to the* Conch *offices tomorrow and I'll tell you everything.* But a surly-looking guard barred the front entrance. Getting past them would be tricky.

But with her Tide-blessing there was always a way.

The doors opened. A man came out. No good. He was almost twice her size—her clothes wouldn't stretch that far.

A short person in a nettle-green coat. Also no. Ista's coat was a hand-me-down from Pa, long and black and baggy.

A woman all in black, her collar pulled high. Not much taller or broader than Ista. She smiled at the guard as she left, and the guard smiled in return.

Perfect.

Ista dipped, minnow-quick, into a nearby alley. She unrolled her trouser hems, loosened the sash at her waist, and flicked up her collar so it looked more like the woman's. She took a breath. Focused. Glittery stabs of power rushed up her limbs.

Less than a minute later, she walked up to the *Conch*.

"Back so soon, Mab?" said the guard. He was a grandfatherly sort, now that he wasn't trying to be ferocious.

"Forgot my gloves," Ista murmured, her throat scraping slightly; Mab must be coming down with a cold.

She strode across the checkerboard floor of the lobby, nodding to the receptionist at the desk. She could have come in as herself, she realized. Left a note for Nat. But, no, it would be better face to face. A note might go missing. Besides, she was here now.

In the elevator, a column of buttons waited, marked

B, G, and 1 to 5. Ista scrambled for inspiration. Nat had expected her to recognize his mother's name. That meant she was important. Probably. And important people had rooms with views, to help them think their important thoughts.

So 5 it was. Ista punched the button. The elevator rose, a soft chime sounding with each floor it passed. The fifth floor was exactly how she'd imagined a newsroom, all intense faces and busy feet. At the center of the bustle was the gigantic copper print terminal. Ista had seen a picture of one before, but up close it was truly impressive, looming over everything like a huge mechanical octopus— except distinctly less knobbly and with at least twenty arms. Each limb ended at a typing station with a reporter hunched over it, frantically hammering the keys. A clear pipe, not unlike a drainpipe, spouted from the crown of the octopus's head, and every few seconds a metal canister would shoot through it, whiz around the ceiling, and disappear down the far wall and into the floor.

"Watch it, Mab!" The words were slung at her sideways by a purple-haired girl wielding a stack of leather binders.

"Sorry," Ista said, but the girl was already plowing past.

"Got those records you want, Priya!"

Priya. The girl carved a path through the chaos, and Ista hurried after her.

Priya Shah was poised over one of the typing stations. It was unquestionably her. She had Nat's thick eyebrows, and the same stubborn juts of chin and nose, although on her the effect was more eagle than owl. Also, Nat was perched beside her.

Ista felt wrong-footed. She'd thought Nat would be alone, doing homework in a corner somewhere, but he was glued to his mother's side, peering over her shoulder.

"Have you finished sorting that data for me, Charlie?" Priya called, spinning her chair to one side.

"Not yet, Priya, sorry," replied a young, pasty-faced man at a desk in the corner. Ista saw that his fingers were moving unnaturally quickly over the keys of his typing station. "Give me another half hour. I'll be at triple speed once the Tide's a touch higher."

Priya twisted to glance at the week's Tide-table, which was pinned to the wall, gave an almost satisfied nod, then saw Ista loitering and sat upright with interest.

"Mab? You're back fast. Did you get it?"

Ista shook her head. Whatever *it* was, she definitely did not have it. "Sorry." She took a step backward, edging toward the door.

Priya's eyes narrowed. "Not stopping?"

Being the subject of her full attention was like being under a searchlight. "Um," Ista said, fighting the urge to shrink away from its beam. "Um, no. I . . ." Her throat convulsed with a cough. "I don't feel well." True. Shivers ribboned up and down her body.

"Oh." Priya straightened. The searchlight feeling

dimmed. "That explains it. You should go home. It'll be a disaster if we all catch it three days before the election."

She returned to her work. Ista looked at Nat, willing him to notice her coat, which was a baggier cut than Mab's. Her scuffed boots, which were far too wide for Mab's feet. But his gaze fell back to whatever task he'd been engaged in before.

Sink this, Ista thought. She had to do something. She couldn't just leave. He was the kind of person who noticed *everything.* If she could only catch his attention.

Priya must have sensed her lurking. Her focus snapped up again. "What is it, Mab?"

"Well . . . ," Ista began, then burst into a coughing fit that made Priya wince but bought a few precious seconds of thinking time. "Have you heard of a restaurant called the Fabulous Fletwin? It's in the artists' quarter, just north of Shipwrights' Square."

"Of course. Everyone knows the Fletwin. Excellent little place." Priya reached for a pen. "Why? Have you had a tip about something?"

"Oh, nothing like that," Ista said. "I just heard they have an excellent *early-morning* breakfast deal at the moment." Which wasn't true. The Fletwin didn't even open until lunchtime. "I thought Nat might like it." She sank extra weight into his name. Nat looked up, his forehead crinkling in confusion.

Come on, Ista willed him. *There's something strange*

about this, you know there is. You met a girl who could change shape last night, and now here's Mab acting oddly in a coat that looks a bit like hers but definitely, definitely isn't.

"Nat?" Priya's eyebrows drew halfway toward a frown. She looked from Ista to Nat, who was in turn staring at Ista.

"Yes," Ista plowed on. "You were saying *yesterday,* weren't you, Nat, how much you like . . . um, breakfast?" She ran a hand down the front of her coat. *Look at the buttons, Nat. Are Mab's buttons like this? Is her coat this shabby?*

Understanding sparked in Nat's eyes. "I do," he said. "I do like breakfast."

Ista could have hugged him. "Excellent. Well, I really think you'll like the early-morning deal at the Fabulous Fletwin. You could even try it before school tomorrow."

Priya's eyebrows completed their journey. "Thank you, Mab, for the recommendation," she said in the same voice she might have used if Ista had climbed onto one of the workstations and done a little dance. "You get on home now. We'll see you when your fever's gone down."

Magic spiked the air, closing over Ista's head as she traipsed back to the Fletwin. Worry needled her. What if Nat hadn't actually understood? Tomorrow would tell, she supposed. For now she had to hurry, or she'd miss the start of the dinner rush. Not only that, but it would soon be dark. Moonlight pooled between swirls of mist as she sped back through the artists' quarter, Tide-lanterns illuminating shuttered shop fronts plastered in election posters. VOTE HETTLE! VOTE BROOK!

Rounding the corner, she found the restaurant dark, the dining room deserted, the CLOSED sign on the door. That was odd. Very odd. The Fletwin closed at Moon Tide, but it was extremely rare for it to shut on any other evening. Dread fluttered in Ista's stomach.

She wove between the tables and through to the kitchen. "Padley? Giddon?"

"Ista?"

It was Cauldi who answered. Cauldi who sat alone at the table, where they had all been together just a few hours before, her face streaky with tears in the lamplight.

"It's the grilks," she said. "They took Padley."

9

GONE

Not Padley. Anyone but Padley, with his stories and his kindness and his naps by the fire.

"When?" Ista said.

Cauldi's eyes were as bleak and dark as caves. "Not long after the sundown chimes began. We were short on lamp oil. Giddon was upstairs resting, so I said I'd go, but Padley insisted. He'd only been gone a minute when Giddon came hurtling down the stairs, faster than I've ever seen him move. He was shouting for Padley. I said Padley had gone to the lampers, and Giddon . . . It was so strange. He ran over to the coats on the hooks, and then he said, "I'm too late. It's too late! They'll have him already!" And he ran out into the street and straight round to Pinch Alley. It was as if he *knew*."

"Pinch Alley?" Ista felt as if she were floating away, up

toward the ceiling. Pinch Alley was a grimy squeeze of nothingness running down the side of the printmaker's shop. Padley used it as a shortcut sometimes, when his knee was hurting. "Is that where . . . ?"

Cauldi nodded. "I ran after Giddon—and we met Kip the potter running the other way to find us. They'd been closing up when Padley passed by. Said he waved to them, then disappeared into the alley, and then the mist came, and by the time we got there, there was nothing. Just that awful smell."

"But where's Giddon now?" Ista said.

"I don't *know*." Cauldi's last word unfurled into a wail. "He asked me to wait for you here, and he just went. Oh, it's all *my* fault." She looked so wrung out it was a wonder there was any water still in her, but she began to cry again.

"No, it isn't," Ista said firmly. "But didn't Giddon say anything about where he was going? Anything at all?"

A sniffle. "No." Cauldi sat up, found a handkerchief in her pocket, and blew her nose. "Only that we should stay here until he came back."

Ista was grateful for that; if she'd had to wait by herself, she thought the loneliness of the Fletwin would crush her. They lit a fire and sat in front of it, leaving Padley's rocker empty as they made and then ignored a plate of toast.

The wood burned down, the Tide climbed to its peak, and Giddon didn't come home. Cauldi nodded in her chair, her eyelids drooping. Ista sat stick-straight, watching the door, willing it to open. Her heart was hollow, but her head was crammed with magic and her feet itched with waiting.

Still no Giddon . . .

Ista stood. Moved around, mouse-quick, cat-quiet. She put the guard over the grate. Draped a blanket across Cauldi's knees. The hinges sighed as she opened the door, but Cauldi didn't stir. When she eventually did, she'd see the note Ista had left, fixed in place by a salt-spoon on the table: *Gone for help. Back soon.*

Ista wasn't confident that either statement was true, but if there was any help to be had, there was only one place she'd find it—and it wasn't by the dying fire.

Out on the street, it almost felt like Moon Tide still. The magic was all teeth and claws, the Tide-lanterns so bright they were dazzling, while the regular streetlights jittered on their poles. Nimble Lane seemed jittery too. Three times Ista caught its snuffed-birthday-candle-and-salt-water smell, and three times it slipped away, shy as a fish darting down into the reeds. The fourth time, she was lucky, catching the scent at the same time that she spotted a blur in the wall to her right. She leapt sideways, air rushing past as if the bricks were zipping back up behind her.

The lane was . . . different. The sky was clear, as it always was in this strange, secret place, no matter the weather in the outside world, but the houses were blurry like the backdrop of a dream, and the cobbles seemed to sink beneath her, as if lingering too long would send her falling through them.

Ista picked her way forward, treading lightly, practicing what she would say.

Alexo, my friend is gone.

I will make you a new bargain.

I will do twenty more errands.

Fifty.

More. Enough to fill one hundred jars with shells.

If you were lying before, if you do know something, anything, please tell me. It may be too late for Pa, but perhaps we can still save Padley.

She set her hand to the wood of the Shrieking Eel's blank front door. Nothing happened. She lifted her hand. Tried again.

"Not tonight, wanderer" came a growl.

"No," Ista said. She would not be put off. Not now. "Please, please let me in. Please."

Inside, something thumped, like a bag of flour hitting the floor. A curious meow filtered out.

"Terrible?" Ista leaned closer. "Terrible, it's me. Please make the door let me in."

Another meow. Followed by what sounded like a harrumph. Above her fingertips, the line appeared in the wood. The circle formed. The door swung inward. Terrible gazed up at her.

"Hello." She bent to greet him. "Thank you. Thank you so much."

He flicked his tail and went back to his chair. Ista turned to the elevators. PLEASURE was barricaded by a thin green rope and a sign that read OUT OF ORDER. There was a notice by BUSINESS, too: EMERGENCY ACCESS ONLY.

Well, this was an emergency, wasn't it?

As if it agreed with her, the grille slid open, the metal tentacles untangling to let her in.

"Wish me luck," Ista said to Terrible, but he'd already gone back to sleep.

Down rattled the elevator car. Down, down, down. Ista had never noticed before quite how deep it went. The hallway below was ocean-trench dark.

"Alexo?" she called.

The Tide-lantern sputtered awake, illuminating his door. She raised her hand to knock. "Alexo?"

Silence. Could he be sleeping? He must sleep sometimes. She tried the handle. It turned. Inside, the fire was lit, pink-and-green flames making shadows dance over the muddle of furniture and towers of knickknacks.

"Alexo?" Doubt was creeping in. She was venturing into unknown territory, being here if he wasn't. Bookcases and cupboards jutted like crags. "Hello?"

Nothing—except the strum of the magic and the crackle of the fire. Against the far wall was the cabinet.

Pa's clarinet case. But that hardly seemed to matter now. Before she knew it, Ista was further into the room than she'd ever been before, so she saw that one half of it extended, tapering into a narrow corridor. *Don't,* whispered a voice in her mind, but she picked her way forward, round a card table and a hat stand, a tarnished mirror in a shabby gilt frame. The floor sloped as it tapered, and soon the clutter was behind her, the walls squeezing tighter, smelling of briny water and chalk. An underground smell, but laced with freshness, definitely not grilkish.

A Tide-lantern hung from a hook, turning the walls a sickly blue. Beyond it, the floor curled back on itself, spiraling down into darkness. A stepless staircase, its core an open drop.

Down Ista went, following the coil of stone, her hand tight on the spindly railing that traced the wall. Each time she reached the edge of the light, a new lantern flickered awake, shedding its glow a little lower, while the one behind her snuffed out.

At the bottom of the spiral was a door. It was slightly ajar, and cold air seeped out, the briny smell sharpening.

Fear curdled in the pit of Ista's stomach. Only for Padley did she keep moving—then froze as her eyes adjusted to the darkness beyond.

A vast cavern stretched around her. Water dripped from the ceiling, and strands of rock dripped with it, reaching down in calcified vines toward a wide green pool. All the light seemed to come from below, shimmering like steam against the jagged outline of the bank.

A shadow crossed the pool. *No.* Ista's breath hitched. It wasn't a shadow; it was a *something.* A coiled shape, small at first, but growing with every kick of her pulse.

Not growing. Rising.

The pool juddered, brackish water sloshing. Scales glinted as a great, smooth head broke the surface, then went under again. A long body followed, arching up like the curve of the trundle-track.

An eel. It had to be. The clue was right there in the name of the inn—although this was easily two hundred times bigger than any eel Ista had seen before. The head reemerged, two rows of vicious teeth glinting like blades as the eel opened its mouth and shrieked.

Ista ran. She ran and didn't stop until she was almost back at Alexo's room, her muscles burning and her breath coming in tatters. Voices sounded behind her, far down the spiral of stone, and she froze. Two people, their conversation floating up in cloudy snatches. They must've been in the cavern too, or in another room beyond it. Hope swelled in her chest; one of them had to be Alexo.

The first voice she didn't recognize, although it was young, and reminded her of the reed pipe Pa had tried to teach her to play when she was small: low and tuneful but with the occasional scratch and squeak to it.

"What a night, boss! Not one haul but two!"

"Yes, very impressive." That was Alexo. She could hear his smirk. "You'll be paid finely, as always."

"And what about that man Giddon?" The stranger's tone became anxious. "He was very upset when he got here."

Giddon? Was this where Giddon had come for help? Ista's hope withered, confusion blooming in its place.

"That was . . . regrettable," Alexo said. "But I spelled him to sleep. He won't even remember most of . . ." His voice faded out, muffled by the contours of the building.

The stranger sniffed. "And the little face-changer?"

With a jolt, Ista understood they meant her.

"I told you. Keep an eye on her."

"And if she suspects?"

A pause, as if Alexo was deliberating. "She won't. But if she does, you know what to do."

They fell silent, the last words echoing off the stone. Ista felt as if a cold hand had closed around her heart. She hadn't thought it was possible for everything to crumble twice in one night. She'd come to Alexo for help, trusted him despite his tricksiness. But now . . .

Their footsteps grew louder. They must be only a turn or two from the top of the spiral. It took a second for fear to trickle in, for her to realize how alone she was, how easy it would be for her to disappear.

Never stay too long. Never get caught. Wasn't that what

Alexo was always telling her? She turned. Slowly. Precisely. Like a figure in a music box. She crept, as quickly and carefully as she'd ever crept in her life. Back past the Curiosities and the pink-and-green firelight. Up, up, up in the elevator, begging it not to rattle. Out to where Terrible dozed in the hall.

He opened his eye. The front door opened too.

"Go safely, wanderer."

But Ista wasn't sure she would ever feel safe again.

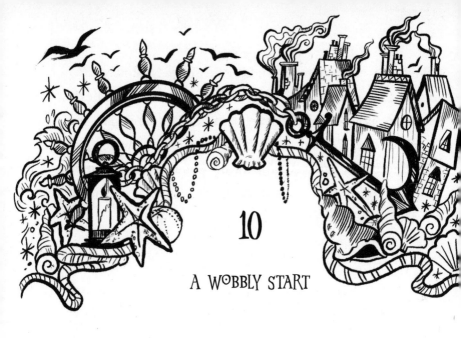

10

A WOBBLY START

Ista woke in her attic at the Fletwin, purplish light peeking in through the gaps in the shutters. For a few heartbeats everything seemed normal. The softness and warmth of the mattress. Her jar of shells on the bookcase. Pa gazing at her from his photo frame . . .

Then she remembered.

And the little face-changer . . . if she suspects?

If she does, you know what to do.

She shut her eyes again, replaying it all. The cavern below the inn. The giant eel. Alexo and the stranger. Already her memory was muddling the pieces, making her doubt herself. She'd crept back into the Fletwin to find Cauldi still dozing in the kitchen and told her she could go home—that Giddon had sent word he was on his way, which of course wasn't true.

Alexo's voice rose like a ghost in her mind. *I spelled him to sleep.* The Tide gave you *one* blessing and one blessing only. Everyone knew that. But Alexo existed outside the rules somehow. All Ista knew for certain was that his magic was as slippery as it was rare—her best guess was that he'd found a way to siphon the power from some forgotten branch of the river running deep beneath the inn.

How long does a sleep spell last? she wondered. She'd lain awake listening out for Giddon, just in case, but her eyelids had grown heavier and heavier. As the magic had drained toward Low Tide, she'd sunk into restless dreams that had left her feeling as though her head were full of cobwebs.

She needed air, she decided, swinging her feet to the floor, but when she opened the window, Alexo's glass-bug chest seemed to lurk menacingly below the sill instead of simply sitting there as it normally did. The magic was an insistent throb, the sun barely up, the shadows laced with frost. She hoped Nat *had* understood she'd meant for him to come to the restaurant that morning. She'd already been desperate to find out what he knew, to find out whether he had any information that might lead her to Pa. With Padley gone too—and *he'd* only been gone for a few hours—it felt more urgent than ever to speak to Nat. If he knew anything at all, she needed that information *now.*

It might already be too late, of course. But she couldn't

think like that. Not about Padley—not about Pa, either, although he'd been gone for ever so long.

Giddon definitely wasn't back. The building pulsed with emptiness as she dressed and went downstairs. On a normal morning, there would already have been something delicious-smelling puttering away on the stove or turning golden in the oven, but now there was only the ashy tinge of last night's fire. Yesterday's cozy lunch felt like a distant dream.

Thinking about it made Ista's stomach gurgle demandingly. *Empty belly, empty mind,* Pa always said, and like him, she couldn't think when she was hungry. She rummaged around and found some leftover shortcakes. They weren't as good cold, but they would do for a quick breakfast. She was halfway through her second one when there was a loud knock at the restaurant's front door.

"Hello?" Nat's voice. "Is anyone there?"

Ista went to let him in and found him bundled up against the cold, a satchel slung across his body and a copy of the *Daily Conch* tucked under one arm.

Nat saw her and sagged with relief. "Phew, you *are* here. I wasn't sure I had the right end of the stick." He peered past her, into the darkened restaurant. "Do you work here? I, um, I still don't know your name."

"Yes, I work here." Ista was surprised by how glad she was to see his nosy face. "I live here, too," she told him. "I'm Ista. Ista Flit."

"Ista." Nat tested it out, stretching the *S* sound. "You know the victim who lived here, then? Padley?"

Ista's throat grew tight. "How'd you hear about Padley?"

"Oh, Mum's got contacts everywhere, and strangers leave information for her at the *Conch* all the time too. She's always one of the first to find out when a grilk comes." Pride threaded through Nat's voice. "Here." He passed her the newspaper. "Hot off the press. You're practically the first to read it."

TWO TAKEN IN ONE NIGHT!

Only six days after the previous attack, the grilks struck again last night. Padley Mattheson, co-owner of the Fabulous Fletwin restaurant, was taken at sundown from an alley in the artists' quarter. The other victim, who cannot yet be named, was taken from the top of Boardstar Street between tenth bell and eleventh bell.

More on this story in the late edition.

Padley. In the paper. Ista's heart clenched. Seeing it in print made the fact that he was gone more real somehow. Could the second victim be Giddon? Her errands had never taken her to Boardstar Street. She wasn't even sure exactly where it was.

"I'm so sorry," Nat said. He left a pause, just long enough for her to reply if she wanted to, then went on. "You've changed your mind, then? About helping."

"Depends." Ista wanted to find out everything he knew about the grilks, that was for sure. "What is it you want me to do?"

"I don't exactly know yet." Nat shrugged. "Like I said before, loose threads are all we have. We've found out everything we can about anyone who's gone missing since the grilks were first sighted, but there isn't a single thing that links them. Not age, or who they know, or where they live or go to work or school, or even how much magic they have."

"Well, Padley doesn't have much magic," said Ista. "He moves little metal things, like teaspoons and thimbles, but he can't move them far, and he mostly does it by accident, to be honest."

Nat took off one glove and pulled out his notebook, which had recovered from its encounter with the lake, although the pages looked stiff and crinkly. He jotted down what she'd told him. "We can't prove the missing people were *all* taken by grilks, of course. There weren't always witnesses, and Mum says people sometimes have their own reasons for vanishing—but over sixty people have vanished since the grilks were first sighted."

Over sixty. Ista was quiet as that sank in. She hadn't

realized—hadn't let herself realize, perhaps—that it was quite so many. "But why is your mum so sure that someone *is* controlling the . . . the creatures?" If there were no connections between the victims, surely the grilks were just preying on people at random. "You said she gets 'hunches.' Is that her Tide-blessing?"

"Yes." Nat looked impressed. "She says the magic gives her a nose for a story."

Better a nose for a story than a nose for trouble, Ista thought. "And these hunches never lead her off on a wild goose chase?"

"Never." There wasn't a drop of doubt in his voice.

Ista wondered about that. Magic was as tricksterish as a marsh-spinner sometimes. Priya Shah hadn't seemed like a wild-goose-chase type of person—she'd seemed, in fact, like the kind of person who saw straight through to the truth of everything—but her nose couldn't be *that* accurate. After all, she and Nat had no idea who was doing this supposed "controlling."

"This story might be the hardest one she's ever had to break," Nat said, as if he'd read her thoughts. "Mum says all we can do is keep asking questions, but people are so scared of the grilks that the witnesses won't always talk to her. But with *your* blessing, you could sneak into all kinds of places—follow people, listen to their conversations, maybe even talk to them, if you can do it as someone they trust."

"All right," Ista said.

A smile pulled up one corner of Nat's mouth. "All right, as in you'll help?"

"Yes." She owed it to Padley—and to Pa. And though it did sound a bit risky, it was no riskier than her "errands," and for a far better cause. "Just don't ask me to borrow anyone else's blessing again. The magic didn't like that." Even at full moon and when her life had depended on it.

"Deal." Nat reached to take the newspaper from her.

"Wait." Ista was scanning the article again. "*Six* days after the last attack? What about the grilk that attacked *us*? That was only two nights ago. Didn't you tell your mum about it?"

Nat's expression clouded. "Yes, but I had a terrible time getting back into the Moon Tower. The man on the front gate was a proper jobsworth. He said my name had been checked off the guest list already, and I don't think he even believed me about the grilk. By the time I found Mum, there was no sign of anything having happened in that courtyard. And we don't know who that grilk was meant to attack before you and I interfered, so she said we should keep it all to ourselves. Between just me and her, I mean," he added when Ista frowned. "I haven't said a word to her about you. Don't worry."

Ista was grateful for that. Still, her frown squeezed tighter. "But why did your mum want to keep it a secret?"

"She's scared," Nat said simply. "Ista, we escaped, but

whoever's controlling those creatures might not know that. If they find out, they might come after us again."

Ista remembered the figure in the Moon-Tower window, the feeling of being watched. She stifled a shudder.

"Who's the other victim from last night?" she asked, glancing down at the newspaper. "Why can't they be named?"

A shadow flitted across Nat's face. "Because she's so young. The family has to give permission first. They own the pickle shop round the back of the market." He perused his notebook as he went on. "Mallard's Pickles, it's called. It's run by Patrice Mallard—although everyone calls her Granny Mallard. Her daughter and son-in-law live with her, but they're away visiting relatives at the moment, apparently. Patrice's granddaughters, Ruby and Saffron, known as Saf, stayed behind with her. It's Saf, the younger one, who was taken last night." He looked up at Ista. "What?"

"I . . . I met them—Saf and Ruby." Ista could barely take in what she was hearing. "At the Moon Tower. I helped them with a cart. Saf has a strength blessing, I think. She wanted to use it, but Ruby wouldn't let her."

The day might have been chilly, but Ista's brain was warming up, and with that warmth an awful suspicion surfaced. Pieces of the conversation between Alexo and the stranger swirled like fallen leaves in the wind, refusing to let her catch hold of them. *You know what to do. . . . Not one haul but two . . .*

Two hauls—and two people missing.

"Nat," she said. "I heard something. Last night. It might be important."

"Really? Great. You can tell me on the way." Nat took the newspaper back, folding it so it fitted into his satchel. "To the pickle shop," he added when Ista looked at him blankly. "Mum's going there now to speak to the family, and she said I should come too and see if I spot anyone suspicious lurking nearby. You know how it is—grown-ups are careful around other grown-ups, but they don't always pay much attention to people our age."

Ista was torn about leaving before Giddon came home, but as there was no knowing when he'd return, she scrawled him a note saying she'd be back soon, and within a minute she and Nat were walking down the road. The sun strained higher, watery light spilling over the rooftops. The entrance to Pinch Alley stood out against the clean morning like an oily fingerprint on a newly washed sheet.

"That's where they got Padley," she said, not wanting to look but unable to stop herself.

Nat gestured with his notebook. "Let's cut down it. Check for clues."

But there was nothing to see. Just grime and dank walls and the grate to the sewer.

"What do you think happens?" Ista asked softly. "When the grilks . . . when they get you?"

"Well, that's just it, isn't it? No one knows. They just get you and *grilk* you and you never come back. There has to be more to it, doesn't there?"

Did there? Ista didn't even let herself think about it most of the time.

"Now, what did you want to tell me?" Nat asked as they walked on again.

"Put your notebook away first." As long as her suspicion was only a suspicion, she wasn't letting Nat make a record of anything to do with Alexo or her errands. "I don't just work at the Fletwin. I work for someone else too. Have . . . have you heard of the Shrieking Eel?"

"Of course." Nat's mouth twitched in puzzlement. "You work for Alexo Rokis?"

"He has something of mine. I'm earning it back." Ista couldn't bear to explain about Pa. Her skin already felt too thin that morning.

"What's he like?" Nat looked as if he was itching to reach for his notebook. "Are the rumors about him true?"

"Probably," Ista said. *Which particular rumors do you mean?* she wanted to ask. She'd heard everything and anything said about Alexo. That he tended the Shrieking Eel's upstairs bar all night on Tuesdays, that he was a thief and a gambler and a monstrous cheat at cards. That he sent anonymous food parcels to families who were struggling. That he was old, that he was young, that he was a ghost, that he was an angel. That he offered a free bed and hot dinner to any weary traveler who found their way to Nimble Lane.

"Last night . . ." She made herself go on, though telling it made her heart thump as if she was living it all over again. "When I found out Padley was taken, I thought Alexo might be able to help, and . . ."

Once she'd started, the words pulled themselves from her in one long thread. Nat didn't interrupt, although his eyes went wide when she got to the part about the cavern and the eel, and she could see his thoughts whirring every time she glanced over.

"Tide's teeth!" he exclaimed when she'd finished. "And you have no idea who the other person was?"

"No, but I'd recognize their voice if I heard it again." Ista was sure of that. "Whatever they'd done, they were pleased they'd managed to do it twice. And they obviously knew about Padley being taken, because they'd spoken to Giddon—he must have gone to the Shrieking Eel for help, like I did, but then . . ."

But then Alexo had spelled him to sleep. She still didn't understand why.

"Alexo has to be involved." Excitement sparked in Nat's eyes. "I'm surprised Mum didn't think of it. Alexo Rokis could probably find a way to lure a grilk to wherever he wanted it."

"I wouldn't be surprised," Ista said.

She'd wanted to believe some of the good rumors

about Alexo. Wanted, despite everything, to believe that he was slippery but not entirely bad. A tiny part of her still did—and, after all, a snatch of overheard conversation didn't prove anything conclusively.

"You must've also heard that Alexo almost never leaves the Shrieking Eel for long, though," she said, because she could sense Nat's certainty snowballing. "His power fades when he's away from Nimble Lane—it hurts him, I think. So I'm not sure he *could* lure the grilks all around the city. Besides, why would he bother?"

Nat shrugged. "Maybe someone offered him something in exchange for his help. He isn't exactly known for his morals."

A deal. Ista had to admit that sounded like Alexo. "But why would anyone want to hurt Saf or Padley?"

"Maybe they weren't the targets, and the grilk got them by mistake. Maybe they just walked down the wrong alley at the wrong moment."

"But that doesn't explain why anyone would go to so much trouble with the monsters in the first place," she said.

"It might not be much trouble for *them,* though, if Alexo's doing the dirty work. It's the perfect crime, in a way. No bodies. No evidence." Nat had picked up his pace. There was a gleeful hunger in his eyes, as if he'd been starved for a good theory and was relishing sinking his teeth into this one.

"This isn't a game, you know." A surge of anger snuck up on Ista. "People are missing. Real people." *Not just stories for your mum to write about in the paper,* she would have added, but her throat clogged, and she couldn't speak anymore.

"I know that." Nat turned back. "I know it's not a game, believe me." He sliced the last words at her.

Of course he knew, Ista thought with a rush of guilt. He'd been right there with her in the mist at the Moon Tower. He knew exactly how real this all was.

"Sorry," she said.

"No need," Nat replied, clearly wanting to breeze past it. "The pickle shop's just round the corner. Follow me, and keep your eyes peeled."

He beetled off, his satchel bouncing against his hip.

Ista stayed put, needing a moment to collect herself. It was almost High Tide. Magic crackled over her, hot and cold.

A peculiar prickle crept up the back of her neck.

She turned. A shadow twitched in the alley opposite, a cloaked figure whisking away in the direction of Bell Street.

There was nothing sinister about a cloak. Plenty of people found them more practical than coats. But the certainty that this person had been watching her remained like a cold hand on Ista's shoulder as she hurried after Nat.

11

A FINE PICKLE

Ista had never visited Mallard's Pickles before. The shop was a skinny, chalk-blue building that teetered between a cheesemonger's and a chocolatier's as if in serious danger of toppling over without their support. *MALLARD'S—We Pickle Anything,* declared a large duck painted on the left of the main display window. *Just kidding,* said a smaller painted duck on the right. *Some things we ferment.*

The jokiness seemed eerie this morning. Mallard's was locked up like a fortress, the awning reeled in and a CLOSED sign on the door.

"Psst." Nat beckoned from a side gate a couple of doors down. "Round the back. Come on. Where've you been?"

Ista opened her mouth to explain about the person in the cloak, but before she could, he beetled off again, leaving her no choice but to straggle along behind him.

There was a standoff in progress at the back of the pickle shop. Outside, packed between the courtyard wall and a large, well-tended greenhouse, stood a knot of reporters, notepads and cameras poised. Framed in the lopsided doorway, glowering at them with a ferocity that would have made most unwanted visitors turn and scarper as fast as their legs would carry them, was Ruby.

"I've told you," she was saying, extremely slowly and extremely loudly, "my gran's said all she has to say to Priya Shah, and we're not talking to any of the rest of you leeches."

"Shut the door, Ruby, my duckling," someone called from inside.

"No, Gran." Ruby was firm. "I'm explaining to them how pointless it is them hanging around." She leveled an even more powerful glare at the huddle. "Shall I spell it out for you? *P-O-I-N...*"

"Mum's already been and gone, then," Nat murmured. "Ruby's grandma can't have had much to tell her."

"I suppose not." Ista studied the crowd. Nothing suspicious, just one large seagull watching curiously from the roof as the reporters jostled for space.

"Tell us about your sister, Ruby," one of them, a weaselly man with a thin black mustache, called. "Tell us about Saf. What was she like?"

Ruby stared at him the same way someone might stare at something sticky they'd found on the bottom of their shoe. "There's no *was*. Saf *is* . . . Look, you don't know anything. You weren't even there." Her voice cracked down the middle. "You . . ."

Camera shutters whirred like insect wings.

"You . . ." Ruby tried again, but her bravado had disintegrated. She stepped back and was almost immediately replaced by a deeply wrinkled woman in a brightly patterned head wrap, who scowled and slammed the door so hard the windows rattled.

"That's more like it." The weasel grinned to himself in a way that made Ista want to stick a knife in something. "Right," he said to his photographer. "Let's swing by the Fletwin and see what we can dig up there."

Soon the courtyard emptied. Nat was right about grown-ups not paying attention. Not one of the reporters had given him or Ista so much as a glance.

"Well, well," he said as soon as it was safe to talk. "That was extremely interesting. Now, are you ready?"

"Ready for what?" Ista hadn't found it interesting. She'd found it sad. Ruby had been terrified the grilks would get Saf, and now they had.

"To talk to Ruby, of course. Didn't you hear what she said?"

Ista frowned. "Which bit in particular?"

Nat's expression made it plain he knew she didn't have a clue what he was getting at. "She said, '*You* weren't even there.' She was obviously talking about when Saf was taken—which means Ruby *was* there. We need to talk to her." He dug out his notebook and a pencil, then peeled off one glove so he could write. "She and Saf must have snuck out somewhere. The newspaper article said Saf was taken between tenth bell and eleventh bell. That's awfully late to go for a walk."

Ista thought about that for a moment. "You're right." Ruby might have seen or heard something crucial that would lead to the truth about what had happened to Pa and Padley. "I don't suppose she'll talk to us, though," she added.

"No, she most likely won't," Nat agreed, jotting something down. "But I bet she'll talk to my mum again." He looked up at her, his eyes full of meaning. "How high's the magic, would you say?"

More than high enough was the answer. Only a minute or two past High Tide would have been Ista's guess. The magic had settled from its full-moon peak two nights ago and was bubbling at a perfect glittery simmer. She should have been able to use her Tide-blessing as easily as plucking a daisy from a lawn.

However, she wasn't used to having Nat Shah watching her while she borrowed someone. They were squashed into a gap between the greenhouse and a rainwater barrel, and the intensity of his sharp-eyed stare was making her extremely self-conscious.

"Give me some space, can't you?" she grumbled. "It isn't easy using a blessing with someone gawping at you."

"Sorry." Nat smiled a sad smile that made something twist in Ista's chest. She thought again of how the bullies at the Moon Tower had called him *dropless*. He shuffled away, turning his back for good measure.

"Thank you," Ista said. She wanted to add that it didn't matter a bean to her whether he was Tide-touched or not, but she sensed that would only embarrass him more. "You can look now," she added a few seconds later, adjusting the drawstring on her trousers. Her clothes felt snug across Priya's shoulders and hips, but hopefully no one else would notice. "What do you think? Is my coat all right?"

"A bit scruffy" was Nat's verdict. "But Mum is scruffy sometimes, and her coat is black too."

It would have to do. They approached the door again. With the crowd dispersed, Ista noticed a neat mailbox with an *M* painted on it, and a metal bootjack in the shape of a duck. This must be the Mallard family's main route in and out of their home—which made sense, seeing as the shop occupied the front of the building.

"What do I say?" Ista whispered. Normally when she borrowed someone, she went out of her way to speak as little as possible.

"Just get her talking to start with," Nat whispered back. "Then we can ease into it."

For Pa, Ista told herself.

A pouch of herbs was tied to the door knocker—a charm to ward off marsh-spinners. She'd insisted on Pa putting a charm like that over her bed when she was small, after he'd read her a story about the tiny, glowing spiderlike creatures that supposedly snuck in at night to sour the milk, give children bad dreams, and get up to all sorts of other small mischiefs. Granny Mallard must be superstitious.

The charm rustled as Ista knocked.

"Go away." Ruby's voice came through the wood at waist height, as if she was curled up against the other side of the door.

Ista cleared her throat. "It's Priya Shah here, Ruby."

She'd barely finished the sentence before there was a scuffle of shoes and limbs, and the door flew partway open, catching on its chain. Ruby's face appeared in the gap.

"Have you found something already?" Hope and dread were mixed in her eyes, like sunlight through foggy river-glass.

"Not exactly," Ista said. "We wanted—"

"Who's we?" Ruby's gaze flicked to Nat.

"Oh yes!" Ista turned. "This is my son, Nat." She gave his head a clumsy pat.

"Hello," said Nat. "I'm so sorry about Saf."

"Thank you." Ruby drew her arms round herself as if she needed a hug. "*Is* there news?" She directed the question to Nat. Ista snuck a glance at him, wondering if Ruby might trust a child more than a prying grown-up. He looked back at Ista expectantly.

Just get Ruby talking, Ista reminded herself. She made herself stand straighter, trying to channel Priya Shah's trustworthiness and confidence. "Actually, I've got a few more questions."

It was the wrong thing to say. The hope in Ruby's eyes was snuffed out, replaced by a glint of suspicion. "Like what?"

Ista could feel the conversation slipping away from her. "Well, um . . . were you there? When Saf got taken."

Ruby gave an exasperated sigh. "Yes, I *just* told you that, a minute ago. . . ." She trailed off, her suspicious expression solidifying into the same distrustful glare she'd given the gaggle of journalists. "Look, come back if you find something. I'm done answering questions for now." She stepped back, closing the door with another window-rattling bang.

"Tide's teeth!" Nat marched away, clutching at his hair, then spun back to face Ista. "What was *that*?"

"What was what?"

"You think Mum wouldn't have asked Ruby that already? You completely gave the game away. She knows something's up."

"But you said . . . never mind." Ista changed back into herself, quickly rearranging her clothes. "I'm sorry, all right? I did my best. I'm not a journalist, am I?"

Nat didn't deign to answer. Ista couldn't decide if she was more annoyed with him for not preparing her better, or with herself for doing such a terrible job.

"What now?" she asked as they made their way back to the street.

Nat's tone was spiky. "Well, I don't know about you, but I've got to go to school, so—" He jolted to a stop, then tugged Ista under the awning of the stationery shop opposite. She threw him a questioning look, and he put his finger to his lips, tilting his head toward a man who strode past them.

There was something oddly familiar about the stranger's face, though Ista thought he was the kind of person she would have remembered if she'd seen him before. You could almost smell the money coming off him. It was in every line of intricate stitching on his coat, and in the sparkling silver buckles of his freshly polished shoes. A sleek-as-an-otter man, a short wave of steely hair smoothed back from his moon-pale face, his steps light but purposeful, his profile stern.

The proud jut of his chin jogged something in Ista's memory. She *had* seen the man before, not in person, but on one of his election posters. BRINTAN BROOK FOR A PROSPEROUS SHELWICH! What on earth was he doing here?

Nat must have wondered the same thing. He turned with deliberate casualness toward the stationer's window in a way that left no doubt that he meant for Ista to do the same.

They both stared hard into the glass, pretending to admire a display of Tide-charts but actually watching Brintan Brook's reflection as he walked up to Mallard's Pickles. He tried the door despite the CLOSED sign, found that it was locked, and rapped on it hard.

Granny Mallard opened it.

"Mr. Brook." Her voice was clipped with displeasure. "This isn't a good time to talk business."

"I'd have thought it the perfect time, given last night's sad events." Brintan Brook didn't sound sad. He placed each word like a tile on a gaming board, methodical and certain, as if he'd already played out every possible move in his mind.

Granny Mallard seemed to deflate, the fire in her eyes dimming. She hadn't looked especially old before, despite her wrinkles, but she looked very old and very tired as she stepped back and gestured for him to follow her indoors.

"Nat." Ista thrummed with adrenaline. "He's a loose thread." She kept her voice low, aware that Brook might leave the shop again at any second. "Your mum said we should look out for anyone suspicious loitering around. Well, *this* feels suspicious. What he just said . . . it almost seems like Saf's vanishing is *good* for him somehow."

Nat tilted his head, considering. "If Brook wants something done, he doesn't need grilks to help him do it. He's the richest man in Shelwich."

Ista's gaze flew to the notebook and pencil in his hands. "Then why did you just write down their conversation?"

"Because I'm nosy. Didn't you hear my lovely schoolmates the other evening? Besides, it never hurts to keep tabs on what someone like Brook is—" Nat broke off, a smile tugging at his mouth.

Ista narrowed her eyes. "What?"

"You're making up theories." He pointed his pencil at her. "You believe me. That someone's behind this."

"Well, suppose someone *is*—just suppose, mind." Ista pointed a finger back at him. "It seems to me that Brintan Brook makes a better suspect than Alexo. I'm going in after him."

Mallard's Pickles was a shop, after all, and if Brintan Brook could ignore the CLOSED sign, so could a potential customer. Ista changed as she walked, borrowing a short man with an extravagant mustache who she often saw on her market trips with Padley. Granny Mallard hadn't locked the door behind her. The handle turned easily.

But the door swung inward to reveal Ruby Mallard's scalding glare.

"I'm sorry, but we're closed today."

"I just . . ." Ista groped for an excuse to enter. She was sure she could hear voices in the room beyond the shop.

"You'll have to come back later." Ruby held firm. Then, for the second time that morning, she slammed a door in Ista's face.

"Forget Brook," said Nat as Ista returned to him dejectedly. "The person we really need to talk to is your friend Giddon. We should ask him what happened at the Shrieking Eel last night." A nearby clocktower gave the single chime that signaled quarter to the hour. He sighed. "I've got to go, or I'll be late for school. I get out just after third bell, though. I need to check in with Mum at the *Conch* straight afterward, but let's meet at quarter to fourth bell, and we can plan what to do next. I mean, if you want to."

"Yes, that's good," replied Ista. "Shall we meet at Shipwrights' Square?" That was as central as anywhere.

"Great." He put his notebook and pencil away, hitching his satchel up on his shoulder.

"Nat," Ista said as he turned to go. "Don't tell your mum the stuff I said about Alexo. Not yet." She wanted far more solid evidence before they brought Alexo into it. He really wouldn't take kindly to reporters snooping around Nimble Lane.

"All right," he said, although his frown told her he didn't like it. "Be careful, though, won't you?"

She lifted her chin. "I can look after myself."

"I didn't say you couldn't." Nat drew in a deep breath. "All I meant was . . . just go to the *Conch* if you do run into any trouble, okay?"

Ista rolled her eyes. "I promise."

But as she watched him hurry away down the road, she found that she felt a little lighter. For so long she'd been trying to figure things out on her own. Now, even though the mystery had become a truly terrible tangle, at least they had some obvious threads to pull. And it was nice to have someone to share it with—even if Nat was as bossy as a beagle.

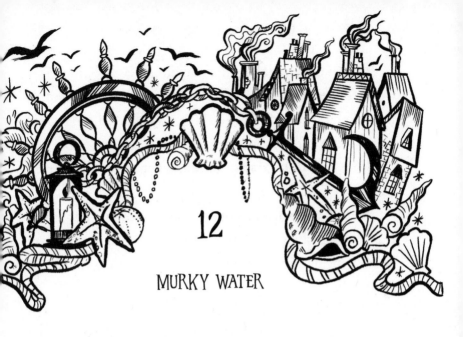

12

MURKY WATER

It was strange how the world could turn upside down for you but keep spinning on as normal for everyone else. The awning of the tea shop Padley liked on Finfroth Street was still the same shade of purple. The market traders still barked like seals. It was the smells that hit Ista the hardest—the yeasty warmth from the bakeries, the briny tang of the harbor. She urgently wanted to see Giddon and didn't want to see him at all, as if the two of them being in the same room together would only make Padley's absence stand out more.

But the Fletwin's kitchen was as empty as she'd left it. Ista waited and paced and made a sandwich and waited and paced some more. The Tide ebbed away until the magic was barely a whisper, lapping at the edge of her senses.

Still no Giddon. She ate an apple. Paced. Waited. Her worry intensified, coiling like a reed-snake in her gut. It was almost second bell. Half the day had dripped away. Surely he should've been home by now.

What if he didn't come at all, and she'd lost him as well as Padley?

No, that was silly, she told herself, squashing her panic. But she was so used to the clockwork precision of Alexo's plans that just waiting and not *doing* anything made her wriggly with impatience.

She should go back to Nimble Lane! The idea went straight to her feet, catapulting her out into the cold again. Giddon must still be at the inn—must have been there when she went last night, sleeping in some tucked-away corner—and though she really didn't want to see Alexo, she wanted answers more.

But the Low Tide magic could be as capricious as a cat, and today it didn't want to know her. She reached the honeycomb of streets where the entrance to the lane was usually found, but no amount of walking and pausing and sniffing would summon the telltale smell of smoke and brine. *Come on.* Ista planted her feet and scrunched up her eyes. *Where are you?*

Nothing. It was useless. Wicka Honeyball's faded face looked down on her from a poster on a noticeboard. Ista felt a flicker of recognition, as if she'd seen the woman before. Tide's teeth, her brain was full of knots today.

If only she knew how a sleep spell worked. Would Giddon even have woken up yet? Perhaps he was groggy and disorientated. Perhaps he'd begun walking home and then fallen unconscious on the way—in which case she might not find him for hours.

And then it came to her. There *was* one place she could try now. If someone had found him and sent for the healers, Ista knew exactly where he might be.

Shelwich Hospital was way out beyond the university and the clocktower known as West Tower, close to the city's western edge, and was a big, practical-looking building, with a smooth stone facade and a spotless lobby. A quick query at the reception desk revealed that no one under Giddon's name had been officially admitted. Neither was he in the short queue of new arrivals waiting to be assessed.

Which meant there was only one ward to check. The ward Ista had visited over and over, looking for Pa.

She hurried to the bank of elevators and, when one arrived, pressed the button for the lowest basement level. The car descended with a polite shush, as if asking her to create as little disturbance as possible. Not that the patients she was coming to see would notice if she arrived accompanied by a full orchestra.

Even by Shelwich standards, *strange* was a consider-able understatement for the cavernous space that greeted her when the elevator doors opened. Tide-lanterns dotted the bare rock walls, illuminating rows of beds arranged in a circle round a mossy-edged pool. On each bed lay a per-son, eyes closed, hands peacefully at their sides, a crystal-line sheen coating their skin.

None of the patients so much as stirred. Not one twitch. Not one breath.

Stone Sleepers, people called them.

A young man had pulled up a chair and was reading softly to one of them, although it was generally accepted that these particular patients were oblivious to every-thing. They were unmoving and rigid as statues, their faces slack and calm as the neatly dressed healers moved between them, making notes on charts.

Ista had found the ward eerie when she'd first vis-ited, but she'd grown to like the stillness of it. She wound her way among the beds, searching each face carefully, though she knew from experience that any new admis-sions would be on the beds nearest the pool.

No Giddon. No Pa, either. Her heart sank.

She stood for a moment, gazing into the water. It was fresh water, not river water, said to come from a mineral spring in the hills, although no one had located the source. It had a rich purple color that reminded Ista of blackberry tea, and a delicious smell rose from it—sweet and spicy at once, like stewed fruit and cinnamon. Lily water, people called it, because neither its color nor its scent was its own. Pointy-tipped lilies floated serenely on the surface, their pads larger than the serving trays at the Fletwin. The flowers were white, but the lilies' roots were deep purple, and it was from them that the color and fragrance seeped into the pool. Ista wondered, not for the first time, how the lilies managed to thrive down here, without any sunlight—although that was far from the most extraordinary thing about them or the pond.

When the Tide was high, the color wasn't all that seeped from the plants to the water. Magic passed through too.

It was the lily water that kept the Stone Sleepers sleeping, that stopped their bodies from needing to do anything else while they healed. It couldn't regrow a limb or make someone walk again, but it sped up the recovery process, saving a good deal of time and pain, and—in the gravest cases—giving the body a chance to fight.

The plants were as rare as they were powerful, impossible to cultivate anywhere they didn't grow naturally. Only three other cities had pools like this, although the water was bottled and delivered up and down the country. This was probably for the best, for, despite its healing properties, lily water was incredibly dangerous. A splash on your skin would leave you unconscious for days, and if so much as a drop of it went in your mouth, the only way to reverse the effects was with the antidote.

That was where the lilies came in again. Their seeds, crushed into a powder, woke the Stone Sleepers from their slumber. As Ista turned, one of the healers came past, carrying a sealed glass jar of antidote toward the patient to whom the young man had been reading.

The crushed seeds looked like pale blue sand. In sharp contrast to the delicious sweetness of the lily water, they had a bitter, scorched smell. It was incredibly pungent, crawling into Ista's nostrils and coating the back of her throat, even though the jar was still closed. She'd heard people claim that wafting just a pinch under a Stone Sleeper's nose would wake them, although onlookers were forbidden during such a private moment, so she'd never seen the process in action.

"Excuse me." Another healer signaled for her attention. "I'm afraid we have to ask you to leave. It's family only when we're bringing someone round."

Ista nodded to show she understood, but something of Nat's nosiness must have rubbed off on her. Her curiosity spiked, and she couldn't resist turning to peek back at the preparations as she hurried to the elevator.

Unfortunately, this peeking—combined with the fact that she hadn't considered anyone might be coming the other way—meant she bumped straight into a tall woman who was stepping out of it.

"Sorry!" Ista leapt back. The woman's coat was cut

from the sort of fine-woven dove-gray fabric you could get dirty simply by looking at it wrong.

"No, no. That's quite all right, child," said Betrika Hettle.

Ista had never been so close to the governor before. She tried to apologize again, but her mouth just goldfished uselessly.

"Truly." Sincerity warmed Governor Hettle's smile. Ista had never heard her speak before either. She had what Pa would have called a "good" voice: calm and clear, her accent a softened version of what people called the Shelwich dip. "It's lovely to see another visitor here. We're so often the only ones."

Ista had been so focused on the governor that only now did she notice the two people with her. One was a bearded man who looked older than Pa but younger than Giddon. The other was the woman who'd shown Nat and Ista to the courtyard at the Moon Tower. She gave Ista a piercing look, as if she knew they'd met previously but couldn't place her.

Which was impossible, Ista reminded herself, because she had been borrowing Jarmak. *No*—they had first met at the gate when Ista was "delivering" linens. A rush of guilt quickened her pulse. What if the woman somehow connected her to the stolen telescope?

"We come to read to the patients sometimes," Governor

Hettle went on. "It was a tradition of my grandfather's, you see. He said that just because no one remembered their Stone Sleep once they woke, it didn't mean people weren't aware of what was happening while they were under. But today we're here for one of my advisors, who's being brought round after six weeks' sleeping."

"We're ready to begin, Governor," called a healer.

"Of course." The governor acknowledged them with a small bow. "I mustn't delay. It was lovely to meet you, child," she told Ista.

One more smile and she swept away, her companions falling into line behind her.

13

A PAPER TRAIL

You'd think, Ista mused as she trudged back the way she'd come, *that the founders of Shelwich might have set the city's center a little closer to the magical lily pond.* Her feet were already complaining, and she really needed to try to find Nimble Lane one more time before she met Nat, just in case Giddon was still there. She had a better chance, at least, of finding the lane now. The Tide was pouring back into the afternoon, its magic a determined hum vibrating up and down her bones.

But as she wove through the streets, who should be coming toward her but Giddon himself.

"Where have you been?" Ista cried, relief bursting over her so hard it almost felt like fury.

"Well, for the past hour I've been looking for you, young'un," Giddon said. "You weren't at the Fletwin when

I got home. Ista, I'm sorry I didn't come back last night. I didn't mean to worry you. I've been at the . . ." The aftereffects of the sleep spell must not have fully dissipated; he trailed off, his eyes glazing over.

"Giddon?" Ista prompted gently. "Are you all right? Is there any news? Where did you go?"

He shook himself. "Oh yes. I mean, no. No news. That is, I went to get help, but . . ." It happened again, as if he were peering through a layer of mist. He gave another shake, his gaze turning serious. "Ista, the important thing—the really important thing—is that we *will* be all right, you and me."

Without Padley, he didn't add, but Ista felt the unspoken words like little stabs between her ribs.

"But *you* must be famished," Giddon went on, changing the subject. "Shall we see what we can rustle up for lunch?"

Ista was ravenous, actually, despite the sandwich she'd had earlier. Wolfishly so, in the way you can only be when you've been carrying an enormous ball of stress in your stomach and then it vanishes and leaves you empty. But the clocktower on the corner chimed for quarter to the hour, and she didn't want to keep Nat waiting.

"I can't," she said. "I've promised I'll be somewhere."

"Oh! Are you meeting a friend?" Surprise and pleasure brightened Giddon's face. He and Padley had been trying to encourage her to spend time with people her own age.

A *friend*. Ista turned the word over in her mind. She'd only met Nat Shah two nights earlier, but friendship wasn't something that could be measured out in days and weeks. Nat was a monstrous know-it-all and took himself far too seriously, but he was clever and kind, and he'd worried about her staying safe while they were apart that morning.

"Yes," she said. "I s'pose I am."

Nat was already waiting when Ista arrived in Shipwrights' Square. She spotted him opposite old Betrik Hettle's statue, by the clocktower known as Pond Tower. This was a name Ista found a little confusing, because there was no pond nearby, although a stone toad and a stone newt stood guard at the tower's base. She liked the toad particularly. It had kept its warts despite decades of salt air and fierce weather, and there was a long crack down its spine where a stripe of lichen grew.

Nat sat astride the newt, looking as if he meant to ride it off toward the river. He clambered down when he saw her, and they both spoke at once, their voices overlapping.

"You'll never guess who—" Ista began.

"I've got something very important to show—" Nat held up his hands. "Sorry. You first."

"Well . . . ," Ista started, but immediately trailed off with a shiver. "Nat." She dropped her voice to a whisper. "I think someone's watching us."

Think wasn't the right word. She *felt* it, just as she had early that morning near the pickle shop. A deep, cold certainty that settled in her stomach like a slab of ice.

Nat glanced surreptitiously around. "I don't see anyone."

Ista didn't either, but the feeling had trapped her in its jaws, and she couldn't wriggle free. "Still. Let's go somewhere less . . . open. Then we can decide properly what to do next."

"Good idea," said Nat. "What about the library?"

This was an excellent plan. The library was free and open to all. It was also only a few streets away.

Ista used the short walk to recount her failed attempt to find Nimble Lane, her unsettling conversation with Giddon, and her unexpected meeting with the governor at the hospital.

"I thought she wasn't very popular," she said as they climbed the gentle ramp to the entrance, "but she seemed nice enough to me."

"Niceness isn't enough to make a good leader, though, is it?" said Nat. Ista suspected he was echoing something he'd heard from Priya. "If Betrika Hettle really wants to honor her grandpa, she should stop spending time reading to people who can't even hear her and start listening to the people who can vote for her. She's done nothing to even try to stop the grilks—not unless you count blathering on about how scary they are."

Ista felt almost sorry for Governor Hettle. She remembered what Padley had told her about old Betrik Hettle so cleverly catching Lightning Lucy. It couldn't be easy trying to live up to such an extraordinary legacy.

They bypassed the information desk and the queue for the clackety elevators, heading straight for the vast, dim labyrinth of bookstacks. It was two labyrinths, really, with a wide aisle of blue carpet running like a river between them. Down this they padded, breathing in the scent of ancient paper, while a gentle glow of Tide-lanterns and oil lamps lit the way.

Nat tilted his head toward the furthest end of the room, which was exactly where Ista had been thinking they should go. They walked past banks of tables where people huddled over their reading, past PRE-TIDE ARCHITECTURE and HERBAL LORE—HISTORY AND PRACTICE, to where the carpet narrowed and the stacks squeezed closer like trees in a thickening forest.

"Here," she whispered. "Your turn now. What did you want to show me?"

"Well." A quiver of excitement wobbled Nat's breath. "Governor Hettle's making *another* speech later this afternoon. Mum went early to get a good seat, so she'd already left the *Conch* before I got there, and I couldn't ask if she knew what business Brintan Brook could have wanted to talk to Granny Mallard about. But it was still lucky I stopped by. There was a message for me at reception." He rummaged in his satchel and pulled out a piece of paper, which he passed to Ista.

It was a very strange message indeed. Nothing but the words *Please help. I'm so thirsty* written in the middle of the page. Ista turned it over, peering at it in the lamplight. *For the attention of Nat Shah,* someone had scrawled on the reverse—which would have been the front when the paper was folded. There was something else too: a duck's head, stamped in green ink.

Ista squinted. "Is that the Mallard's Pickles duck?"

"Yes." Nat leaned back against the bookstacks. "No one saw who left it, but it must be from Ruby, mustn't it?"

"Must it?" She turned the paper over again. "Why?"

"Because she came to *me.* If it was a grown-up, they'd have wanted my mum."

That, Ista had to admit, was an extremely clever deduction. "Ah," she said, as if she'd only been a step or two from it herself. "So, what does it mean?"

"No idea." Nat sounded genuinely flummoxed. "I was hoping you might know."

Ista was touched he had faith in her, especially as decoding secret messages seemed much more in his skill set than hers, but though she stared and stared at the paper, her mind remained as blank as the white space around the writing.

"I don't know either," she admitted, "but it'll come to us, I'm sure, if we give it time. Sometimes you have to let an idea come to you."

That was what Pa would have said. As well as playing

music, he wrote it too—Ista pictured him sitting at the piano, a pencil tucked behind his ear. He said he could sometimes feel that a piece was on its way and that it would come quicker if he gave it breathing space rather than crowding its arrival.

Nat clearly wasn't someone who believed in breathing space. He took the paper back from her, his gaze boring into it, as if he could will it into revealing its secrets.

"It's another loose thread—for now," Ista said. "Tell me what you *do* know. You and your mum, you're two of the smartest people I've met. You must've figured out something."

"That's just it." Nat pulled out his notebook, flicking through the pages but not really looking at them. "We've found out as much as we can. We've made all these lists and charts—every victim, every place they were taken from—and we still don't know anything. It's like I told you: there's nothing that links the victims. Lots of magic, no magic, old, young, rich, poor. It's everyone, the whole city. And the grilks were barely even *here* a year ago. It's as if they've come from nowhere, and now people are being taken practically every other night." He sank into a crouch. "Mum's Tide-blessing's never wrong—*never*—but this time . . ."

Ista mirrored him, leaning against the shelves. "Padley said they've come because the Tide's getting stronger. He said *his* mum believed the magic works in bigger cycles than we realize. Like, centuries bigger—millennia, even. She used to tell him stories about all kinds of magical creatures that she said existed once upon a time—"

She let out a gasp, flying to her feet.

"Ista?" Nat stood too.

"What if Padley's mum was right?" Ista said. "What if the grilks are *old* creatures? Really old creatures? Don't you see?" His perplexed silence said that he absolutely did not. "Think about it. We're in a whole building full of books. I'm sure I've seen a section on myths and legends here before."

"Yes, it's just over there." Nat pointed. "But—*oh.* Hey, wait for me!"

A quick search later, they deposited a small tower of books on one of the communal study tables. Some were tiny, some huge. One was so heavy that Ista had almost pulled the rope for the help bell, which would've brought one of the librarians hurrying over.

They set to work as fast as they could, Nat beginning with *Legends of Old Shelwich* and Ista with the equally promisingly titled *Mythical Monsters of the Hills and the Rivers.* But there was nothing more than promise—unless you wanted a recipe for a kelp-based love potion, which Ista most certainly did not, or instructions for sprinkling salt on the threshold to keep marsh-spinners out when you were throwing a party.

A musty smell rose from the pages. These were lonely

books, she thought. Perhaps people didn't need the old tales when so much magic was around day after day.

"I don't think whoever drew this had even listened to the stories properly," she said, holding up her book to show an illustration of a tall, winged man gazing longingly through a window. "Look at this. These marsh-spinners look just like people, but in all the stories I know they're meant to be tiny, insecty things, like—oh what's the name for those little glowing bugs that you see in the trees sometimes in the summer?" She and Pa used to go out at dusk to try to spot them, back in her old life, before sunset meant needing to get home and lock the doors.

"Fog-sprites. Those actually exist, though." Nat snorted softly, then frowned as he turned the page. "Let's hope all these monsters *aren't* coming back—or we'll have much scarier things than grilks to deal with."

There was nothing about the grilks themselves, or anything even vaguely similar, in either of the first two books. *The Compendium of Magical Creatures* was no better. Neither was *One Hundred Terrifying Tales for Children*.

Soon enough, only the almost-too-heavy-to-carry book remained. *The Complete Alphabetized Treasury of River-lore and Riverfolk* was its title. It was as fragile as it was large, the pages moth-wing thin and edged in gilt, the text inside teeny and cramped. At least the library provided tool trays at every table. Nat selected a magnifying glass and Ista took up a pair of silver tweezers so she could turn each leaf without any oil from her fingers damaging the paper.

It was more of what they'd already seen, not in the least bit useful—although there was an extraordinarily detailed etching of a huge freshwater cephalopod that could have swallowed the mechanical octopus at the *Conch* in one gulp.

"I'm sorry," Ista said, carefully going through all the *G*s again, in case she'd accidentally turned two pages at once and missed something crucial. "I'm the one who's taken us on a wild goose chase, and . . ." She trailed off, unease trickling through her. "Nat."

"I'm looking at it," he said.

An image of a creature filled the page. Time had faded the colors, but the lines remained distinct.

It was an eel.

An enormous eel, exactly like the one beneath the inn on Nimble Lane.

14

THIRSTY WORK

Ista felt as if a piece of her had been transported back to the cavern beneath the inn. She tried to laugh, but all that came out was a small choking sound.

"Is this what you saw in the underground pool at Alexo's?" asked Nat. "Well, at least we know what it is now. What does it say it's called? A gelkin?" He peered through the magnifying glass at the word under the drawing. "Or jelkin. Depends if it's a hard *G* like *goose* or a soft *G* like *giant*."

Ista considered it. "A hard *G*, I think—like you said it the first time. Read out what it says, then."

Nat cleared his throat. " 'The most ancient and powerful of all the magical creatures, gelkins roamed the waters from the marsh flats to the sea. They had razor-sharp teeth and were said to be deadly if cornered, with the power to mesmerize their enemies before they struck, although they were also rumored to grant wishes to sailors and fisherfolk who showed them kindness.' Look. That wavy line must be a river or the sea—oh, and that's a boat."

It was the large, three-masted type of boat that crossed the great oceans. The gelkin almost matched it in size.

A fingernail of dread scraped the back of Ista's neck. She turned to the next page, finding another picture of a gelkin, this one with a boat balanced precariously above the creature's sharp-toothed mouth.

Nat went completely still. "Ista."

Ista said nothing. She knew what had made him freeze. A previous reader had been less careful than her, and the accompanying text had been water-damaged into an indecipherable blur, but inside the gelkin's long throat was the unmistakable shape of a person, legs braced and arms reaching as if they were straining to climb back out.

"I think you might be in terrible danger," Nat said quietly. "If there's any chance, any chance at all that Alexo knows you snuck into the inn last night . . ."

"What?" Ista couldn't hide her smile. "He'll feed me to a gelkin?"

"He threatened you," Nat insisted.

"You mean what he said to the stranger?" *Keep an eye on her . . . you know what to do.* Her mind flitted back to the feeling of being watched she'd had that morning, and again, not so very long ago, in Shipwrights' Square. "Nat, come on," she said. "Alexo is a lot of things, but he isn't evil. He wouldn't hurt me." She felt a sudden tiny prickle of doubt about that and quickly smothered it with a laugh. "Seriously, you're worrying too much."

Nat's mouth flattened. "Well, forgive me, but the last time I didn't worry enough, my brother went missing." Then he pushed back his chair and strode off into the bookstacks.

"Nat?" Ista hurried after him.

He had his back to her; his shoulders trembled. He was either crying or trying very hard not to.

"Your brother?" she said gently.

"Yes." His voice was a perfect blank, as if he had painted over his feelings. "Ravi. It was last autumn, almost four moons ago. He was only seven. Two grilks took him. Our neighbor saw it. My mum . . . she'd already had her hunch and been asking questions by then. She thinks it's her fault, that it was a warning, to stop her digging around. It did the opposite, of course."

"I'm so sorry." Ista remembered the cloth mouse Nat had been carrying at the Moon Tower, the limp ruin of its body after the lake. No wonder he and his mum were so desperate for answers.

Nat turned to face her. "It's like you said: this isn't a game."

Ista felt wretched. She'd flung those words at him that morning thinking she was the only one who'd lost people she loved.

"My pa's missing too," she said, not to score points but because Nat looked so hopeless and she wanted him to know that she really did understand.

His jaw fell. "Your father?"

That was the trouble with sharing secrets. They often required you sharing more of yourself to explain them. Ista picked at her thumbnail, trying to decide where to begin. "Pa was living in Shelwich without me while he found work and saved up enough money for a place for us to live. But then a letter came saying he had disappeared. That's why I came here. To find him. My village . . . it's so different from here. So much *smaller.*"

She hardly ever let herself think about it, but memory after memory tumbled down on her now. The water meadows and the hawthorns and the wide-open sky. The trees Pa had helped her climb. The stream where he'd taught her to swim. How he'd pretended to be a frog, then a duck, then a dolphin, croaking and quacking and laughing as they'd splashed around in the shallows.

"I've been so, so . . . lost since I got here. Everything's strange. Even the Tide seems stronger. And without Pa, I don't know how I . . . Well, that's why I came to find you after I'd thought about what you said. In case there was any chance . . ."

"I'm sorry." Nat wiped his nose with his sleeve.

"You didn't know." Ista felt like a hedgehog that had pricked up its spikes and didn't quite know how to smooth them back down. A whole day of running around, and what had they achieved? Nothing but impossible riddles and useless water-stained books.

And, just like that, the answer dropped into her thoughts.

"Tide's teeth," she breathed. "It's *thirsty*."

Nat cocked an eyebrow. "I'm sorry?"

"Ruby's message. The paper." The certainty was electric. "It's *thirsty*. It needs . . ."

Understanding filled his eyes. "Water! Oh, you're brilliant. That's brilliant! Come on. There's a drinking fountain outside."

He darted out of the stacks and into the low-slung sunlight of late afternoon. Ista had to race to keep up with him. The drinking fountain was the kind dotted all over Shelwich, with a shallow stone trough to catch spills. Nat ran some water into it and set the paper on the surface.

A second layer of words bloomed over the first, like limecress across a pond.

I have something important to show you.
Come to the corner of Crook and Crinkle
at tenth bell. If you tell your mum,
the deal's off.

Bring your friend from this morning.
We'll need her.

"But what if it's a trap?" Nat asked for the third time.

"I don't know," Ista said, also for the third time. "Do *you* think it's a trap?"

They had taken shelter from the wind in the porch of a music shop that was closed for the afternoon.

Nat hunched in his coat. "No . . . I don't know."

Ista peered through the glass door at the instruments displayed. There was a particularly fine vespalin, which Pa would have loved, its body decorated with swirls of white, its delicate strings well oiled, ready to be plucked. "Why does Ruby want me, though? 'Bring your friend from this morning,' the note said. Do you think she knows what I can do?"

"She must do—somehow." Nat chewed his lip. "We have to go, don't we?"

"I think so." *Please help,* the unsecret part of the message read. If they didn't go, Ista knew that the *please* would haunt her. "The Tide won't be high at tenth bell, at least."

They were both studiously avoiding, however, the fact that it *would* be well after dark.

"What's on the corner of Crook Street and Crinkle Row, anyway?" Ista asked.

The top end of Crinkle Row was where the lampers, candlemakers, and jewelers worked. She loved the bustle of it, from the heat and hammering of the lantern forge to the neater labor of the silversmiths, and the pearl-combers wandering between the workshops, selling their pickings. But her shopping trips with Padley never took her as far as Crook Street.

"Houses, mainly," Nat said. "But it's close to Boardstar Street, where Saf was taken. If Ruby wants to show us something important, it must be to do with that. Unless the note isn't from Ruby at all, and the whole thing *is* a trap. Maybe we should tell my mum."

"We can't. It said so, remember." They'd been over this several times too, and Ista was standing firm.

"But—"

"If you say 'How will Ruby know who we've told?' one more time, I am going to scream."

"All right." Nat made a zipping motion across his mouth.

In the late-afternoon light, Ista noticed how deep the shadows were under his eyes, as if he hadn't slept properly in a very long while.

"You can't blame yourself," she said. "For what happened to your brother."

"I can, actually." His voice was small. Careful, as if he were tiptoeing past a sleeping dragon. "I was meant to be watching him that day. My dad . . . I'm named after him, you know. Nathaniel. He and Mum split up when Ravi was a baby. He doesn't live in the city. It's always been just the three of us—Mum, Ravi, and me."

Ista nodded. "It's always just been me and Pa, too. My ma left when I was little." She swallowed, trying to chase a sudden dryness from her throat. If Pa's vanishing was a loose thread, her mother's absence was a knot. "I stayed with my aunt sometimes, when Pa had to travel. That's where I was when he came here."

"Won't she be worried about you now? Your aunt?"

"No." Ista drew her arms around herself. "She believes in one of the old religions. They teach that only demons can change their shape. When she found out what I could do, she was scared. She never said anything, not while Pa was living with us—I could just see it in her eyes." Which had been worse, in a way. You couldn't defend yourself against a look. "Then one day, after Pa left for Shelwich, we were arguing." Aunt Abgill had always seemed to want to argue about something, no matter how hard Ista tried to be tidy and quiet. "And . . . she called me a monster."

Ista had never told anyone that, had carried it inside her like a stone. But Nat had a way of listening that made it easier to let secrets out than keep them in. With him steady and silent beside her, she told the whole story. How she'd thought she could stick it out until Pa sent for her. How Mikkela's letter arrived, and everything changed. Running away. Arriving in Shelwich.

"I was so sure I'd find Pa, but I didn't even find Mikkela

that first night—or anywhere to stay. So I tucked myself into a corner of Shipwrights' Square to wait for morning, but as I was drifting off, I smelled it. The grilk smell. And I had this feeling—like every drop of my magic was draining from me. And then *it* was there. The grilk." The drag of the wings. The pointed teeth glinting.

"You've escaped a grilk *twice*?" Nat said. "Why didn't you tell me? No, don't answer that. How did you get away the first time?"

"Alexo rescued me." Ista pulled herself from the memory. "That's how I met him."

His eyes narrowed. "I thought you said he had something of yours and you were earning it back."

She should have known she couldn't sneak that half-truth past him. "It came into his possession while he was rescuing me."

"You mean he stole it while you were vulnerable and now he's making you pretend to be other people so you can steal more things for him."

"I suppose, if that's how you want to see it." Ista felt hedgehoggy again, her prickles out. "But he also sent me to Padley and Giddon—he made sure I was looked after."

Nat waved her last sentence aside. "How did Alexo fight off a grilk, though?" He fixed her with a searchlight stare that was uncannily like his mother's.

"I don't know. . . ." Some bits of that night were etched into her memory, but other bits kept swimming out of reach. "He was just there, suddenly, and the grilk went away. Look, I'd better go. I don't want Giddon to worry."

"All right. See you." Nat sounded as bristly as she felt. "We're still meeting later to see Ruby," he added. "Aren't we?"

"Of course," Ista said. "Let's meet ten minutes before tenth bell, by the silversmiths at the top of Crinkle Row— that'll give us plenty of time to be at the corner of Crook and Crinkle at tenth bell."

"Oh good." Nat brightened. "Great. I'll see you later, then."

Honestly, he was ridiculous, Ista thought. Just because she was grumpy with him didn't mean she was going to derail their investigation, especially not when they finally had a proper lead.

The gloomy afternoon was tipping into a crisp and pretty evening, with the sundown chimes singing over the beat of the incoming Tide, and what Pa would've called an ice-cream-sundae sky. Ista made sure to check the eel shack again, relief twisting through her when the awning remained handkerchief-free.

There was still one errand left, though. Alexo would summon her eventually.

She walked on, but she'd only gone a few steps when awareness scuttled up the back of her neck.

Someone was behind her. Someone who didn't want to be seen.

Veering off the river walkway, Ista stole a glance to her right. The hem of an algae-green cloak flicked up as its owner whisked away round a corner. This was puzzling. She could have sworn they'd been following her, but now they seemed to be running away, as if they were as scared of her as she was of them.

Be careful, Nat's voice echoed in her mind. But the need for answers burned through her caution, and she set off in pursuit.

Ahead of her, the figure ducked into an alleyway, their cloak billowing like a green sail. Ista felt a surge of triumph. She knew that alley. It led to a tiny shoebox courtyard, with nothing in it but a rickety shed that the pearl-combers used. She slowed, sticking to the shadows, arriving just as the shed door banged shut.

Without making a sound, she grabbed an old rake that had been left propped against the wall, and crept forward. The door was slightly ajar, as if the figure had slammed it so hard that the latch had bounced straight out of its groove again. Ista gripped the rake tighter, reaching out her foot to give the door a bold kick, then leapt back, knees bent, ready to defend herself if she had to.

Nothing happened. She edged forward, her heart knocking against her ribs.

The shed was empty. No cloak, no figure, no cupboard where they could be hiding. No window or trapdoor by which they might have escaped. It was as if they had evaporated.

In a day of strange and troubling events, this was the strangest and most troubling of all.

15

ON THE CORNER OF
CROOK AND CRINKLE

At this hour, the Fletwin would normally have been bustling, with the lamps lit, the cutlery shined to a wink, and the day's specials chalked in friendly letters on the board. Instead, Ista arrived to find the restaurant looking even bleaker than it had that morning, its front door firmly closed and its sloping timbers seeming to droop like wilted flower stems in the dwindling light.

"Tide save you, Ista!" Kip the potter called from a few doors down. "A bad business, this. Our poor Padley. Feels like the heart's been carved out of the neighborhood."

That, Ista thought, was exactly how it felt. The painters and makers of the artists' quarter usually sold their wares well into the evening, but today they had pulled their shutters down early, and the little music café on the corner was closed too, leaving the street shrouded in a mournful hush.

"As for young Saf Mallard," Kip went on, "just the other day I saw her lift a whole wagon off the ground like it was nothing more than a basket of onions. If a girl with her strength couldn't fight off a grilk, what hope is there for the rest of us?"

Ista didn't have an answer for that. She remembered Padley telling her Kip's story about a youngster with an astonishing strength blessing; at the time, she hadn't made the connection with the girl she'd met at the Moon Tower. Had that shopping trip with Padley really only been yesterday morning? She felt exhausted suddenly. Excusing herself from Kip, she hurried round to the back of the Fletwin.

Muffled voices drifted under the heavy kitchen door. Inside, Giddon was at the worktop, where he would have been on a normal night, although without his apron on. That, however, was as far as any illusion of normality went. Warming himself at the fire stood Brintan Brook, his smart coat and newly polished shoes out of place against the ancient hearthrug and the worn brick floor.

"And who do we have here?" Brook asked, turning a shrewd gaze on Ista.

"A chef in training," Giddon answered before Ista could. She had the distinct impression he didn't want Brook to pay any attention to her. As for Brook, Ista felt as if he was banking her face in case it came in handy in the future.

"A chef." He nodded to himself, as if he was filing that information away too. "Well, I must be going, Giddon.

Read over the contract, but you'll find it's more than generous. I'll return tomorrow night for your decision. No, no." He waved Ista aside as she moved to hold the door for him. "I can see myself out."

His voice was as measured and polite as it had been at the pickle shop that morning, but his eyes gleamed with a cold satisfaction that sent unease shivering through Ista's belly. The door shut behind him, but she nudged it back open a crack, watching him saunter away under the bruise-colored sky.

"You'll let the cold in," Giddon said.

Ista shoved the door closed. "What did he mean? About a contract? Is that it?" On the counter was a rolled-up document, bound with a blue ribbon.

"Nothing important." Giddon gave a wry smile. "He wants to buy the place."

"To buy the Fletwin?" Panic bloomed in Ista's chest. "But—"

"I'd never sell to him, of course." Giddon cut her off. "No need to worry, young'un." He slid the papers into a drawer and closed it with a firm click that said the subject was closed too.

Ista believed him—and he seemed very much like himself again, much sharper than he had earlier, so perhaps she could ask him about Alexo and the sleep spell.

"You never did tell me where you went last night," she said, sidling nearer. "Who did you ask for help?"

"Last night? I went to . . ." It was exactly like before. He went all foggy, the end of the sentence slipping away from him. Then his eyes refocused, a pained expression flicking across his face. "It doesn't matter. I didn't find anything."

Ista clenched her fists. This wasn't the aftereffects of the sleep spell. This was something else. No, not something. Some*one*—and she had no doubt as to whom.

She wanted to press for the truth, because surely Giddon must remember at least a few details. But he looked . . . older, as if the loss of Padley had etched new lines between the wrinkles she knew so well. He sank into the little armchair opposite Padley's rocker, his eyes now so hopeless and empty that she could hardly bear it.

I'm going to find him. And Pa. I'm going to find them and I'm going to bring them both home.

The words died on Ista's tongue. She couldn't reveal what she and Nat were up to. Giddon would make them stop.

"You mustn't worry," he said, glancing up as if feeling her gaze. "I promise, whatever happens, you and I really will be all right."

But later, as she crept downstairs to meet Nat, Ista paused by the drawer where Giddon had put the contract, and she wondered, just for a second, if that was true.

"Brintan Brook wants to buy the Fletwin?" Nat stopped in his tracks.

"Yes." Ista had explained it all in a breathless tumble as they hurried along Crinkle Row. "And it can't be a coincidence, can it, Brook going to see Granny Mallard *and* Giddon about business today, so soon after they both lost someone to the grilks?"

"No," said Nat, walking on again. "I don't think it can. We'll have to ask Ruby what she knows. What about the person in the cloak? Do you reckon they're the same person you heard Alexo talking to at the Shrieking Eel?"

"They must be, mustn't they? He told them to keep an eye on me." *You know what to do.* She shuddered at the memory. "It was so strange today, in the shed. They just vanished, but there was nowhere for them to go."

Nat sucked in a sharp breath. "What if they didn't go anywhere? The Tide was rising by then, wasn't it? What if they were still there?"

"You mean they might have an invisibility blessing? Maybe. I don't know."

Thinking about being watched was like thinking about fleas or the little red mites that lived in the sand. It made her itch. Ista turned, sure she felt eyes on the back of her neck, but no one was there.

"There's something else about Alexo," she said. "I know I said he couldn't leave the inn for long, but he has these . . . well, I call them glass-bugs. They're like beetles, except I'm not even sure they're alive. Anyway, they go wherever he sends them. So if he could use them to lure the grilks somehow . . ."

"He wouldn't even need to leave the Shrieking Eel." Nat didn't miss a beat. "He could get the grilks anywhere he wanted—and then send the glass-bugs away when the real target arrived."

"He's done something to Giddon, too," Ista said. "I'm sure he has. Every time I ask Giddon what happened at the inn, it's like he can't talk about it. I thought it was just the sleep spell wearing off at first, but it's more like Giddon's been hypnotized." A thought struck her so hard that she gasped. "Nat, what if it's the gelkin? The library book said that gelkins could mesmerize people. What if Alexo's keeping it under the inn so he can use its magic?"

Nat made a considering noise. "But then couldn't he just mesmerize everyone, all the time? In which case, why go to the trouble of getting you to do his errands?"

Ista didn't know, but it kept nagging at her like a thorn.

They reached the meeting place. Crook Street sprouted sharply from one side of Crinkle Row like the branch of a skyrocket tree. The night was steeped in mist, with occasional slivers of lamplight peeking out of upper-story windows. At street level all was still. Silent, save for the rustle and fizz of the magic.

When the magic sparks upon your skin, and the mist is high, and the night creeps in . . .

"Maybe we shouldn't have come," Ista murmured. What if it *was* a trap?

But, as she spoke, a clocktower chimed, and a shadow detached itself from the opposite wall.

"Whew," said Ruby Mallard. "You two don't half make a racket."

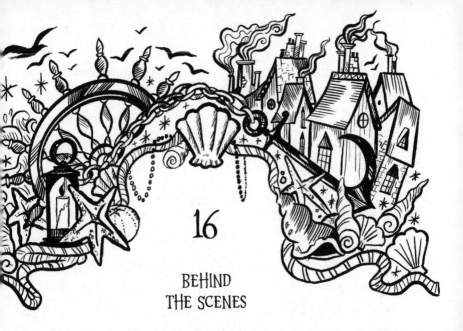

16

BEHIND
THE SCENES

"Hello, Nat Shah. Hello, girl from this morning and from the Moon Tower." Ruby stepped forward, into the puddle of blue light that fell from the junction's only Tide-lantern. She was dressed in black from head to toe, her braids coiled high on her head, her long coat brushing the tops of her boots.

It was a bit overdramatic, frankly, Ista thought. She folded her arms. "You said you had something to show us."

"First things first." Ruby stalked toward her. "What's your name, and do you copy people's blessings or only their faces and bodies?"

Ista and Nat exchanged a glance.

"She *does* know, then," said Ista.

Ruby shrugged. "Thought there was something strange about your mum the second time she knocked on our door this morning," she said to Nat. "So I watched the pair of you through the letterbox. Turns out it wasn't your mum at all that second time." Her gaze flicked to Ista. "Was it?"

"No," Ista said.

Nat aimed a glare at her.

"Well, there's no point pretending," Ista told him. "She needs us for something." She turned to Ruby again. "I'm Ista. And, yeah, I get people's blessings when I borrow them. But only if the Tide's high enough, and . . ." She didn't know if Ruby would believe the explanation that the magic didn't like it, that it sent the Tide-song off-key. "It doesn't last long," she settled on saying.

Another shrug. "We won't need long." But Ruby's voice trembled, like a flame caught in a draught.

She might act confident, but she must be desperate, Ista realized, *to ask strangers for help.*

Nat's expression softened, as if he'd had the same thought. "It was risky leaving us that note. How could you be sure we'd work out what it said?"

"Your mum told us about your brother," Ruby said simply. "Figured you'd want answers as badly as I do."

With that, she turned and strode off down Crook Street.

Nat frowned after her. "I still don't see why she didn't want us to tell any grown-ups."

Because this is going to be dangerous, and grown-ups would probably mess it all up by trying to stop us, Ista thought.

But there didn't seem much point saying that out loud, so she kept her mouth shut as they followed Ruby.

Crook Street was named for its shape rather than because anything particularly nefarious happened on it— to the best of Ista's knowledge, anyway. Ruby headed for the point where it began to curve. A padlocked gate stood between two houses. She vaulted over it without breaking stride, leaving Ista and Nat to clamber after her.

"Where are we going?" Nat whispered as they struggled along a path that was overgrown with prickly weeds.

Ista had no idea. The dark shape of a building loomed into view, a pair of empty stone pedestals guarding the entrance, as if the statues that should be in residence had snuck off for a late-night stroll. Ruby took up a position between them, tossing a large blue Tide-pearl from hand to hand as though she'd been waiting there for hours. Above her, two faces were carved into the portico, one mouth smiling, one turned down.

The Muses. Ista recognized them from a book. The smiler was Comedy and the frowny one was Tragedy. Which meant . . .

"Is this a theater?" Nat got there first.

"It *was*." Ruby threw the Tide-pearl again, letting it arc through the air before catching it. Then she opened the door and reached inside to extract a strange-looking clay pot studded with tiny holes. She placed the Tide-pearl into it. Streams of pale blue light washed from the holes, picking out the details of what must once have been a foyer.

"That," said Nat, "is clever."

It really was. A makeshift Tide-lantern.

"Saf thought of it." The words were spiked with pride. "Watch your step. The floor's rotten." Ruby padded forward, leading them past the old ticket counter and through another doorway.

Ista couldn't hold in her gasp as a huge auditorium opened up in front of them, rows of seats curving partway round a low, circular stage, which, in the blue glow of the lantern light, looked almost like the Stone Sleepers' pond. Ruby stopped at the edge of it.

Nat pulled his notebook from his pocket. "How did you find this place?"

"My gran knew about it from when she was a kid. I needed somewhere to practice."

"Practice?" Ista said.

"Yes." Ruby turned, raising her eyebrows at Nat's notebook.

"Sorry." He put it away again. "Habit."

"We won't tell anyone," Ista said. "Whatever it is."

Ruby placed the lantern on the floor. "You ever seen the acrobats when they've come through the city?"

Ista hadn't, but Nat nodded. "Mum took us for my birthday. They're incredible."

Ruby lit up with enthusiasm. "Right? I was only six

when Mum and Dad first took us. Saf was too little to be into it, but I *knew*, right then, that that's what I wanted to do. I made Dad take me round to talk to them after the show, and they said they had this training program for people our age, but you had to practice really hard just to get in it. So I did. And I got good." She shrugged. "I'm not being . . . I'm just saying. Anyway, the next time the troupe came through, I asked if they'd let me audition."

But. There had to be a *but,* Ista thought. Or else what did this have to do with Saf and the grilks?

"What happened?" she asked.

"The Tide happened." Ruby sighed. "The magic was high when I did my audition, and the acrobats thought I was cheating."

"Cheating?" Nat pursed his lips in confusion. "Why? What exactly is your Tide-blessing?"

Ruby laughed, but it was a hollow kind of laugh, as though the joke was on her. "I'll show you." She crossed to one side of the stage, where a metal ladder ran up the wall to a railed walkway near the ceiling.

"What's she doing?" Nat murmured as Ruby began to climb.

"I don't know." Just looking at the walkway made Ista's feet tingle.

Ruby completed her ascent, the metal bouncing under her feet as she stepped onto the walkway. She made her way round until she was directly above center stage, then ducked under the railing. Ista's stomach plummeted. Ruby was holding on, but she'd twisted so she was facing outward, her toes hovering in the air.

"Sink me," Nat breathed. "She's going to jump."

Ruby did not jump. She dived, headfirst and arrow-straight. Ista's horror spiraled, conjuring twisted limbs and jutting shards of bone and . . .

"You can open your eyes," Ruby said. She stood on the floor, unscathed, one corner of her mouth twisted up with amusement. "That's what the Tide gave me. I always land on my feet. Well, when the magic's in. Wouldn't want to try too close to Low Tide."

Ista swallowed. "No. Probably best not." It was two hours past the night's High Tide peak, and Ruby had made that leap without so much as a quiver of worry. Her magic must be as strong as, if not stronger than, Ista's own.

Nat opened his mouth, then shut it again. Then opened it.

Ruby looked at him. "Yes?"

"It's just . . . Why was that a problem? With the acrobats? I'd have thought they'd have made you their star performer."

"They thought that if the magic was helping me do that, it was helping me with the rest of my flips and tumbles, too. Which it wasn't." Ruby's eyes were fierce. "It's my own fault. If I hadn't been showing off . . ." She kicked the air with her foot, then straightened, disappointment apparently banished. "It was for the best, probably. I'd have had to go away for the training, and I would have hated leaving

Saf. Anyway, I only showed you that so the rest of it would make sense. Come on."

Grabbing the lantern, she strode off, her coat billowing behind her.

"She knows how to make an exit," Nat whispered.

And an entrance, Ista thought. Ruby would give Alexo a run for his money.

Her lantern light led them behind a thick curtain to another large space, strewn with abandoned pieces of scenery and rails of mildewy-smelling costumes. The blue light gave everything an underwater feel, old bits of half-broken furniture rising like twists of coral.

"Welcome to the scene dock." Ruby swung the lantern. Ista sensed fragility under her showiness, as if she was gearing up to something unpleasant. "Saf always wanted to mess around back here—but the floor's dodgy, so I hardly ever let her."

They wove onward, past an ancient piano and some even more ancient-looking crates overflowing with coils of rope and cable. At the end of the scene dock was a pair of doors as tall as the grain store in Ista's village. Ruby halted in front of them.

"This is where they used to bring the set in. We never came down this far, me and Saf." She cleared her throat. "I should explain. About last night. It happened so quickly. We'd had this fight—I don't know if you know that Saf had a strength blessing. . . ."

"I'd heard about it, yes," Ista said, bending down to remove a piece of moldering paper that had attached itself to her boot. It must have been a flyer for some kind of children's show. The words *The Incredible Kettle* swirled across it in curling black script.

Ruby gave a soft snort. "It's a miracle anyone didn't, the way she kept showing off about it. And I've been getting really worried. There've been so many attacks lately, and Mum and Dad are away visiting my auntie and her new baby. We have Gran to look after us, but I feel like I have to look after Saf too. Anyway, she was showing off again yesterday, and I really yelled at her. Told her that the grilks would definitely get her if she used her magic outside again. I . . . I really scared her. I felt so guilty—I mean, she just wanted to enjoy her magic, and what's wrong with that?—so I brought her here last night so we could both let off some steam someplace where we'd be safe from grilks."

"Hang on." Nat was doing his searchlight stare again. Ista felt rather relieved that it wasn't directed at her. "How do you get here safely in the first place? We were nervous about being out after dark tonight."

"Ah," Ruby said. "Well, you know how grilks don't fly. Not properly, anyway . . ."

"Yes, but neither do you or Saf." Ista couldn't fathom where this was going at all. "*Do* you?"

Ruby choked out a short laugh. "No, we go over the rooftops. There's an easy route from our house to here.

Easy for the two of us, anyhow—all the way from my bed-room window to the gate on Crook Street. But then last night, we were halfway home, and Saf dropped one of her gloves. They're her favorites, and we both knew Gran would be cross if she lost them. I said I'd jump down and get them, but Saf said she should do it because it'd be quicker for her to climb back up. I shouldn't have let her, but she's so stubborn sometimes, there's no point arguing. Anyway, she climbed down, and I lost sight of her, just for a second. Then she screamed. I saw it, the grilk, just a flash of it—a shadow, really. And then she was gone." Her breath hitched, like fabric catching on a stray pin.

"It wasn't your fault," said Nat, and Ista knew he was thinking of Ravi, just as she was thinking of Pa.

Ruby acknowledged Nat's words with an awkward one-shouldered shrug. "I always thought you vanished if the grilks got you," she said after a moment. "Vanished for real. Like you'd never existed in the first place. But this morning everything was so weird at home. I needed to get out for a bit. I don't know why I came back to the theater. Just because it's me and Saf's place, I suppose. And I found . . . this."

She dipped a hand into her pocket and produced a small stripy glove.

"It's Saf's. It's one of the ones she was wearing last night. And this morning it was right here, just inside these doors."

17

THE TRUTH BELOW

"You're sure it's Saf's?" Nat asked, staring at the glove in Ruby's hand.

Ruby's voice turned steely. "I know my own sister's glove. Gran knitted it for her."

"But . . ." He raked his hands through his hair and held them there as if he needed to stop his head falling off. "But that would mean . . ."

"That Saf didn't vanish," Ista said in wonder.

Ruby's fierceness melted slightly. She turned to the double doors at the back of the scene dock again. "I didn't believe it at first either, so I tried these doors. Didn't think I'd get them open, but I did."

"What's out there?" Nat asked.

"Just a yard." Clearly not *just* from the way Ruby's voice

trembled. "But there's a gate at the end. I'll give you one guess where it leads."

"Not Boardstar Street?" Ista said.

"Very good. Ten points to you," Ruby told her. "Only a little way down from where Saf was taken."

"So, the grilks got her on Boardstar Street." Nat gazed around. "And brought her through these doors, here, where she dropped her glove. But then what?"

"Then *this*." Ruby led them onward, the lantern light shivering over a long-abandoned pile of Incredible Kettle posters. Trails of painted steam rose through the swirling writing, almost obscuring the *K* completely. She stopped by a stack of crates near a wall, reaching into her pocket again.

"The other glove?" Nat took it from her as if he needed to touch it to be certain it was real.

"It was just here. Right where I'm standing." Ruby glanced at the floor. "If it was only one glove, I'd think she'd dropped it by accident again. But it's both of them. And Saf's clever. Not just at school stuff. She's practical. Like how she came up with the idea for this lantern."

Understanding flared, bright and sharp, like a match striking in Ista's mind. "Wait. You think Saf dropped the gloves on purpose? You think she was conscious?"

Ruby nodded. "I think she was trying to leave a trail."

"A trail to where?" said Nat as they approached the wall. "There's nowhere else to go."

"Yes," said Ruby. "There is."

She stood to one side, angling the lantern so they could see what was beyond the crates. A large patch of floor had given way entirely, leaving a hole like a ragged mouth, emptiness yawning below it.

Nat crouched down. "You think that's where they took her?" His question fell into the dark and echoed back like a birdcall: *took her, took her . . .*

"I don't know." Ruby's voice was grave. "But I'm going to find out."

She stepped toward the hole, and Ista realized what she was planning to do. "Ruby . . ." She swallowed. "Are you sure you'll be able to land?"

"Hang on," said Nat. "You're going to *jump*? Into the terrifying chasm? There could be anything down there. We don't even know how far down it is."

Ista couldn't have put it better herself. Even standing several steps away from the hole made her entire body clench with nerves.

"I tested it." Ruby took a stone from one of her pockets and held it over the hole. "Listen."

She let go of the stone. Ista counted in her head. *One . . . two . . .* Before she reached *three,* there was a distant clunk. Her palms went slick.

Ruby turned to Ista. "Can *you* pull me up again?" she asked. "That's the real question. Can you be Saf? Can you use her blessing?"

She unbuttoned her coat, and Ista saw that she was wearing some kind of harness over her trousers, a coil of thin rope hanging from the belt.

Ista paused. Magic pulsed in glittery waves against her skin. She'd have no trouble borrowing Saf. Borrowing Saf's blessing, though . . . What if the Tide wouldn't let her use it for long enough? She remembered the feeling of snapping back into her own body, the fall into the lake at the Moon Tower. And that had been High Tide and a full moon. It was two days after the full moon now *and* well past High Tide.

"What exactly do you need me to do?" she asked Ruby.

Nat flung his hands in the air. "Are you both out of your minds?"

Ruby ignored him, speaking only to Ista. "Wear these." She threw a pair of leather gloves at her, then set the lantern down and secured one end of the rope to a nearby pillar and the other to her harness. "Right, that should hold. Don't touch the rope until you're sure I'm down safely. I'll signal by blowing on this"—she held up a whistle—"once when I'm down, twice when I'm ready to come back. That's when you do your thing and pull me up. All right? Look, if it goes wrong and I get stuck down there, you can both run and get Nat's mum and bring a crew of people to get me out."

"Oh, sure," said Nat. "Because there are teams of people just ready and waiting to come leaping into underground abysses. Let's at least wait until the Tide's all the way up again."

He was right, Ista thought, they *should* wait. But the magic wouldn't climb to its highest point again until tomorrow morning—and they had no time to lose. She put on the gloves, then reached for the magic, testing, holding Saf's face in her mind.

Ruby gasped as she took in Ista's transformation. "Wow, that's . . . It's hard not to believe you're actually her." She rolled back her shoulders. "Right, then. You keep the lantern. I've got a spare Tide-pearl with me."

There was nothing else to say. She threw Nat a cocky smile and offered Ista a small nod.

Then she jumped.

One . . . , Ista thought, staring down into the dark. *Two . . . three . . . four . . . five . . . six . . .*

Nothing. Only a bottomless silence that chilled her blood.

"What should we—" she began, but from beneath her feet came a faint snapping sound, like a twig breaking.

Another—louder—snap. A hairline crack appeared near the toe of her left boot.

"Ista," Nat breathed. "I think—"

Before he could say another word, the crack widened and multiplied, the entire floor splitting open. For an infinitesimal fraction of a second, Ista hovered, the terror in Nat's eyes a mirror of her own.

Then they both went tumbling into the chasm.

Two and a bit seconds feels like forever when you're falling. *Jarmak*, Ista thought as the empty air rushed past her. *Wings*. No, it was too late for wings. But she had to do something. And what about Nat? Where was he? They were going to die, and Ruby . . .

Ruby!

She changed. The magic gave an off-key groan, and the ground soared toward her like a cold stone wall, but power crackled in her toes, and then somehow her feet were down and her head was up and she was standing unscathed in what, as far as she could tell, was some sort of cavern.

One under the Shrieking Eel, one under the hospital, one here, Ista thought. So many secret spaces beneath the Shelwich she knew. Dim light filtered in from one side, and there was a warm, sweetish smell that reminded her of planting tomato seeds with Pa in Aunt Abgill's greenhouse.

"Nat?" Ista changed back to herself, whirling round, ears and eyes straining. "Nat? Ruby?"

Fear slithered in her belly. It had been a long way down. A long, long way. Nat didn't have any magic to protect him from the impact. As for Ruby . . . Ista scoured the gloom. A large part of the cavern ceiling had collapsed. There was no sign of the Tide-lantern, and debris had fallen everywhere, lumps of rock and chunks of broken furniture scattered like meteorites. What if something had hit Ruby when the floor caved in?

Ista tried again. "Ruby? Nat?"

An answering groan made her shudder with relief. "Ista?"

She spun back. "Nat!"

"Ista, up here!"

He wasn't far from where she'd landed, although a fair bit higher, on a ledge that protruded two-thirds of the way down the cavern wall. Above him, a slope led up to a narrower ledge. He must've broken his fall on that and then rolled down to where he was. Below him was another bank, steeper and pitted with stones.

It didn't look climbable—not easily, at any rate—but Jarmak's blessing would come in handy now. Ista borrowed him, magic dancing eagerly over her. She sank into it, focusing on the tingle between her shoulder blades, letting his great wings burst from her back in a tumble of feathers. The Tide did *not* like her borrowing another blessing so soon. Its off-key moan rose almost immediately to a howl.

"Hold on, Nat!" Ista called as she flapped and strained. "I'm coming." Collapsing onto the ledge, she found him clutching his ankle. "Are you all right? Can you stand?"

"Let's find out." Nat took the arm she offered, hissing as he put his weight on his feet. "Ouch. But it isn't that bad. Are *you* all right? Have you seen Ruby?"

As if in reply, a whistle split the air. They both turned, Nat with a wince—his injury obviously worse than he was letting on.

"It came from that way, I think." Ista pointed across the mountain of rubble.

"Ruby!" Nat shouted.

Two whistles, shrill and firm. A tiny light glimmered, like a fog-sprite or a marsh-spinner.

"There! That's her with the spare Tide-pearl." Ista waved, not sure if Ruby could see them, then turned back to Nat. "Grab on to me. I'll fly us."

She had to wrench the magic to her. Nat clung on like a limpet as they swooped over the rubble. Ruby *had* seen them—she whistled again, waving the Tide-pearl to guide them.

Ista was prepared, this time, for the magic to desert her; she could hear that it was already preparing to pull away. She took them lower, avoiding the chunks of debris.

"Ista . . ." Nat's voice was a wobble.

"We have to land." Jarmak's pebble-polished vowels rolled from her mouth and echoed around the cavern.

She swooped lower still, until their boots almost scraped the ground.

"Now," she gasped. They landed at a stagger, tumbling into a heap as the magic went silent, ripping Jarmak's wings away from her.

Ruby's footsteps thundered toward them. "Ista? Nat? Are you all right?"

"Yes." Ista sat up, disentangling her legs from Nat's. The magic returned to her in a cautious flicker, as if it didn't trust her not to break the rules again. "I think so. Nat, is your ankle okay?"

He gave a soft hiss. "It's fine."

Liar, Ista thought, peering up—and up, and up—at the ragged hole they'd fallen through.

She hoped Nat could still walk, because there wasn't a whelk's toe of a chance she'd be able to fly him back up to the theater safely anytime soon. She wasn't actually sure the Tide would let her borrow Jarmak's blessing again. Not without a fight, at any rate.

"I thought you were goners when the ceiling collapsed," Ruby said, looking up too. "I was only just down when I heard it crack. Hardly had time to unclip myself and get clear. So . . ." She turned to Ista. "Jarmak Hettle can fly. Interesting. Do you think you'll be able to get us out of here?"

"I think so. In a while." Ista clambered to her feet, speaking with more confidence than she felt. There was no point burdening the others with her worries yet. "But there has to be another way out, doesn't there?" All these caverns underneath the city. At least some of them had to be connected.

"Yes." Nat was up too. "Look."

An archway was set into the cavern wall, an inky silence lurking beyond it.

"It's either a way out, or it'll take us right into the grilks' lair." Ruby bounced on her toes, as if she needed to keep moving or her courage might drain away. Ista knew what she was thinking—if it did take them to the grilks, it might also take them to Saf. "Don't suppose the lantern survived the fall, did it?"

Ista shook her head. "I looked, but I couldn't see it." It must be buried under the rubble.

Ruby allowed herself a very small sigh, then turned to face the archway. "Good job I brought this extra pearl."

A very good job, Ista thought. They'd come for answers. It was time to find some.

At least the magic seemed to have forgiven her. It curled round her again, flickering brightly as the archway led them to a tunnel, narrow and low-ceilinged. Without the pot to magnify it, the Tide-pearl's light didn't stretch far. They huddled together, feeling out each tentative step in case of any unexpected holes in the ground. Eventually, round a bend, a Tide-lantern sputtered on the wall, coating everything in a greasy sheen. Ahead was another archway.

Ruby and Ista both froze.

"What?" Nat stopped too. "What is it?"

"I don't know," Ista said. "It's . . . quiet."

The Tide suddenly seemed to have dimmed to a whisper, as if it were calling to her from behind a wall of glass.

In its place, a little voice took root in her mind, murmuring, *Gogetoutnowrunaway.*

"Do you feel it?" she asked Ruby.

"Yes." Ruby wrinkled her nose. "It's like something's smothering the magic. And look." She lifted the Tidepearl higher. Its glow was waning, the darkness of the tunnel pressing in tighter.

But there was no turning back now. Ista made herself keep walking, dread pouring into her as the imaginary voice grew louder, like an out-of-control typewriter printing words into her brain: *Gogetoutleaverunnowrun.*

Murky yellow lantern light spilled over an enormous circular chamber. Three other tunnels branched off it, the archways at their entrances each marked with a different symbol. In the center, a cluster of jagged rocks, person-sized or a little taller, huddled together like roosting birds or bats.

"Which way, do you think?" Nat wondered.

Ista opened her mouth to answer—but the air had changed, a new scent prodding at her nostrils. No, not new. Fear crashed down on her. The smell was familiar, a cold mineral tang mixed with a sour odor of rot.

Limestone. And leaf mold.

"Nat," she breathed, pointing at the cluster. "Stop. They're *grilks.*"

But Nat kept going. "No, they're not. I mean they are, but . . . look."

"Tide's teeth!" Ruby brushed past him. "*No.* No way."

Ista's chest was tight, but her head felt loose, as if she were outside herself and gazing in. Why weren't the others running away? Why did neither of them sound scared? The grilks were motionless in their huddle. There were about ten of them, maybe more. She couldn't bring herself to count. Time seemed to unwind, taking her back to that first night in Shipwrights' Square. She could hardly see or think straight through the smell and the fear.

"We've had this so wrong," she heard Nat saying, though his voice was all fuzzy and far away. "We've been wrong about the most important thing! Ista?" He spun back to her, the most peculiar blend of worry and excitement playing across his face. "Ista, *look*."

And this time Ista did.

Before, she'd only ever seen the grilks at night and in the mist—only ever when her eyes and her judgment were clouded with terror. She had only ever seen the creatures moving.

Now, it wasn't that her fear was gone. It still beat inside her like a second heart. But through it—past the jaws and the wings and the smell that threatened to choke her—she saw the truth. She saw stitches. She saw poles. She saw the same web-fine strings she and Nat had seen on the vespalin at the music shop.

"They're . . ." Her mouth wouldn't form the words.

"Yep." Nat went right up to them, prodding the bottom of one limp wing with his finger. "They're puppets."

18

THE MONSTERS
THAT WEREN'T

Puppets. And not magical puppets that needed the Tide or someone's blessing to bring them to life. *Puppet* puppets, with rods and strings, propped up on wooden frames. A strange feeling bloomed between Ista's ribs as she watched Nat inspect each one in turn.

"Saf's alive!" Ruby was trembling, as if she had so much energy coursing through her that she didn't know what to do with it. "I knew it. We have to find her. She must be here somewhere."

"Maybe they all are," Nat said. "All the missing people."

Saf, Ravi, Padley . . .

Pa.

Hope. That was what the feeling was, Ista realized. A window opening in an airless room. A path where there had been a dead end.

"Your mum was right, Nat," she said, still struggling to wrap her mind around it. "She was right from the start—just not in the way you thought, because the grilks aren't real. But someone *has* been controlling them."

"Let's go." Ruby looked round at the archways.

"Hang on a second." Nat poked at a wasplike torso. "We should see what we can find out here first. These things are seriously clever. There's almost nothing to them, just material and wire. Anyone could lift them. Oh, and look, this bit has a glove built into it, and this other bit's a sort of harness."

"You mean someone's been wearing them?" Bile rose in Ista's throat.

"Yes. Oh, and it's so clever. The wires connect all the parts together—and with the way these rods are angled, you'd be able to control all the movement from almost right down on the ground." He demonstrated, crouching and spreading one of the wings, making it drag against the earth with a sandy scrape. At the same time, the grilk's head gave a horribly lifelike twitch.

"That *is* clever." Ista inched nearer. The magic seemed to grow quieter with every step she took.

"Yeah, yeah, very impressive," Ruby muttered, striding away toward one of the archways. "Shame they smell like death."

"I think it's the cloth." Nat studied the wing. Sniffed. Frowned. "It's like it's been dipped in something."

"You're right." Ista knelt beside him to get a better look. A fine layer of grit or dust coated the material. "What is that stuff?"

She reached out, touching her fingertip to the rough surface. The last whisper of the Tide snuffed out like a candle. With a gasp, she snatched back her hand. A faint pulse of magic returned.

"What?" Nat turned his frown on her. "What's wrong?"

"It's the wings. They're what's draining the magic." Ista reached out again, smoothing the fabric with her palm. Tideless quiet smothered the world. "Ugh, it's making my skin go numb—and what are these weird ridges? It's like there's something in the cloth, or under it. Wire or thin rope or something. Does it feel strange to you?"

He shook his head. "I feel the ridges, but no strangeness. But I wouldn't, would I? No magic to start with. Ruby, come over here and see what you think."

"Um . . ." Ruby was examining a row of shadowy alcoves carved into the cavern wall. "You should both come and see this first."

Ista and Nat hurried to join her. One alcove was full of broken grilk parts: wings and heads and limbs piled up in a grisly heap. The next contained tools; the one after that, a clutch of tall barrels.

In the last alcove, something shimmered, bright and slick as a barrow of fish. Ista drew level with it. Every last drop of magic seemed to drain from the air. It was a large basket, full to the brim with a tangle of weblike silver netting.

"It looks like metal." Ruby scowled at it, then turned to Ista. "Horrible, isn't it?"

"Yes." It was *wrong,* that metal. It muffled the Tide completely, so that the quiet scuttled over Ista's arms and curdled her stomach. "If you had to, do you think you could use your blessing now?" she asked Ruby.

Ruby's scowl deepened. "I *know* I couldn't."

"But what is it?" Nat edged past her. "Oh, it's in sheets. Wow, it's really light." He inched further into the alcove, apparently not affected by the metal at all. "This must be what's in the wings. That explains the ridges."

"And it explains why Saf wasn't able to fight off the grilk that took her." Ruby's voice was steely with fury. "Her blessing wouldn't have worked."

"No one's would," Nat said. "It's ingenious, really. Magic-proof monsters. What's in the barrels, do you think?"

He went over and pried one of them open. A foul stench poured out, hitting Ista squarely in the gag reflex. It was grilk stink multiplied by twenty, like chalky stale sweat and fish left to rot in the sun.

"Tide's teeth!" Ruby backed away, coughing.

Nat rummaged through the tools and pulled out a thick-stemmed ladle, which he dipped into the barrel and then held up with a flourish. "Look! Crystals."

They were all shapes and sizes, some honey-colored, others a deeper orange. Every one of them was streaked with slender gray veins, like the filigree of mold that develops on blue cheese; the larger ones were riddled with webs of thick black lines.

"These are what's making everything reek, then." Ista could barely choke out the words.

"They're doing more than that," Nat said, pointing. Above the ladle, a fine haze floated. "Remind you of anything?"

"It reminds me that we should get out of here," said Ruby. "Oh, but hold on, is that . . . ?"

Ista gasped. "It's like the mist that comes with the grilks." She moved closer, wincing as a fresh wave of foulness attacked her nostrils. "Isn't it?"

"Only one way to find out." Nat flipped the ladle upside down. The crystals scattered like rotten stars, shattering as they hit the ground. Each impact was a tiny detonation, creating burst after burst of mist until a thick cloud formed.

"Seriously?" Ruby spluttered. "That was the only way?"

"Come on, Nat," Ista said. "We're wasting time here." Pa and all the other missing people might be just round the next corner.

"Sorry." Nat didn't sound sorry at all. "It's brilliant, though, isn't it, when you think about it? Like an extra layer of disguise for whoever's operating the puppets. We should take some. And some of the netting. I bet Mum knows someone who can analyze it for us."

He stepped deeper into the alcove and reappeared clutching a sack and a small metal box.

"This'll do." Half a ladle's worth of crystals went into the box. "Get one of the puppets, would you? Or one of the heads, at least."

"Fine." Ista picked a grilk head from the pile of parts and tucked it under her arm. The broken piece was almost worse than the complete puppets, strips of fabric hanging like shredded skin. "Now let's go."

"Seriously, Nat." Ruby snorted. "Anyone would think you didn't want to find Ravi."

"Of course I do!" But Nat still hesitated. He was worried, Ista realized, that they might already be too late. "This blasted stuff's all tangled together," he said, glaring at the netting as he tried to tease out a sheet.

"Okay, so which way?" Ruby asked Ista, ignoring Nat's complaining.

Four archways. The one they'd come through, which was marked with the shape of an arrowhead, and three others: one marked with an *X*, one with a wavy line, one with a circle. Ista had no preference. She just wanted to go. This quiet was making her itchy.

Except it wasn't quiet anymore. Not completely. There was a sound. So faint she might not have heard it if the netting's wrongness hadn't been drowning out the magic.

Nat stiffened. "What *is* that?"

"I don't know." Ruby looked as puzzled as Ista about which way the sound was coming from. "It sounds like—"

"Wheels." Ista clutched the grilk head tighter, a chill creeping over her. "Someone's coming."

The sound grew louder, solidifying into an unmistakable *clack-clack-clack* of wheels traveling over the uneven cavern floor.

"Run!" Ruby hissed. "This way!" She hurtled toward the archway marked with the wavy line.

"Come on, Nat!" Ista urged as he gave up trying to separate sheets of the netting and scooped a great armful of it into the sack.

They took off after Ruby, Ista running and Nat stumbling along in her wake. Behind them, the clacking rose to a clatter, echoing off the stone. There was no time to look back, no way of knowing if they'd been seen. They flung themselves through the archway, darkness closing round them like a fist.

19

THE HUNGRY POND

No one spoke. No one chanced so much as a whisper. Ista pressed her back to the rugged tunnel wall, sensing, without seeing, that Ruby and Nat were doing the same. Back in the grilk cavern, the sound of wheels stopped, quiet pouring in like ink.

Then footsteps. A soft crunch of boots moving across the ground. Someone cleared their throat, then coughed louder, then louder again.

Keeping her body glued to the stone, Ista turned her head. To one side of the puppets there was now a peculiar-looking cart with high wooden sides and a strange metal mechanism under its base. A person with their back to her was hunkered down beside it, their clothes dark and nondescript, a toolbox next to them on the ground.

Ista shuddered a soundless breath into the cup of her

hands. A tool clanked as the person shifted position to tinker with the mechanism under the cart. Their face was veiled by shadows, but Ista could tell that they were tall and broad. They coughed again. Twice. A third time. It was a nasty, rasping, rattling cough that seemed to always strike in threes, as if something was stuck in the person's throat.

Ista used the noise as cover, turning quickly, speaking low. "Recognize them?"

"No," Ruby whispered.

"Me neither." Nat spoke more quietly still. "We have to go."

He was right, Ista knew. If they were discovered, they'd be in serious danger.

They'd chosen this tunnel at random, but they'd have to stick with it now. Onward the three of them crept, Ista carrying the grilk head, Nat with the sack containing the netting and the box of crystals. Bringing the netting meant they had brought the magic-muffling wrongness too. The Tide was barely a murmur, the darkness absolute. When a flickering Tide-lantern came into view high on the wall, they stopped beneath it, sucking in gulps of air as if they'd been underwater.

"We have to find out who that was," said Nat. "I don't suppose they're your person in a cloak, Ista?"

Ruby raised her eyebrows. "Person in a cloak?"

"Someone's been following me," Ista explained. "But, no, the person in the cloak was shorter and slighter than that. Younger, too, I think, judging from their voice. Are you all right, Nat?" He had bent to assess his ankle.

"Yes." But his wince said otherwise. Having to run must have made it worse.

"How's the Tide-pearl, Ruby?" Ista asked, acutely aware of the vast weight of rock hanging over them, of the stillness and emptiness stretching ahead.

"It's snuffed it." Ruby opened her palm, revealing what looked like a normal gray pebble. "Don't think it likes the nets."

Above them, the Tide-lantern sputtered as if in agreement. Fortunately, there was another lantern not far along from the first, and then another, and another. Ruby took the sack and the grilk head, and Ista offered her arm to Nat, who was moving more gingerly with each step. They followed the lights like bread crumbs, trying to keep track of each turn they made, although the path forked and twisted and curled back on itself so often that Ista worried they were going in circles.

We'll find them, she told herself. *Just round this next bend. Or if not this one, the next.*

But they didn't. Ista focused on putting one foot in front of the other. In the shadows, time turned to liquid.

"We're lost, aren't we?" Nat was the one to say it.

"I wouldn't say *lost,* exactly." Ruby slid the sack to the ground. "We just don't have any idea where we are. Or where we're going. Or where we've been."

Ista put her head in her hands. "Sink me, we're so, so lost." And Nat's ankle must be unbearable; he had been leaning on her hard. She shook herself, trying to shuffle practical thoughts to the top of her mind. "We need to find somewhere safe to rest for— What was that?"

A flash of green had hopped across the edge of the lantern light.

"What was what?" Ruby spun round.

Nat turned too. His eyes narrowed in confusion. "Is that . . . a frog?"

It was. A frog, green as a grape, and almost as small. It hopped back across the pool of light, then leapt off down a path that forked from the one they were on.

"Let's follow it," Ista said. Her throat felt suddenly desert dry, and where there was a frog, there might be water.

Sure enough, the air became moist, tinged with an earthy sweetness as if some underground plant had come into bloom. Another frog, slightly bigger than the first but still no larger than Ista's thumb, leapt out in front of them, zigzagging ahead as the tunnel thinned and then widened, sloping softly downward. Intricate swirls of Tide-pearls studded the walls, and a chorus of ribbits and insect sounds rose from the shadows. Tide-song rushed into Ista's ears too, as if whatever they were walking toward had so much magic that even the netting in the sack couldn't silence it.

"What *is* this place?" Ruby murmured.

"I don't know." Ista sniffed. The smell intensified: a pinch of spice cut through the sweetness as the tunnel opened into a mossy, high-ceilinged cavern. Tide-lanterns dangled over a series of rough-hewn stepping stones that led across a huge pond. The water stretched from one side of the cavern to the other. Ruby dropped the sack and wandered down the path to investigate.

"It's beautiful," Nat said, following her.

It really was. The Tide-lanterns hung like moons, and magic danced over Ista's skin. There was so much life here. Pale-crested newts and more tiny frogs, even a great warty toad gazing solemnly from a rock as Ruby bounded across the stepping stones. Nat trailed behind her, wobbling on his sore ankle. A jewel-winged dragonfly hovered near his feet, then darted away above the lily pads.

Lily pads.

Ista started, taking in for the first time the pointy-tipped flowers, the purplish water that swelled gently toward Nat as he took his next step. Another lily pond, like the one at the hospital. *Impossible,* her mind insisted. But here it was, all the same.

"Smells amazing too, doesn't it?" Ruby leapt from the last stone to the bank, the grilk head tucked under one arm. "Like fruit pie or something. Sink me, I'm starving."

She crouched down, wafting her free hand over the water, as if the fragrance alone could fill her stomach.

Nat took another step, tottering on his injured ankle. Around him, the water stirred, sloshing upward. Ista felt its magic like a thousand invisible tendrils reaching out, searching.

"Stop." The command shot from her mouth. "Both of you, stop moving. Don't touch the water."

Ruby straightened, backing away from the pond.

Nat turned on his stepping stone. "Ista, what is it?"

Think, Ista told herself. What did they have? The netting that smothered magic—and the water *was* magic, wasn't it? She walked down the slope, grabbing the sack from where Ruby had left it.

"Have you heard about the pool in the hospital basement? The one that freezes people to heal them?" She didn't let her voice shake. Didn't want to spook Nat into making any sudden moves.

Ruby nodded. "The Stone Sleepers' room. Gran says even a splash of that water'll knock you out."

Nat's brow furrowed. "But that pond's under the hospital. This can't . . ." He trailed off, looking down. The water bubbled softly, as if someone had set it to simmer.

"I think this is the same kind of water," Ista said. "I think it knows you're hurt—and it wants to heal you."

"But if it touches him . . . ," Ruby began.

"It'll freeze me." Nat's smile was grim. The simmer

rose to a boil, the lily pads bobbing as tiny waves scuttled across the pond. "But there's an antidote, right? The lily seeds. We'd only need a pinch of them, wouldn't we, if they were crushed up?"

"Yes, but . . ." Ista surveyed the pool. All the flowers were too far from the edge to reach without a pole or a hook. "Let's think of that as a backup plan."

He gave a short, bleak laugh. "Okay. What's the main plan, though?"

"Well, I'm working on that." Ista opened the sack, the wrongness of the netting washing over her.

"Let's see what we're dealing with first," Ruby suggested. "Try to take another step, Nat."

"All right." Nat looked as if he'd rather stay exactly where he was, thank you very much, but he shuffled forward, inching his foot over the edge of the stepping stone.

A wall of water rose like a blade, barely missing his toes. There was no time for a proper plan. No more time to think at all. Ista wrenched a handful of netting from the sack and flung it into the pool.

The water stilled. Then began churning softly again.

"Run!" Ruby yelled.

Hoisting the sack over her shoulder, Ista launched herself across the stepping stones. "Go, Nat, *go!*"

There was a limit to how fast Nat could move. She caught up with him by the final stone, water raging after them as they flung themselves clear. The bank sloped up toward an archway. Ruby was already there, shouting for them to go faster.

Nat stumbled, and Ista caught him by the waist, pushing him ahead of her, conscious, with every step, of the water frothing and surging like a crocodile at their heels.

"Don't look back," Ruby said when they reached the top.

So, of course, Ista and Nat both did.

The cavern was almost completely underwater. A lily pad floated where Ista's feet had been only seconds before.

Then, as if the magic knew it couldn't have what it wanted, the water fell back again, retreating until the pond was as still and quiet as when they'd found it, gleaming innocently under the Tide-lanterns.

"That," murmured Ista, "was a little too close."

"Um, yes." Nat's eyes were still wide with fright. "Just a little."

And there was no way to go but onward. Through the archway they found a tunnel that unrolled into black nothingness, the only light a faint overspill from the cavern they'd just fled.

Ruby peered into the dark. "We should check it out. I'll go. You two stay here."

Ista didn't argue. They'd all have to go eventually, but Nat was flinching with every other step and obviously needed to rest. He slumped down against the tunnel wall, and she sank into a crouch beside him.

"You know what I don't get?" said Nat as Ruby padded out of sight. "How the grilks manage to show up all over the city."

Ista was tired down to her bones. She leaned back, closing her eyes. "Well, these tunnels go all over, don't they?"

"Yes, but we're a long way underground, and I haven't seen any stairs or paths leading up to the surface. Not even a ladder."

We need to find a way out soon, though, Ista thought. They were lost. Nat was injured. And no one would be coming to save them, because no one knew where they were. She wanted to leave so badly she could almost taste the outside, a stab of cold and salt piercing the stink of the grilk mist that lingered on her clothes along with the cloying sweetness of the lilies.

A yelp echoed off the stone.

She flew to her feet. "Ruby?"

"I'm all right! I'm all right." Ruby's footsteps pattered back, accompanied by the low, scraping sound of wheels rolling over the ground. "I bumped into this. Thought we could push you along in it, Nat."

She was towing a cart almost identical to the one the person with the toolbox had been working on.

"If you're sure." Nat hauled himself upright, then stopped, bending to look under the cart. "Hey, there was metal like this on that other cart—that's what they were fixing."

Ista squatted beside him. He was right. A zigzag of thick metal rods was concertinaed on the cart's underside. "They look like they should move."

"There's a handle on this side," Ruby said. "Let's see what happens if I turn it."

From deep within the mechanism came a reluctant creak, followed by a series of clicks as the metal rods began to move, unfolding like long limbs, lifting the cart higher.

They'd be very, very long limbs, Ista thought, *if they straightened out fully.*

She looked upward and gasped, understanding rippling through her. "That's why there aren't any stairs anywhere!"

"What?" Nat followed her gaze. "Oh. *Oh.* Stop, Ruby!" he cried. "We need to get lined up first."

Ruby clamped her hands to her hips. "Lined up with what? What in the flood are you two going on about?"

In answer, Ista pointed toward a gap in the cavern ceiling, where moonlight shone through a circular grille of the type found in streets and courtyards all across the city.

And less than two minutes later the three of them crawled out into the middle of Shipwrights' Square.

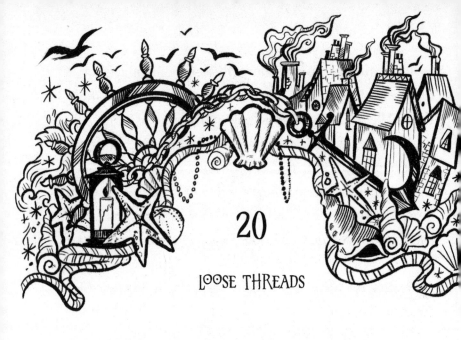

20

LOOSE THREADS

"We'll be safe here, won't we?" Ista said. She was sitting on an upturned bucket in a shelter that the pearl-combers used when the weather was bad. Shipwrights' Square had been empty—which was no surprise at this time of night and so soon after Moon Tide. They'd needed somewhere to talk, and they couldn't risk hanging around the grate through which they'd just crawled, so they had fled down Thumb Lane to the river path. This was the first hiding place they'd spotted, and she was already regretting their choice. The thin walls weren't enough to properly fend off the chill, and being in a confined space with the sack of netting was giving her a serious case of the jitters. A Tide-lantern the combers had left behind was flickering resentfully, as if it felt jittery too.

"I hope so." Nat fidgeted on a crate beside her. "At least

we don't need to worry about grilks getting us anymore, I suppose."

"But what are we going to *do*?" Ruby peeked through the shelter's tiny window. The sky was starless, thick with cloud, as if the moon had gone into hiding too. "Saf's down in those caverns, I know it."

"I think all the missing people must be," Ista said. She could hardly bear to think about Pa down there in the stillness and silence. He was such an *un*still, noisy person— always humming or whistling or tapping his fingers. "But there are so many tunnels. We could search for days and not find anyone."

"We need to show everyone what we've found tonight," said Nat.

"Will people believe us, though?" Ista lifted the grilk head, gazing deep into its empty face. Even in the distorted light the puppet was obviously not a real monster.

"My mum will believe us." Nat was firm. "And everyone will believe her if she writes about it in the paper. That won't tell us where the missing people are, but if we prove the grilks are fake, it should stop more people being taken."

"And it might scare whoever's behind this," said Ruby, sounding very much as if she'd enjoy doing some scaring. "It might even frighten them enough to let everyone go."

"If it doesn't scare them so badly they make the missing people disappear for good!" Ista pointed out.

"If those missing people aren't already gone." Nat's voice was hollow. "Well, someone has to say it," he went on when Ista and Ruby both flinched. "And we still don't know what links any of the victims."

"But something *has* to," Ista said. "Now that we know the grilks are puppets, we know all the attacks must have been planned—none of them can have been mistakes. Well, except for the grilk that attacked us at the Moon Tower. That one must've been waiting for someone else."

"And we've no idea who." Nat's tone was bleaker than ever. "For all we know, some of the other people who got taken might not have been the intended victims either."

"Wait." Ruby stared from him to Ista. "*You two* were attacked? And you got away? I didn't know anyone had ever escaped them."

"The night I bumped into you and Saf," said Ista, nodding. "And I was attacked by a grilk the first night I arrived in Shelwich, too. I only got away that time because Alexo Rokis saved me."

"Alexo Rokis!" Ruby's voice shot up. "Alexo Rokis of the Shrieking Eel? How on earth is he involved in this? And how come neither of those attacks was in the papers?"

"I'd better explain from the beginning," Ista told her. "I came to Shelwich looking for my pa. . . ."

Recapping it all didn't take as long as she thought it might. Nat chimed in, and Ruby listened without interrupting, although she took a sharp breath when Ista reached the part about the gelkin, and another when Ista mentioned Brintan Brook and the contract he'd offered to Giddon.

". . . and then we met you," Ista said. "And you know the rest. Theater, tunnels, puppets, pond—I bet that's how Pond Tower got its name, you know. The lily pond we found is probably right underneath it. But I can't fathom what the tunnels would have been used for. Anyway," she finished with a shrug, "here we are."

The atmosphere between them, though, felt very different to how it had been a few hours earlier. Ista couldn't put her finger on exactly when it had happened, but the frosty mistrust between them had thawed. They might disagree about the details of what to do next, but they were a team now, and they would muddle on together.

"Well, I can solve one mystery for you," Ruby said. "Brintan Brook does want to buy the pickle shop. He's been trying for a while. I know Gran worries about money—you don't exactly get rich from pickles—but she's always turned him down before."

"What about this time?" asked Nat.

"This time . . . she said she'd think about it." Ruby pulled her arms around herself. "She's different since Saf . . . since yesterday, and Brook was so persuasive. He said we could all still live there and run the business, only he'd own it and we'd pay him a small rent. Gran looked so sad when he'd left. That's why I snuck out. I couldn't stand it. I just hope Mum and Dad get back before Gran signs anything. We've sent word to them, of course, about Saf, but it'll take a couple of days for the message to even reach them."

"So Brook wants to buy the pickle shop *and* he wants to buy the Fletwin." Nat sat forward. "He's targeting the victims' families while they're vulnerable. I bet the deal he's offering isn't nearly as good as it sounds."

"That doesn't prove Brook's behind the attacks, though," Ista said. "Only that he's happy to take advantage of people who are in trouble."

"What about Jarmak?" said Ruby. "What if it wasn't an accident that the grilk at the Moon Tower went after you when you were borrowing him? He's the governor's son. The governor is Brook's opponent. And didn't—what's her name?—Wicka Honeyball get taken by grilks too? What if Brintan Brook's using the grilks to get ahead in business *and* politics?"

"That would make sense," said Ista slowly. "Padley said that loads of people started supporting Brook after Wicka Honeyball got taken. And once she was out of the way, it might have been too obvious for Brook to go after the governor herself, but maybe he thought that going after Jarmak was the next best thing?"

"I don't know." Nat took out his notebook, flicking through the pages. "If we find out about any other businesses that Brook's bought recently, we can see if they have connections to the victims or their families. All we really have so far is a lot of coincidences."

Which was true, Ista conceded, but the more coincidences that stacked up, the harder it was to believe they *were* coincidences.

Nat turned to her. "What about our other loose thread?"

"You mean Alexo?" She frowned.

He nodded. "That weird conversation you overheard, the 'not one haul but two' one. That was in a cavern under the Shrieking Eel. All these caverns under Shelwich have got to link up, right? And Alexo must know about them, because there's one under his inn. It's got to be him who's doing Brook's dirty work—if it *is* Brook behind it all, and it's looking likely that it is."

"The night Alexo saved you from the grilk," piped up Ruby. "How did he get there so quickly?"

"Exactly," said Nat. "Don't you think it's strange that Alexo Rokis, who almost never leaves Nimble Lane for long, just happened to be strolling through Shipwrights' Square at the exact moment the grilk attacked you?"

"I don't understand," Ista said. She could feel a theory brewing like a storm in Nat's mind.

"Did you borrow anyone?" he asked. "That first night."

"Yes." She cast her mind back. "Quite a few people."

She'd been desperate to find Mikkela and learn the truth about Pa. Lots of the music venues didn't admit children, and she'd had to borrow faces instead of asking questions as herself. The city had been chaotic to her raw country eyes; she'd changed without caution, over and over, never once thinking that anyone might be watching.

"I didn't change back into myself until I'd settled down to sleep," she said.

Nat's stare took on its searchlight quality. "Who was the last person you borrowed?"

"I didn't exactly ask for her name," Ista said. "I just chose someone strong-looking I'd seen that evening, who I thought would put people off from trying to rob me. But I can show you."

Not easily, though, at this particular moment. Pond Tower chimed for second bell, as if to remind her it was almost Low Tide. Ista willed the magic closer. She could do this. It wasn't as if it weren't there. It was just a duller fizz than sometimes, its bubbles more spaced out. She reached for each one of them, pulling the power to her.

Tall and broad, the woman had been. The details of her face were a blur in Ista's memory, but Ista's magic never forgot anyone once she'd had a good look at them.

Another breath, another reach . . .

Done.

"Tide's teeth!" cried Ruby. "That's her. That's Wicka Honeyball."

"Wicka Honeyball?" Ista jolted back into her own body.

"Possibly the most important victim of all, if Brook is behind this," said Nat. "Worth Alexo leaving the inn for, if he's been helping him. You said you only changed back just as you were about to go to sleep. Suppose they set up the attack thinking you were Wicka Honeyball and then saw at the last moment that you weren't really her. . . ."

"I . . ." Ista stopped and thought about it.

She'd borrowed Wicka Honeyball just before exiting a tavern, changing quickly in the dimly lit porch and leaving the real woman inside at the bar. If Alexo—or someone working for him, such as the mysterious cloaked figure— had been watching the building from across the street, waiting for Wicka . . . of course they would have believed the actual Wicka had just left.

"You're right," she said. "He wouldn't have known till the square. And then he'd have seen what I could do and realized I'd be useful."

So Alexo had pretended to rescue her, and in the confusion he'd stolen the clarinet. She should have guessed. Everything with him was a trick or a trap.

"Why would Alexo help Brook, though?" she said. "What could Brook offer him? He doesn't need power. He doesn't need money."

"But Alexo collects *stuff,* right?" said Ruby. "Like old gadgets—that's what he gets you to steal?"

"Yes. He's fascinated with how things work. He's always taking them apart and putting them back together again." Flashes of the Curiosities jumped to life in Ista's memory. The shell-encrusted corkscrew she'd slid into her pocket in a bar just two streets from here. The tiny coffee grinder she'd nabbed from the windowsill of one of the houses near the heath.

"Well . . ." Ruby spread her hands. "I know they say money can't buy happiness, but it can definitely buy stuff."

"And Brintan Brook's the richest man in Shelwich." Ista felt numb.

"Why does Brook need Alexo if there's no magic involved, though?" Ruby said. "That's what I don't understand."

"Maybe Alexo's the only one who knows how to get around the tunnels," Ista said.

"Maybe," said Nat. "Or maybe he's putting the missing people under a sleep spell like he did with your friend Giddon. Or maybe . . ."

Something in his voice trailed ice down Ista's spine.

"What do you mean?" she asked. "You don't think . . . not the gelkin?"

People were vanishing, and a people-eating monster lived underneath Alexo's inn. She saw it rise from its pool, saw its bladelike teeth flashing.

"No," Nat said. "Not that. I hope not, anyway."

Then why does he sound so sad? Ista wondered. So sad, and so sure about something.

"When did you get here?" he asked. "To Shelwich. How many moons have you been here?"

"Three. And a half. Almost." He was watching her so intently she couldn't think straight. "What?"

"Have another look at the victims." Nat passed her the notebook. "Just see what you notice. Just in case. Start here." He gestured to one of the dates. "That's when Wicka Honeyball got taken."

Ista stared at the page. "That's two days after I got here, isn't it?"

"Um, Nat, what's going on?" said Ruby.

Nat ignored her. "What do you notice, Ista?"

"I don't know," Ista said. "I guess there are people whose businesses Brintan Brook might have been interested in, but it's hard to know, Nat. Like with Saf—she didn't own the pickle shop, did she?"

"What else?" Nat's voice was threaded with excitement—and with worry, as if he knew he was right but desperately didn't want to be.

"Well . . ." Ista read on. "The attacks get closer together, like they're building to something. But like you said before, there's nothing to connect the victims. They're all kinds of people, and the places they go missing from are all over the city." Outside a concert hall, near a late-night bakery, in the little park next to the university . . .

A gasp leapt from her throat.

"What?" said Ruby. "Will someone please tell me what's going on?"

"I . . ." Ista could barely shape the words. "A lot of these people, I think I've borrowed them for my errands."

"You think?" Nat said. "Or you're sure?"

She scoured the list again. She couldn't remember the exact dates, but the places, the names . . . "I'm sure."

"And when you say 'a lot'?"

"Not anyone who vanished before I got here, obviously, but since then . . . half. Maybe more. Give me your pencil, Nat. I'll mark them."

The numbers went up much more quickly after her arrival. Not every disappearance matched an errand, but every errand matched a disappearance. Each location and—yes, she was almost sure now—each date too.

"Tide's teeth, it's me." Ista flew to her feet. "I'm a loose thread, aren't I?"

21

ONE LAST ERRAND

"Let me get this straight." Ruby began pacing again. "So we're saying that Brook's using the grilks to steal people who might get in the way—of his business, or of him winning the election? And he's been paying Alexo in . . . gizmos. And you've . . ." She looked at Ista.

"I've been helping them." Ista felt as if her own voice were coming from very far away. "Not with all the disappearances. Twenty errands, that's my bargain with Alexo—and there's still one left."

But nineteen times. Nineteen shells in the jar in her attic—and it could easily have been nineteen victims had she not been in the courtyard instead of the real Jarmak. He might not have managed to take flight before the puppet drained his magic.

Guilt filled her stomach like thick gray sludge.

"What I don't understand is exactly what Alexo's using you for." Nat had the expression of someone trying to unpick a particularly troublesome knot.

"I do," Ista told him. "I'm a distraction. I don't know how exactly, but that must be it . . . mustn't it?"

"I guess." Ruby made a thoughtful noise. "To make sure no one's watching the real victims closely in the run-up to them vanishing."

"Yes, that must be it," said Nat. "Like a magic trick—and Ista's the part that distracts the audience while the crucial pieces are being moved into place."

Ista's chest was tight, as if she couldn't get enough air, and the little shelter suddenly felt oppressively cramped. The sack of magic-draining netting wasn't helping. It was impossible to order her thoughts with the quiet stifling everything.

"I need . . . ," she began, reaching out to open the door. "I just need . . ."

She didn't know what she needed. Only that she couldn't bear to have Ruby and Nat looking at her the way they both were. She poked her head outside, and Tide-song trickled over her, gentle as ointment on a burn. With it came a clicking sound.

Ista froze. Listened.

Somewhere nearby, tiny footsteps scuttled, halting and then starting up again.

Glass-bugs.

"Ista?" Nat murmured.

Ista waved for him and Ruby to be quiet and stay back.

The scuttling moved again. Paused. Moved. She gave chase, striding after the sound, drinking the salt-sour air down in gulps as the magic rolled over her, lapping at her greedily as if it didn't like that they'd been separated.

A few paces ahead, a single glass-bug lay motionless on the ground. Then another . . . and another—a whole string of them, making a trail, as she'd half known they would. Leading to the eel shack.

A blue handkerchief dangled from the folded awning. Pinned to the handkerchief was a roll of paper tied with a loop of string.

Ista reached for it. When she looked round, the glass-bugs were gone and Ruby was hurrying toward her, sack in hand. Nat limped behind, carrying the grilk head.

"Hey!" Ruby cried out, letting the sack fall to the ground. "What's going on?"

Nat's gaze flicked straight to the paper. "What's that?"

"An errand." Ista untied it, wandering over to the nearest Tide-lantern so she could read. "It's for tomorrow night. Well, tonight, technically." The instructions were as intricate as Alexo's instructions always were. "I have to go to a tavern called the Sunken Chandelier and ask for a woman called Emleen and order a drink called a Pelican's Grace, and then I'm to sneak to one of the back rooms and steal a wooden fish—"

"But *who* do you have to pretend to be?" Nat cut her off.

Ista read the instructions again. "That's the strange part. It says I should go as myself." Which was not just unusual but unprecedented—although it explained why Alexo hadn't summoned her to the Shrieking Eel to show her the person she needed to borrow. "Maybe it isn't as risky as some of the other errands, or maybe Alexo doesn't mind me being spotted, as it's my very last errand."

Or maybe, whispered a sinister voice at the back of her mind, *you're about to become the next victim.* What if he saw her as a loose thread too, now that her work for him was ending?

"A wooden fish, though?" Ruby scrunched her nose. "This is Alexo's last chance to use you. You'd think he'd want something really special."

"Oh, the fish'll be special." Ista was in no doubt of that. A mechanical fish. A musical fish. A fish that doubled as a cocktail maker. This was Alexo, after all. If he really intended to honor their bargain, he wouldn't waste this last errand. She pictured his cluttered study, stuffed to the gills with Curiosities, the fascination in his eyes whenever he investigated an item he hadn't seen before. Whatever this fish was, he must want it very badly indeed.

"Tide's teeth, that's it!" Ista started. "I know how we can do it!"

She felt the same crackle of certainty she'd felt when she'd solved the mystery of Ruby's note, so strong that even the wrongness of the netting in the sack couldn't dull it. She turned toward the river, seeing the whole plan bloom like duckweed on the surface of the murky water, letting a slow smile spread across her face to match it.

"I know how we can catch Alexo."

"Catch Alexo?" Nat gave Ista an extremely hard stare.

She chewed her lip, gazing out to Glass Island and the shadowy columns of its ruined towers. "Do you both know the story of how old Betrik Hettle caught Lightning Lucy?"

"Um, the most famous story in the whole history of Shelwich?" said Ruby. "Yeah, I'm familiar."

"Ingenious thief plaguing the city. Elaborate trap involving a Tide-pearl-studded vase. Local nobody becomes local hero. Thief lives out her days in prison." Nat rattled off the plot points. "We did a play of it at school last year. I was a cabbage seller."

"Alexo gets weak when he's away from Nimble Lane. He never leaves unless he has to." Ista thought back to the night she'd met him, the way he'd doubled over in the street, as if he physically couldn't bear to be so far from his home for so long. He might have been following Wicka Honeyball for a while, she supposed. "But, like we said, this is my last errand—the last one he knows I'll do for sure—so he must really want this wooden fish. And if he's desperate, he'll be reckless. If I ask him to meet me somewhere else to collect it . . ." She dropped a glance at the sack, then shrugged, letting them play it out in their minds.

"We use the netting to trap him!" Ruby slapped her hands together. "Oh, that's *good.* Think you could get him to the theater? There's all kinds of ways I can rig it up there."

"Will Alexo definitely come, though?" asked Nat. "And is the netting powerful enough?"

Ruby huffed a laugh. "Oh, it's powerful enough. I reckon the more magic you have, the worse it makes you feel."

"Exactly." Ista nodded. "And neither of us has a fraction of the magic Alexo does. It *is* a gamble. I can't say for definite that he'll come, but I think it's the best chance we have, and if it works, maybe we can make him confess publicly, and give up Brintan Brook and anyone else who's been helping them!"

"And tell us where the missing people are," added Ruby.

"Yes," Ista said, although saying it felt almost dangerous, like running a blade over her own palm. But if this worked, if they could catch Alexo and trap him and keep him until he squirmed on their hook, everything and everyone they loved just *might* be restored to them.

Doubt slid across Nat's face. "I still think we should tell someone. A grown-up."

"Your mum, you mean," said Ruby.

"Well, yes." He spread his arms. "I don't see what harm it'd do."

"Other than the fact that she'll stop us doing it!" Ruby exclaimed.

Ista was with Ruby on this. "If your mum starts pointing fingers, Alexo and Brook might panic, and then we might never find out where the missing people are." She took a deep breath, trying to smooth her tangled thoughts. "How about if you write your mum a letter explaining everything and leave it for her at the *Conch* tomorrow night, when it's too late for her to stop us? You can leave her the grilk head and the crystals too. That way your mum has the evidence if something goes wrong."

Ruby nodded in agreement.

Nat screwed up his face. "All right. I should probably tell her to warn the governor, too. If Brook *is* behind this, Jarmak might still be in danger."

"So that's it, then." Ruby yawned. "We've got a plan. Oh, you know what would be useful, though? If we knew what Alexo looked like. For all I've heard about him, I've never actually seen him."

"That," said Nat, yawning too, "is a good point."

They both turned to Ista expectantly. The yawning was contagious. It was hard to keep her eyes open, but she nodded and summoned some scraps of energy, gathering the crumbs of Low Tide magic to her and holding Alexo's image in her mind.

Fox-faced. Wolf-eyed. The twist of his smirk. The curl of his wrist as he lifted the latest Curiosity to the light. She'd never tried to borrow him before. It felt strange. Wrong, as if each of her cells was being pulled in two different directions at once, or his magic was too big for her bones.

"*Stop!*" Ruby yelped, her voice so sharp that it sent Ista tumbling back into herself. "Stop. Your hands!"

Ista looked down. Her hands were normal.

Ruby spun toward Nat. "Did you see? The greeny brown?"

"Yeah, I saw it." Nat frowned. "It was . . . I don't know. It was like fish scales or something. I hope that netting hasn't done anything to your magic."

"No," Ista said quickly. But panic squirmed in her stomach. *Could* the metal have affected her blessing somehow? "I'll prove it."

This time it was Governor Hettle in her mind as she gathered the magic closer, feeling a rush of relief when the transformation swept over her.

"No problem there, then," said Nat.

Ruby wrinkled her nose. "Weird seeing the governor up close. What made you pick her?"

Ista shrugged, her coat sleeves too short for Betrika Hettle's arms. "We were just talking about her." They'd been talking about Brintan Brook too, of course, but the idea of borrowing him made her feel oily all over.

"Your eyes!" Nat was peering at her. "They were gray a second ago."

"And now they're blue," Ruby gasped, moving nearer. "Wow, even at Low Tide. The governor's blessing must be more powerful than people think."

Ista hadn't been able to resist checking, only for a moment, that the netting hadn't dampened her ability to borrow blessings, too. Guilt prodded her. Pa definitely wouldn't approve when there was no need for her to do it.

"Alexo must've done something to stop me from borrowing him," she said, changing back into herself. "As for how he looks, he's . . . well, he's . . ."

It was most peculiar. She couldn't pin him down in words, either. His features kept slipping sideways in her mind.

"He's hard to describe," she said, giving up. "But if you see someone watching everyone else without letting them know he's watching, that's him."

"Great. That clears everything up perfectly." Nat rubbed his eyes. "Ugh, I need sleep. And food. I'm starving."

"Mmm, food," Ruby groaned, bending to retrieve the sack of netting. "What I wouldn't give for some cheese on toast right now. Or Gran's rice. Or roast chicken. Right, which way are you both walking?"

"The same way as you, to start with." Nat tested his ankle, rotating it gingerly. "But Ista's the other way. Will you be all right by yourself, Ista?"

"Course." Ista grinned. "Like you said, it's not as if we need to worry about grilks now." And Alexo needed her safe and sound, at least until she'd completed errand number twenty. "Where shall we meet tomorrow?"

"Somewhere with lots of people." Nat considered. "The library again? After school."

"Look after yourself till then, though, yeah?" Ruby said.

"Yes. Don't go doing anything without us," Nat added.

They both fixed Ista with a look.

"Whatever." Ista swallowed round the pebble that had lodged in her throat. She'd been lonely. Lonely in a deep-down way she hadn't let herself examine too closely. But she wasn't lonely anymore. "You be careful too. Both of you."

The pair of them shambled away, listing more things they'd like to eat. Nat really must have been tired, because he'd left the grilk head beside where he'd been sitting. Ista picked it up. She was still for a moment, gazing down at the grilk's toothless jaws.

It was strange. The thing she remembered most clearly about that first night in Shelwich was the teeth, but she supposed she must have imagined them.

The talk of food had set Ista's stomach gurgling, and it kept up its complaints as she flopped into bed. If she could have chosen anything she wanted to eat and drink, she'd have had apple tea and gingercrumb tart and she'd have sat by the fire while Padley snored and the clock doled out its heartbeat ticks from the mantel.

She wanted all that so badly she could actually hear the ticking, which was strange because there wasn't a clock near the hearth at the Fletwin. *Oh,* she thought, *I'm dreaming.* And she let the dream fly her away, over the slopes of the park and the Moon Tower's great glass dome to the brackish creek near her aunt's house, where Pa had taken her for a picnic the day before he left.

I'll send for you, he promised, his eyes certain in the dappled sunlight.

No need, she told him, over the lazy slap of water. *I'm coming, Pa. No need to send for me. I'm coming for you.*

22

THE PIECES FALL INTO PLACE

Ista awoke to grayish light trickling through the cracks in the shutters, and a black cloak waiting in the glass-bug chest below the window. *For tonight,* read the accompanying note in Alexo's handwriting.

"I could have guessed that," Ista muttered, taking the cloak to the mirror. But she had to admit it was . . . lovely. A cloak for midnight adventures, light as silk but warm as velvet. The finest piece of clothing she'd ever worn. It was practical, too, with a hood that stayed up without drooping over her eyes, and three pockets of varying sizes concealed in the lining.

There was no sign or sound of Giddon, the air sharp with quiet as she washed and dressed, but he'd left a note on the mantelpiece saying he'd left early and might be out late and she wasn't to worry. Ista made a stack of fluffy pancakes, which she smeared in marsh honey and washed down with a whole pot of tea, then idled at the kitchen counter, prickling with nerves as she read over Alexo's instructions, committing them to memory as she always did.

The last errand. Unless that, too, was a lie. *Either way, I'll never get the clarinet back now,* Ista thought dully. Alexo would never forgive her for what she was going to do.

But if it worked, she might get Pa.

The magic rose and fell, the day slipping away under a gull-wing-gray sky. At a quarter to third bell she made one last trip to the attic to tap Pa's photo for luck, then headed out, the new cloak swishing and the grilk head bumping along in a bag over her shoulder.

She was imagining Nat and Ruby making their separate ways to the library, so she froze in confusion at the sight of them both hurtling precariously down the road toward her on a rusty-looking bicycle, Ruby pedaling and Nat riding pillion.

They screeched to a halt, both speaking at once.

"We have to go! Right now!"

"They took Jarmak!"

"Took Jarmak?" Ista felt as if all the heat was draining from her body.

"Grilks," continued Ruby, puffing with exertion. "Well, whoever's . . . operating them. In the governor's own . . .

garden. In . . . broad daylight. Half the city's . . . talking about it." She ran out of puff entirely and motioned for Nat to take over.

"One of the governor's staff saw it happen," he said. "And we have to hurry. Governor Hettle's about to make a speech in Shipwrights' Square!"

Three was too many for one bicycle to carry. Ista had to run behind the others, sandpipers *wheet-wheet-wheet*ing and circling high above her as if they were cheering her on.

A podium had been set up on a platform in front of Shipwrights' Hall, and a subdued crowd had gathered under the glowering clouds. Ista spotted people she knew from every walk of Shelwich life: makers and traders, artists and musicians, shipwrights and fishers, shop-keepers, scholars, and all kinds of other folk. The journal-ists were at the front, Priya Shah among them. She threw Nat a wave, her expression grim, then turned back to the platform.

"Don't worry," Nat said when Ista gave him a look. "I haven't told her. But I snuck out of school early and got someone at the *Conch* to help me dig out the records of Brintan Brook's recent business deals."

"And?" Ista said.

"Well . . ." Out came the notebook. "Brook's definitely

persuaded nine of the victims' families to sell businesses or properties to him. So that isn't conclusive—but some other people might have refused whatever offers he made them, and he might have all kinds of private grudges that we don't know about." The uncertainty bothered him, Ista could tell.

"No Governor Hettle yet," said Ruby, returning from stowing the bicycle in a rack at the side of the square. "What do you think she'll say?"

"That she's going to concede the election, I'd guess." Nat rose to his tiptoes, craning around. "After all, it's meant to happen tomorrow, and how's anyone supposed to believe she'll keep the city safe when she couldn't even protect her own son? Oh, there's Brook. Sink me, he looks smug."

Brintan Brook was in front of Pond Tower, surrounded by a huddle of supporters. He was clearly trying to look somber, but he couldn't quite stop his smirk from poking through. Which made sense, seeing as he was probably about to get exactly what he wanted.

"We'll show him," said Ruby. "If our plan works, we can make Alexo confess publicly, and everyone will know what Brintan Brook's done. He'll never become governor after that."

It was a big *if,* though. Ista's head swam with guilt. They'd suspected Jarmak might be in danger. They should have warned him or the governor straightaway.

She snuck a peek at the grilk head in her bag, wishing she could use it to confront Brook there and then. But a shaft of late-afternoon sun pierced the cloud, and the puppet looked more puppetlike than ever under the sharp slant of light. No one would ever believe that *this* was one of the creatures that had been terrorizing the city and literally snatching people off the streets.

For the moment, Ista, Nat, and Ruby could do nothing except watch and wait.

More people drifted in, until the square was bursting with bodies, a buzz of voices filling the air, almost as if there was about to be a concert or a play.

"There's the woman from the Moon Tower," Nat said, nudging Ista. "The one who showed us to the courtyard before the grilk almost got us. . . . What?"

Ista was scowling, but not because of the woman. She'd seen something else. On the far side of the crowd—an algae-green cloak.

"Hold this." She thrust the bag at Nat. There was no time to explain. She wriggled through the throng of people like a swimmer fighting the current. If it was the same green cloak, and a prickle of instinct told her it was, then this had to be the person she'd heard with Alexo at the inn—the person who'd been trailing her, who'd disappeared down a dead-end street.

It *was* the same cloak. There was a particular sheen to the fabric as it caught the light. And this time its wearer wasn't looking for Ista. They were shaking hands with someone else. A tall white man with a neat brown beard. He turned slightly, and Ista lurched to a stop.

It was the man from the hospital. The one who'd been with the governor and the Moon-Tower woman. And now here he was, sidling into a recess in the side of a building with the person in the cloak. Ista flattened herself against the wall and edged as close as she dared, straining to hear their conversation.

". . . all set up. No need to worry." The reed-pipe voice, the unmistakable scratchy lilt she'd heard at the Shrieking Eel. It *was* the same person. "There's just the matter of payment."

"Yes, yes," said the other voice, which belonged to the bearded man—Ista could just see him, although not his companion, from her position. "As agreed. Half now, half tomorrow night, when it's over."

A rustle and a clink, as if a bag of coins was being passed from one set of hands to another.

Ista scuttled back to avoid being seen as the cloaked figure swept from the recess, their face masked by their hood. They made a swift beeline for Pin Row. The bearded man walked off the other way, almost directly past Ista, although he was thankfully too absorbed in his thoughts to notice her. He cleared his throat as he went—once, then twice, then again with a loud rattling wheeze.

That cough!

Ista's blood went cold. She plowed back through the crush of bodies to Ruby and Nat.

"The person from the grilk cavern!" Her mind was spinning so fast she didn't know where to start. "The one who was fixing the cart. He's here—I recognized his cough. He works for the governor, and he was talking to Alexo's helper in the green cloak, but *they've* gone, and . . ."

"Wait," said Ruby. "Slow down. How do you know the person we saw in the cavern works for the governor?"

"He was with her at the hospital, visiting the Stone Sleepers." Ista scanned the crowd. "Look, there he is! That man with the beard, to the right of the podium."

Nat peered toward where she was pointing. "Is that the Moon-Tower woman with him?"

It was. The bearded man was talking to her, gesturing back to the recess. The short, stern-faced woman broke into a smile—then immediately smothered it as if remembering where she was.

"Tide's teeth," Ista breathed. "*She's* in on it too." She threaded the ideas together as they landed—each with such force that she was sure she was right. "At the Moon Tower, I thought the latch on the courtyard door must have got stuck, but what if that woman locked us out there deliberately? And the bearded man, just now, he was handing over money—I'm sure he was—and he said something about how that was only half of it and the person in the cloak would get the other half tomorrow night, when *it* was *over.* He had to mean after the election, didn't he?"

"Yes," said Nat, "but—"

"And today you said one of the governor's staff saw Jarmak being taken."

He blinked at her. "Yes."

"They were the only witness," said Ruby.

"Or they were the one who took him!" Ista's pulse was beating double time. "Think about it. The puppets don't look at all realistic in the light. That must be why there's never been a grilk attack in daylight—until today. Until Jarmak. If anyone had seen him get taken, they'd definitely have known the monster wasn't real. Unless—"

"Unless they were behind it!" Nat finished her sentence.

"Exactly," Ista said. "Those people might officially work for the governor, but maybe they *really* work for Brintan Brook."

At that very moment, as if on cue, the great front door of Shipwrights' Hall opened.

Governor Hettle walked out to face her audience. She was a shell of the woman Ista had bumped into at the hospital the day before; her gait was slow, the shadows under her eyes so deep they might have been smeared on with charcoal. An expectant hush blanketed the square as she stepped up to the podium. The governor cast a glance at her grandfather's statue before she spoke, as though trying to draw courage from his proud stone face.

"Thank you all for coming." Her voice carried like the tolling of a deep, sad bell. "As you have no doubt heard, grilks took my son, Jarmak, from our home earlier this afternoon."

It was almost dead-on Low Tide, barely a drip of magic in the day. Even so, people didn't like hearing the grilks named. Anxious mutterings blew and swirled like leaves.

The governor nodded. "My friends, I know you are scared. I have been afraid too. But even in our darkest days we must have courage. We must have hope. More than that, we must have action."

"Fat chance of that from her" came a murmur not far from Ista's shoulder.

"Shh," said someone else. "Let's hear what she has to say."

Ista wanted to know, very much. The governor wasn't showing any sign that she planned to give up on the election as Nat had predicted. When she continued, her eyes were steelier than they had been, and the Shelwich dip swayed more strongly in her vowels.

"I know some of you feel I have not done enough to protect our city from these creatures, but that changes today. You see, my boy—my brave Jarmak—is special. The Tide has blessed him . . ." She let the pause hang, as if what she was about to reveal was so astounding that she herself had struggled to come to terms with it. "With telepathy."

"*Telepathy?* He can speak to people—using his mind?"

Ista had the strangest feeling, as though a tidal wave were surging toward her but it was too far out for her to see it yet.

"That's not right," Ruby whispered. "Unless . . . could Jarmak have more than one blessing?"

No, Ista thought. She'd borrowed Jarmak at High Tide under a full moon. She'd felt his wings wanting to bloom even before Nat had told her Jarmak could fly. If he was telepathic, she'd surely have sensed that too.

There was no time to unpick it further. All around them, the skeptical mutters ceased, faces turning attentive as the governor went on, her words clear and crisp over the faint burble of Low Tide magic.

"Jarmak has spoken to me. Since he was taken. That's right," she declared as the crowd seemed to draw in a breath as one. "My son is alive. He has told me how to find the path to the grilks' lair, deep beneath our city. And there is more. Your missing loved ones are alive too! The grilks are holding them captive, feeding on their magic."

"Let's get them!" a lone voice cried.

"Yes, what are we waiting for?" called another. "Get our people back and kill the grilks. Kill the grilks! Kill the grilks!"

The chant took hold, spreading like wildfire from a crackle to a roar, the crowd pressing forward, carrying Ista, Nat, and Ruby with them.

The governor, though, shook her head and raised both

hands for quiet. "We must not be hasty. The grilks are formidable. Remember how they took young Saf Mallard, the strongest girl in the city? And we all know they sense magic. Anyone with a drop of it would be at risk." She turned toward old Betrik's statue again, and this time every head in the square turned with her. "Which is why I must go alone."

There was a collective gasp.

"I have a confession," Governor Hettle said sadly as all eyes swung back to her. "You all believe, I know, that the Tide has blessed me with the ability to change my eye color. The truth is . . . I do not hear the magic at all. I was so ashamed, in fact, that I have been deceiving you using special lenses. Words cannot express how deeply I regret this deception. I feared your judgment—and it is only today that I realize how foolish that was."

A burst of consternation greeted this, and she raised her hands for quiet again. "But now my very lack of magic *is* a blessing. The grilks will not sense me coming. With Jarmak to guide me, I will be able to hunt them down and restore what has been taken from us. And once our people are out safely, I will burn down the grilks' lair, and tomorrow . . ." She inclined her head, acknowledging a flurry of cheers and applause. "Tomorrow, when I return, I hope I will have proved myself to you and that you will trust me with the future of our city."

The crowd surged forward like a storm, the journalists'

hands and notebooks waving. Ista caught sight of Brintan Brook, floundering in the chaos, his mouth hanging open as if he was as astonished as she was.

"I am sorry," the governor called over the din. "I'm sorry, but there is no time for questions. I must prepare."

With that, she swept from the platform and back into Shipwrights' Hall.

Brintan Brook stared after her. Ista looked from him to the bearded man and Moon-Tower Woman, watching for any sign or signal between them, but there was nothing. A fragment of the governor's speech rang in her ears: *I hope I will have proved myself to you and that you will trust me with the future of our city.*

"Sink me!" Ruby's voice dragged her back. "Jarmak being taken has driven the poor governor out of her mind. She must be so upset that she's imagining hearing his voice. Now all Brintan Brook has to do is wait until she heads off to 'save' everyone, and then he can get rid of her, too."

"No." A cold realization swept over Ista's skin. "It isn't Brook. The governor's lying. About all of it. She has a blessing. You both saw me borrow it last night."

She gazed across the crowd at the statue of old Betrik Hettle, Padley's words springing up in her mind.

As for Betrik . . . Like a man transformed, he was . . .

"Tide's teeth," Nat breathed, following her gaze. "She's trying to copy her grandfather. Be a hero like he was. I thought I recognized part of her speech just now. It's because I've read it. It's almost exactly what old Betrik said the night before he won the election."

Ruby shook herself. "Are you saying what I think you're saying?"

"Yes." Ista was more certain with each passing second. "It's *her.* The governor's been behind this all along. She's staged all the grilk attacks—and now she's going to 'rescue' everyone."

23

THE SUNKEN
CHANDELIER

Some people were already celebrating. Shouts and cheers echoed around the square. Other people wandered about half-dazed, as if they thought they might be dreaming.

Ista knew how they felt.

"But will the election still go ahead?" Ruby gestured at the chaos.

"Definitely," said Nat. "Don't you see? That's what all this has been for. Governor Hettle must've been planning this for ages. The very first grilk sightings were basically just rumors, remember—not long before old Betrik died. I bet the governor and her helpers started those. And the first attacks were spaced out, weren't they? And then they started happening closer and closer together. It was all building to tonight."

Ista let out a gasp. "That's why we couldn't work out

what connected the victims! There was nothing that connected them—that's the whole point. The governor needed to take all kinds of people from all over the city to make sure *everyone* was terrified of the grilks—just like how the whole city was plagued by that thief Lightning Lucy before Betrik Hettle caught her. She must have meant to stage her big rescue a couple of days ago, so that everyone would hear about it before the election. But then we interfered at the Moon Tower, and she couldn't exactly pretend Jarmak was guiding her to the grilks when he hadn't even been 'taken.'"

"I'm pretty sure the news will get around in time anyway," said Ruby as more cheers erupted nearby.

Nat nodded. "She'll win by a landslide. She'll be so popular she'll probably end up being in power for even longer than her grandfather."

The three of them stared at each other.

"This doesn't change anything," said Ista. "We stick to the plan. Get the fish, get Alexo to the theater, make him talk. We know he's helping her. I saw that man give Alexo's helper the money—and he said they'd get the rest tomorrow night, when this was all over."

"I . . ." Nat developed a sudden interest in his fingernails. "Do either of you think we should maybe . . . let the governor do it?"

Ruby rounded on him. "What?"

He shrugged wretchedly. "She's going to bring everybody back, right? That's her plan. To stage a big rescue. I just . . . I just want Ravi to come home."

"But then she'll get away with it all!" Outrage scorched Ista's insides. In the background another chant of "kill the grilks" broke into a chorus of cheers for Governor Hettle. "And anyone who's been helping her will get away with it too."

"Yeah," said Ruby. "We can get everyone back *and* get justice."

"Exactly." Ista fixed her eyes on Nat. "We're the only ones who can do it."

He blew out a small sigh. "You're right. We have to try. Do you really think it'll work?"

Ista swallowed. "I don't know."

But there it was again. Hope. Like a star blazing inside her, burning so bright that the gently rising Tide was only a faint sizzle in comparison.

Because one thing was certain. If the governor was planning to stage a rescue, the missing people *must* be alive.

The Sunken Chandelier was almost all the way out by the Great East Bridge, so far from the city center that Ista had to borrow Ruby's bicycle. Her route took her by the cemetery, where Stone Tower tolled its solemn bell, filling her chest with a quiet unease. *Arrive at sundown,* Alexo's instructions had read, and night was gobbling the last tatters of the gloomy afternoon. The Tide was rising, its magic nosing at Ista like a puppy seeking attention as she opened the door.

The tavern was not at all what she'd expected from its name. It was scruffy and almost completely empty, save for two bored-looking customers and an even more bored-looking bartender, who raised their eyebrows questioningly when Ista approached the bar.

"Hello," Ista said, conscious of the stickiness of the countertop and how out of place she must look beside it in her fine new cloak. "Um, I'm here to see Emleen."

The bartender gave a single tilt of their head toward a sparsely filled bookcase that slumped against the wall, then resumed polishing a glass.

Nineteen errands had taught Ista to trust an obvious signal when it was given. She walked to the bookcase, not surprised in the slightest when it slid aside.

A burst of lively music rose to greet her, increasing in volume as it drew her down a sloping corridor that doubled back on itself six or seven times until she came to a cavernous space far greater than the dingy room she'd left behind. An enormous Tide-pearl chandelier hung from the ceiling, turning slow pirouettes as if kissed by an invisible breeze, the light sprinkling down over crisp white tablecloths, a stage where a four-piece band was in full swing, and a marble-topped bar. Here, a second bartender used their Tide-blessing to frost glasses with a touch of their finger, while a team of servers flitted here and there, smartly suited and dragonfly-quick.

One stopped at Ista's elbow. "Welcomethisway ifyouplease."

They spoke so fast that by the time Ista's brain caught up she was at a table near the stage. For the next song, the band was joined by a tangle-haired boy with a vespalin. He couldn't have been much older than Ista, but he played as if he'd known how from the cradle, his slim brown fingers skipping dexterously over the strings. The clarinetist nodded along in approval. Ista frowned. Could Pa have played here? His letters hadn't mentioned this place.

Another server appeared. "WhatcanIgetforyou?"

"A Pelican's Grace, please." Ista wondered what would be in it—then had a flash of worry about how she'd settle the bill. She hadn't brought any money with her, and there was none in any of the cloak pockets.

But when the drink came, in a tall frosted glass with a curly straw and a long metal spoon, it was accompanied by a card that read WITH THE COMPLIMENTS OF THE MANAGEMENT. It was also one of the most delicious things Ista had ever tasted, creamy and chocolaty with crunchy sprinkles on top that popped on her tongue in tiny starbursts of sweetness.

This was an exceedingly strange errand. She caught her reflection in a mirror and realized she was tapping her foot. The chandelier swirled, shedding droplets of light that landed like rain on the dark fabric of her cloak. And all she had to do was sit here as herself for the next fifteen songs, order a toasted sandwich if she wanted one, and then nip down a specific corridor and into a specific room to fetch the fish. If she hadn't known better, she'd almost have thought Alexo wanted her to enjoy herself.

Ista did know better, though. She couldn't help wondering whether Alexo was simply keeping her busy and out of the way while the governor carried out her "rescue."

But there was nothing to be done about it. If she didn't stick to his instructions, something might go wrong and she might not get the fish—and without the fish she had nothing to lure Alexo to their meeting. So she sat and tapped her foot and drank her drink and ate her sandwich.

"Ista!" A lanky figure bounded toward her. It was Mikkela, Pa's trumpet-player friend. They were the kind of person who bounded everywhere, so much energy fizzing through them that even the heaviest days couldn't weigh them down. "Tide keep you, Ista. Wasn't expecting to see you here. I'm so sorry about Padley. I came by the Fletwin yesterday when I heard the news, but no one was in." They pulled out a chair, flipped it round, and straddled it backward, their freckled fingers tapping out a pattern against the wood. "Have you heard about this rescue attempt the governor's got planned? Now, that would be a fine thing. We mustn't float our hopes too high, of course."

Mustn't hope to get Pa back after all this time, Mikkela

clearly meant. But Ista's hope had become a living creature almost separate from her, with wings that could fly
to the moon, and claws to tear anything that stood in her
way. Beneath it she felt a flutter of nerves. The last song
had been the fourteenth since she'd arrived, which meant
it was almost time to wrap up her errand and continue
with the rest of the plan.

"Are you playing tonight?" she asked, changing the
subject, because Mikkela definitely fell into the category
of grown-ups who would try to stop her doing what she
was about to do if she told them the truth.

Mikkela nodded. "With my friend Tamlin, there on the
vespalin. Good, isn't he?"

"Very." Ista felt there must be magic in the boy's playing. The melody rose, then dropped away like a staircase
to nowhere, one phrase glittering and wild, the next soft
and rich. It seemed to have cast a spell on its player, too.
At the end of the set, he looked up, flipping his hair back
from his face and blinking at the audience as if he was
surprised to see so many people there.

Mikkela waved to him as he set his vespalin on its
stand. "Hey, Tam! Come and meet my friend."

The boy's hair flopped into his face again as he loped
over, raising a shy hand in greeting. "Hello. Tide keep you."

It was *him*. Ista would have known that voice anywhere. The tuneful lilt, the scratch underneath it. The
stranger in the green cloak.

A gasp slipped from her before she could stop it, and Tamlin stilled, a half-formed smile freezing on his lips. She saw realizations land like pebbles breaking the surface of a pool. He hadn't recognized her from the stage, but he did now—and he knew she'd recognized him.

"This is Ista." Mikkela beamed, oblivious.

"Tide keep you," said Ista.

"Tide keep you," Tamlin said again. "Mikkela, I've just remembered there's something I need to . . ."

Letting the end of the sentence evaporate, he turned on his heel and fled. This time there wasn't a shadow of a doubt in Ista's mind that he *was* fleeing. She pushed back her chair.

"Well, I never!" Mikkela exclaimed. "I'm so sorry, Ista. He's normally— Hey, now, what are *you* doing?"

Ista didn't know. This was a terrible idea. It might derail the errand, derail the whole plan, but it was as if a switch had flicked inside her. Tamlin hurtled through a door to one side of the stage, and she hurtled after him. A hallway unrolled, drenched in Tide-lantern blue. Tamlin skidded through an open door halfway down it, throwing himself into the room beyond.

Little face-changer, he'd called her, but not only was he about her age, he was hardly any taller—and he certainly wasn't faster. Ista burst into the room seconds later.

"Stay back!" Tamlin was on the far side, in front of a

tall cupboard. "Stay back or I'll do it." He turned away, rooting in his pockets. "I'll do it, and you'll be sorry."

"Do what?" Ista was genuinely perplexed. He reminded her of a species of tree frog she'd read about, which had the same colors as the poisonous frogs so bigger creatures would think twice about eating it. She edged forward.

"You stay there! Stay right there!" It was almost a plea. He was faking. Trying to buy time while he found whatever it was he was searching for.

"Listen." Ista raised her hands, trying to look as unthreatening as possible. "I know what you've been doing. If you know where the missing people are, please tell me. I won't turn you in."

"Missing people?" Tamlin pulled out a red handkerchief and a wooden guitar pick, tossing them both to the floor. "I don't know anything about that."

"I saw you." Ista inched closer again. "With that bearded man in Shipwrights' Square today—the man who works for Governor Hettle. He gave you money. And I heard you with Alexo at the Shrieking Eel. I know you've been following me, and I know you're working for the governor."

"No, I'm not." Sincere confusion flashed across his face. "That money was for a gig. Some big party tomorrow. I hardly know that man. He was in here last week—came up to me after my set." He tried his side pocket again, giving a little bark of triumph as he pulled out a large silver key that was engraved with strange markings, almost like musical notes.

"All right," Ista said. Maybe he really didn't know about the governor. "But you *are* working with Alexo."

With him, or *for* him? It struck her that Tamlin might be running errands not unlike hers.

"If he's making you work for him," she began, but he cut her off with a laugh.

"Making me? He's *helping* me. A boy's got to eat. But, speaking of Alexo, I am under strict instructions."

The cupboard door was ajar. He pushed it shut, shoved the key into the lock, and twisted, first one way, then the other; then he withdrew the key and flung the door open again. A wave of wind crested out, smelling of somewhere cold and far away. It blew Ista backward so hard she staggered.

Tamlin clutched the doorframe, his hair whipping wildly. "See you, Ista Flit."

With that, he propelled himself forward into what every fiber of Ista's being screamed should still be the cupboard but was now unquestionably a waterlogged and overgrown garden with a pocket square of lawn that was more mud than grass. The wind looped around, following him, and slammed the door.

Ista dived for the handle and wrenched the door open again. The cupboard gazed innocently back at her, its shelves groaning with old pots and cups and plates.

Impossible. She stared, breathless with shock. Somehow, there had been—she was sure—a whole other world where now there was only crockery. How had Tamlin done it? Was it something to do with his blessing? With that strange silver key?

She might have stood and puzzled over it for hours—but, behind her, tiny feet scuttled.

She sighed. "Come to spy, have you? Well, I've messed everything up."

The scuttling stopped. Ista turned. Four glass-bugs peeked up at her from the floor. Above them, hanging from a nail on the wall, was a piece of driftwood carved in rough strokes into the shape of a fish.

"Oh," Ista said. "Or maybe not."

It had to be *this* fish, although it was so simple that she couldn't imagine it occupying Alexo for long. Perhaps it had a secret compartment. She unhooked it, gave it a shake, listening for a telltale rattle—but the only sound was the glass-bugs scuttling closer, as if they too were curious.

They froze again when Ista looked up.

"Well," she told them. "As you're here, you might as well deliver a message for me."

With a silent *thank you* to her past self for tucking a pencil and paper in one of her many pockets, she sat down and wrote instructions to Alexo for an errand of her own.

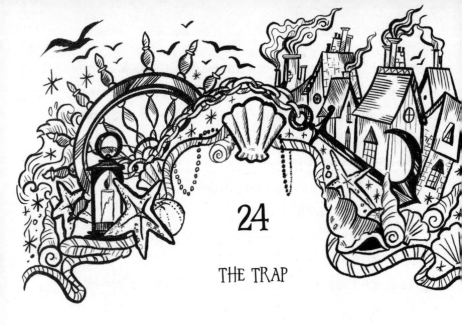

24

THE TRAP

Mist drowned the city like thick, cold soup. Ista pedaled furiously, juddering over the cobbles, magic singing in her blood. Just over half an hour till High Tide. Nat was waiting outside the theater, a Tide-lantern in one hand.

"You're here! Are you all right? Did you get it?"

"I got it." She reached into her cloak, feeling the outline of the fish nestled in the largest of the pockets. "Did you leave the note for your mum at the *Conch*?"

"The note, the grilk head, and the crystals. And everything's ready here. Come on."

Inside, they crept carefully over the precarious foyer floor. There was another Tide-lantern on the ticket counter, a second by the doorway to the auditorium, and a third midway down the central aisle. A trail of bread crumbs to lead Alexo to the stage, where a fourth, unmagical lantern waited, a candle flickering behind its glass.

Ruby's voice drifted down from the walkway. "Ista! Did you get the fish?"

"Yes." Ista halted level with the front row of seats. "Where are the nets?" She could sense them sapping the magic, but the light was so dim that she couldn't see much at all.

Nat chuckled softly. "Right there on the stage. It's one big net now. We sewed them together and painted them to blend in with the floor."

Ista wouldn't have spotted it if she hadn't known where to look. She put one foot on it, wincing as the wrongness flowed up through the sole of her boot. She couldn't feel the ridges, though, so Alexo wouldn't be able to either.

"There's a wire round the edge," Ruby explained, "connected to a counterweight up here. You need to get him as close to the center as you can. Then you leap out of the way, we release the weight, and . . . hey, presto, one Alexo Rokis in a bag. Well, hopefully."

Ista took the driftwood fish from her pocket, running her hands over the roughness of the grain. Would he really come for it? Would the net be enough to hold him? To make him talk? So much depended on him assuming the feeling of wrongness was down to the fact that he'd strayed too far from Nimble Lane.

But it was too late for second-guessing.

"You should go up, Nat," she said. "He could be here any moment."

"Okay." Nat was all shadow, but she imagined him giving her an encouraging nod. "Let's do this."

His footsteps clanked up the ladder. Somewhere in the distance, the half-hour bell chimed. Ista circled to the back of the stage. She had to cross the edge of the net to get there; wrongness scuttled all over her, like insects crawling.

Time dripped to a stop. Her throat was dry. Her palms slickened, the silence pressing in.

Bang! The doors flew open, a sharp breeze whistling into the auditorium. The wind brought magic with it. So much magic—Ista could see it sloshing over the seats and down the aisle like silvery paint.

Alexo had arrived.

"You summoned me." His voice curled like smoke, each word laced with smirk.

"I've got your fish." Ista held it up.

One moment he was at the top of the aisle, the next he had carved down it like a knife. But at the edge of the stage he paused, his expression unreadable in the lantern light.

"Why here, *Isssta*?" Her name was almost a hiss. No—he was slurring. He took another step, heavier than the last. Ista felt a twist of pity. It must hurt him more than she'd thought, being so far from the inn.

She hardened herself. Stepped forward onto the netting, suppressing a shudder at the wrongness radiating from it. "I need to show you something."

"*Sssssshow* me what?"

Panic sliced Ista's spine. Did he know? Was he toying with her? Even if he was, it didn't matter. He was walking again. A few more steps would put him center stage, exactly where they wanted him. He gave a shake, as if trying to clear his head.

"It's this way." Ista gestured vaguely at the dark behind her. "I can't explain. You need to see it. But here, take this first."

She held out the fish.

It shouldn't have worked. It *wouldn't* have worked if Alexo had been his usual sharp self. But he wasn't. He swiped for the fish, and with the swipe came another step.

"Now!" Ista yelled. She leapt away, flinging herself clear as the net whooshed upward, taking Alexo and the fish with it.

There was the sound of thrashing. Then an awful silence, followed by a nerve-jangling howl, raw with hurt and rage.

"Ista*aaaaa*!"

The net dangled just above the stage, and Alexo

dangled within it, as furious as a cat in a sack. Ista picked up the lantern. It took all her courage to make herself walk toward him, and she stopped before she was close enough to see his eyes.

"What . . . have you done?" Half snarl, half whisper. He strained toward her, then shrank back with a hiss. Ista felt the faintest prickle of magic again, as if the wrongness didn't care about her so much now that it had someone with more power to feed on.

"It's worked!" she called up to Nat and Ruby. Then, to Alexo: "We want answers. Starting with exactly where the missing people are."

"And a list." Ruby leaned over the walkway railing. "Of everyone you've taken and everyone who's been helping you."

"And a full confession," Nat chimed in. "A signed one that we can put in the paper."

Alexo hissed again. "*Issss*sta, please. I . . . don't understand. I—" He broke off with a gasp, curling in on himself.

It seemed like the netting was really hurting him. Ista coated her heart in stone, silencing the voice in her head that whispered they'd gone too far. "Stop it. No more tricks. No more lies. We know you've been using me as a decoy to help the governor steal people."

"The . . . governor? To . . . steal people?"

Tide's teeth, he was a good actor. Ista pushed down

another surge of pity. "I came to the Shrieking Eel. The night you took Padley and Saf—I only knew about Padley then, and I thought you might be able to help get him back. I heard you talking to Tamlin. You were pleased because you'd made 'two hauls.'"

"No, Ista, listen to me." Alexo pulled himself upright, anguish straining his voice as he clung to the net. "Tamlin helps me . . . go salvaging. Scavenging treasure from . . . the river. We went over to . . . Glass Island. He has nothing to do . . . with the people, or your . . . errands."

Ista strode nearer, stopping just out of his arm's reach, lifting the lantern closer to his face. "You admit it, then? That you've been setting up my errands to steal people."

"No. No, not stealing. *Saving.*" Alexo's voice was a croak, his eyes half-shut, his face turning gray where it touched the netting.

"Liar!" Ruby cried. "Tell me where my sister is. What have you done with her?"

"Yeah, and my brother!" shouted Nat. "Ravi Shah and Saf Mallard. Where are they both?"

Alexo opened his eyes, his gaze fixing on Ista—no smirk now, just a fog of pain. "Ista Flit, I swear to you, on all my secrets. We've been saving people—taking them to safety before the grilks can snatch them. We've been using you . . . making sure all eyes were on you while we . . . persuaded people to come with us." He wrenched his head up, twisting to look at Nat and Ruby. "I don't know where your siblings are. We couldn't save them. We don't always get the names and places in time."

"Oh, sure. And you're just magically getting these names, are you?" Sarcasm poured from Nat's voice.

From Ruby's too. "Yeah, and where *are* these people you've supposedly saved, and what exactly have you even been saving them from? We know the grilks are just puppets!"

But Alexo didn't. Ista saw the astonishment strike him, clear as lightning splitting the sky. And if he didn't know about that . . . a hundred tiny fragments clicked together in her mind.

The quiet houses leading up to the Shrieking Eel.

The shuttered windows.

The feeling of being watched every time she walked past.

"They're on Nimble Lane," she breathed. "Aren't they?"

"It's the only place . . . I can protect them. It's . . . only temporary, until we learn who's controlling . . . the grilks." He was fading again, his face tight with pain. "But the . . . governor? You said . . ." He crumpled over, his body spasming.

"Let him down!" Ista yelled. "Ruby, he's telling the truth! Now! We're hurting him."

The urgency in her voice must have left no room for doubt. Ropes whooshed, and the net fell, bringing Alexo thumping down with it. Ruby had done almost too good a job with the trap, and he couldn't free himself no matter how much he struggled.

Ista threw herself to the floor, pulling at the strands of netting, ignoring the numbing wrongness that made her shudder with each touch. "I'm sorry," she told him. "I didn't know how much it would hurt you. I'll get you out. Please stop moving. You're making it harder."

Alexo kept writhing, attempting to speak between ragged, gritty breaths. "The governor . . . If it's her, we need to . . . go. It isn't . . . safe . . . here."

"Shh, please." Ista's fingers wouldn't work fast enough. "Help me!" she shouted to Ruby and Nat. "I need a knife or scissors or something. We need to cut him free."

A familiar voice floated from the shadows. "No, no, I think we should leave him as he is for the time being."

"Run," Alexo whispered. "Run, Ista."

But Ista knew she couldn't leave him now. Besides, it was too late.

Governor Hettle strolled out of the wings, smiling as she took in the scene. "Bravo, children. You've saved me a lot of bother by luring Alexo Rokis from his lair."

25

THE FOREST OF STATUES

In another lifetime, Ista thought, Governor Hettle could have made her career on the stage. She had discarded her earnestness as easily as an old shawl, her eyes glinting with malice as she crossed the stage.

"So, it *was* you trying to meddle with my plans, Alexo. I did wonder. I've had spies posted outside Nimble Lane for weeks—a terrible time they've had trying to keep up with it—but they've never been able to spot you leaving. I must thank you, children. His confession has cleared everything up beautifully, and you couldn't have chosen a better spot to stage your ambush." She smiled, as if enjoying a private joke. "It's an ingenious trap, too, although it looks extremely uncomfortable."

Ista was still half waiting for Alexo to spring free, or at

least to bare his teeth and snarl again, but he just gave a soft moan and closed his eyes.

"Yes, quite." Governor Hettle straightened, tilting her head to look up at Ruby and Nat on the walkway. "Come down now, you two."

Ruby folded her arms. "Make us."

The governor's smile sharpened. "If you insist." She pulled a piece of paper from her pocket. "I have a feeling this will do the trick." Unfolding the paper, she began to read. "'Dear Mum, I'm going to start by saying sorry, because I've been keeping secrets from you, but once you've read this, you'll understand why.'"

"No!" Nat lurched against the railing.

"Yes, I thought that might sound familiar." The governor offered him an apologetic wince. "I have to hand it to you: you've worked out almost everything. I really am impressed. The only mistake you made was thinking that Alexo and I were working together, which, as I'm sure you've gathered, is very much not the case. Unfortunately, after she got your letter, your mother decided to go poking around the grille in Shipwrights' Square. I've had one of my staff keeping a lookout there since this morning when I noticed someone had tampered with one of my lift towers. And of course, once we found your mother, we found the letter, and . . . well, here we all are."

Ista didn't know whether to laugh or cry. The letter

was meant to be their insurance, and instead it had led the governor right to them.

"Where is she?" Nat shook the railing, making the whole walkway rattle. "Where's my mum? What have you done with her?"

"Come down and I'll show you," said the governor.

He didn't move. She sighed sadly, as if she were the only reasonable person in the room, then clicked her fingers. Behind Ista, footsteps sounded. A hand clamped her shoulder, dragging her to her feet, and the tip of something pointy jabbed her in the side.

The governor snapped on a smile again and turned the full, bright beam of it onto Nat and Ruby. "How about this? You two behave, and I won't ask *my* friend to fillet *your* friend like a fish. Lovely," she said, smiling wider still as they clanked toward the ladder. "I knew you'd be sensible. What about you, Alexo? Do you plan to behave?"

Alexo's face had turned completely gray. He moaned again, ragged and low.

"I'll take that as a yes." The governor's tone stayed sunny, though her hands twitched with impatience as Ruby and Nat made their way down onto the stage. "Splendid. Well, now that we've all met . . ." She clicked her fingers again, signaling off into the wings.

With a creak and a clack, the floor jerked into motion. Ista stumbled from the clutches of whoever had been holding her, landing on her knees as the entire stage spun like a plate, corkscrewing downward. For a few disorientating seconds, everything was swallowed by darkness, before a final sickening spin ground them to a halt in yet another craggy, Tide-lantern-illuminated cavern.

"Impressive, isn't it?" said the governor. "The theater's been in the family for generations, although it was only Grandfather who really started exploring the tunnels. The revolve was *his* father's design—for his illusions. A bit over the top, I know, but we Hettles have always had a flair for the dramatic."

An illusionist. Of course! Ista remembered what Padley had said about the Hettles being involved in the arts and how the governor's eccentric great-grandfather had squandered the family's money. There'd been those posters and flyers, too. Not the Incredible Kettle, she realized, but the Incredible *Hettle*. Not a play, but a person. No wonder the governor had been so pleased they'd chosen to catch Alexo at the theater. They'd basically served him to her on a plate.

All this time, he'd been working *against* the governor, not *for* her. But how had he been getting the names of the people who were about to be snatched? Perhaps one of the governor's accomplices had been struck by conscience and started sneaking him information—he'd said he'd been working with someone, hadn't he?

And why, oh why, didn't he tell me about my role in it? A tiny part of Ista was furious. If only he'd explained what he was doing, the true purpose of her errands, she'd have helped gladly! But mainly she just felt wretchedly guilty. He didn't speak. Didn't move. She couldn't even tell if he was breathing.

"Come along, please." Governor Hettle led the way down an incline. "No dawdling."

Ista's captor yanked her upright, sharpness pressing into her side again. She risked a look round, determined to meet their eyes, and found Moon-Tower Woman staring impassively back at her. Then another figure sliced out of the shadows. The bearded man who had given the money to Tamlin at Shipwrights' Square! He was carrying a sack, its contents clinking softly as he walked.

Well, Ista thought, *I was right about those two.* If someone on the inside had been feeding Alexo information, it definitely wasn't either of them.

The woman gave her a shove, shepherding her behind Ruby and Nat down a long, winding path. Ahead, inevitably, was a new cavern, which must only have been a cavern or two away from where they'd been the previous night. It was as high-ceilinged as the Hall of Maps at the Moon Tower, lit by huge, ancient-looking Tide-lanterns and dotted with bunches of tall rocks that rose from the floor.

No, not rocks. Statues. There must have been almost fifty of them—human figures carved from strange, shimmering stone. They looked almost like they were dancing, their arms raised in different positions, as if a party had been frozen and magically transported underground, some with their mouths open in what could almost have been laughter.

Or maybe not laughing? Ista's stomach swooped like a diving gull. She recognized that crystalline sheen. They weren't statues. They were . . .

"Stone Sleepers!" Ruby flew forward, her voice tearing out. "Saf? Saf, I'm here! Where are you?"

"Mum?" Nat was off too, weaving between the figures.

He didn't have to go far. There was Priya Shah, her eyes glazed and unseeing. And just along from Priya was Padley, his hands braced as if pushing at an invisible wall, and beside Padley was Wicka Honeyball, her lips pulled back in a grimace.

And beside Wicka was the smallest statue of all, who even with the frosty shimmer playing over his skin was such an exact miniature copy of Nat that there could be no doubt about his identity.

"Ravi? Ravi, it's me." Nat's voice broke, and Ista's heart broke with it. Whereas the hospital patients had been tucked up in bed, cared for and peaceful-looking, these Stone Sleepers were standing exactly as they'd been captured, arms up because they'd been trying to defend themselves, mouths open because they'd screamed, and Ravi's mouth was open widest of all.

"They can't hear you, I'm afraid," said the governor, as Ruby found and flung her arms round Saf, calling her name over and over. "Believe me, I've checked very carefully."

"That's why you were at the hospital!" Ista knew she should keep quiet, but outrage shot the words up straight from her gut. "You weren't reading to those people out of kindness. You were doing it to see whether they remembered you having visited them after they woke up."

There wasn't a drop of a chance the governor's visits would have stayed secret if any of the patients *had* remembered her being at the hospital—and she would have had to be sure. She had a plentiful supply of lily water from the pond in the tunnels, and enough lily seeds to make the antidote, but if even just one of her victims remembered hearing her voice while they were asleep, it would scupper her "heroic" rescue plan.

Ista would have said all that too, but Moon-Tower Woman prodded her with the tip of the knife as if to remind her it was still there.

"Ah, the little shapeshifter." The governor's eyebrows quirked with amusement. "Oh yes, your friend's letter to his mother was most informative about you. You've caused no end of trouble, though I don't suppose we'll have any more problems from you this evening. . . ."

The bearded man had arrived, still carrying the sack

and now also pushing a high-sided wheelbarrow. The front wheel hit a bump, and a groan rose from inside. It was Alexo, still tangled up, limp and gray as a rag.

Governor Hettle's voice dipped down, turning conspiratorial. "I never have found out where those net things came from. Great-Grandfather had heaps of them stashed down here. Terribly useful, though, the way they snuff out people's magic." She glanced at Ista again, assessing. "Still, I think we'd better tie you up, just in case. Bring her down here, please. And Alexo. They should both have front-row seats for this next part."

She strode onward, leaving her minions to do her bidding. The woman hauled Ista between the Stone Sleepers, and the man wheeled Alexo close behind, the barrow jolting loudly over the rocky floor. There was another sound too, like an undercurrent, pushing and pulling—calling Ista forward, then turning her away. Her next footstep landed with a crunch of pebbles, and the air sharpened, tasting riverish.

No, not riverish, she thought. *Salty, like . . .*

The sea! An impossible underground sea, gray waves lapping gently into a flat sheet of water that stopped dead a short swim away at the cavern wall. Water from the estuary, Ista supposed it must be, technically. A crust of seaweed and Tide-pearls marked the high-tide line like a fairy ring. The final few Stone Sleepers stood on the dry side of the boundary. Most were positioned as if gazing out at a distant horizon, but one of them—a man—faced into the cavern. He looked eerily calm, his arms down, his mouth soft, as if he'd accepted his fate.

"Giddon!" Ista jerked in the woman's grip.

Governor Hettle's laugh pealed like a bell as she strode past them to admire this final group of Sleepers. "Yes, we've been busy this evening. I must admit, Alexo, the old man was a clever choice of helper. I'd never have suspected him if he hadn't approached Jarmak at my party the other night. All kinds of tall tales he was telling, about how Jarmak was in terrible danger and needed to leave with him right away. Of course, Jarmak came straight to me. . . ."

Jarmak was in on it! Oh, but of course he was! Ista thought. Presumably, he was safe and snug at home now, waiting to be "rescued."

As for Giddon . . . A piece of hope she hadn't realized she was holding on to shattered. *We've been saving people,* Alexo had said. She'd never have guessed the "we" had included Giddon. Why hadn't *he* trusted her enough to tell her what they were doing? Couldn't one person she cared about be safe and warm and far away from this place?

Well, Pa wasn't here, unless he was concealed deep in the shadows. But Ista felt she would have *known* somehow if he were nearby.

Alexo was wheeled past, eyes closed, one limp gray

hand poking through the netting as the man brought the barrow to a rest. Not a breath or a flicker to suggest he'd registered Giddon's presence.

The governor raised her volume several notches, as if irritated not to have drawn a reaction from him. "I am curious, though, Alexo, how you so often knew where to send your little assistant—and *who* she should be." Her attention flicked to Ista, her mouth hardening with displeasure. "Why is this girl not tied up yet? Honestly, a little initiative wouldn't go amiss! Put her here."

Ista cried out as Moon-Tower Woman yanked her toward the Stone Sleeper next to Giddon, securing her to them with a long piece of cord she must have had ready for such an eventuality. A front-row seat, the governor had promised, but for what?

Near the Sleepers at the tide line was a low stone bench, crumbling and streaked with lichen, on which sat a small metal flask. The governor walked over to it, pulling on a pair of long-sleeved gloves. She removed the stopper from the flask, and immediately a faint fruity sweetness wafted from it.

Lily water. An icy thrill slid through Ista from head to toe.

"Gather round, everyone," the governor said. "Quickly, please, Nat and Ruby. Don't forget: your friend, my friend, very sharp knife. Whereas if you're good, this will all be completely painless."

Run away, Ista willed Ruby and Nat. *Leave me here and save yourselves.* One drop of the lily water, just the tiniest splash, would be enough to plunge them into as deep a Stone Sleep as the silent figures all around them.

But they both crunched forward over the pebbles, stopping on either side of her.

Governor Hettle beamed, running her gaze over them as if deliberating over cakes at a patisserie. "Excellent. Now, then. Who would like to go first?"

26

THE GELKIN

This was the end. Ista felt it, like a bobbin unspooling. She squirmed against the cord, but there wasn't the slightest bit of give. She was bound fast to the poor Stone Sleeper.

"Let's see. . . ." Governor Hettle raised the flask as if making a toast. "I think we'll start with . . . you, Ruby Mallard."

Either stubbornness or fear nailed Ruby to the spot on Ista's left—while on Ista's right, Nat kept craning round as if he was hoping against hope that someone was about to burst in and rescue them. But no one came. Moon-Tower Woman gave an impatient little cough.

Alexo would have had a plan, Ista felt certain, if it weren't for those terrible magic-draining nets. As it was, Alexo did nothing. Said nothing. His skin was changing from gray to a dark greenish brown. The sweet smell of the lily water permeated the air.

"Come along now, Ruby." Governor Hettle lifted the flask again. "No need to make a scene. Just one sip and, before you know it, everyone will be reunited and we'll have a lovely party to celebrate freeing our city from the grilks."

The same party, Ista guessed, for which the bearded man had booked Tamlin. She could practically hear the triumphant speech the governor would make in Shipwrights' Square.

"It won't actually be everyone, though, will it?" Nat piped up. "*We're* not going to the party. You can't let *us* go home. We've seen too much. So has my mum."

The governor sighed to herself. "You really are a very clever boy. What a shame your cleverness made you so nosy. How about this? You take your medicine nicely, and you have my word that I'll let everyone else go. Your brother." She glanced at Ruby. "Your sister." Then at Ista. "Your friends from the restaurant."

"That's hardly much of a bargain," said Ruby.

"It isn't a bargain at all," Ista chipped in. If Nat and Ruby weren't going quietly, neither was she. "You *have* to free everyone else, or this party of yours won't be much of a celebration."

"Exactly," said Nat. "You know what I don't understand, though? This last part's easy enough. You only have to wave the antidote under people's noses, and they'll wake right up again. But hasn't the rest of it been an awful lot of effort? Didn't you ever consider, I don't know, trying to get people to vote for you the regular way? Or did you figure no one liked you enough?"

A dangerous kind of laughter glinted in the governor's eyes. "I know what you're doing. Trying to distract me. It won't work. Fetch her," she ordered the bearded man, jabbing a finger at Ruby.

The man moved fast, gripping Ruby by the wrists and dragging her forward.

Nat nudged Ista in the ribs, tilting his head toward the side of the cavern, where the sack the man had been carrying lay on the ground. She supposed he'd had to abandon it to maneuver the barrow between the Stone Sleepers. It gaped open, revealing glass jars of what looked like blue sand.

The antidote! Ista sniffed, recognizing its bitter odor. If they could only get to it, they could surely wake all the Stone Sleepers. But Nat couldn't run on his bad ankle, and she was tied up, so . . .

It had to be Ruby. And it had to be now. The man had almost hauled her to where the governor waited with the flask. Ruby's feet scuffled wildly. She wrenched round, casting a frantic glance at Ista and Nat. Nat jerked his head and arm toward the jars of antidote.

Ruby's eyes widened. She understood, Ista was sure.

But, though Ruby wriggled like a fish on a hook, the man held her fast. They might not be able to distract the governor, Ista thought, but perhaps they could distract *him*. But how? She could hardly even move, bound to the Stone Sleeper. . . .

The Stone Sleeper! An idea dropped into Ista's mind like a coin falling into a slot.

She screamed, lurching forward against the cord. "Tide's teeth! This one's waking up!"

A bold-faced lie, but either the words or the noise were enough to make the man turn. As he did, his grip on Ruby slackened. Ruby seized her opportunity, striking in two directions at once. A jab with her hand sent the flask flying, missing the governor by a whisker. A kick with her opposite leg went straight into the man's shin.

"Run, Ruby!" Nat bellowed.

Ruby didn't need telling twice. She raced off between the Stone Sleepers while the man lumbered after her, visibly slowed by the kick she'd given him.

The flask rolled to a stop against a rock, the lily water soaking into the ground.

"This is tedious!" snapped Governor Hettle. "Not to worry, though. There's a ready supply of our drink nearby. Well, go on, then." She threw the last words at Moon-Tower Woman, who immediately leapt into action, picked up the flask and stopper, and ran back toward the cavern entrance.

Nat permitted himself a small smile at the disruption, and the governor's attention flicked to him, as if she sensed he was partially responsible.

"I've changed my mind. We'll have *you* drink first."

"Only if you can catch me!" Nat declared. He backed away, stumbling on his bad ankle, and broke into a wobbly run. Ista had thought the governor had already dropped her facade, but it was as if a whole other layer of it fell away now. She shot after him like a kestrel after a vole, the pursuit taking them both beyond Ista's limited line of vision. In the other direction, the man had somehow managed to get ahead of Ruby and cut off her path to the antidote. Twice he lunged for her, and twice she sprang away, until Ista lost sight of them, too, through the forest-like arrangement of contorted frozen figures.

Ista was alone with Alexo and the Stone Sleepers now. She struggled against the cord. She had never felt more helpless. If only she'd been able to use her blessing, but with the netting silencing the Tide . . .

Except the magic *wasn't* quiet. Not anymore. It fluttered in her ears, its tendrils reaching for her, delicate as early spring shoots.

And no one was watching her.

With a surge of pure joy, she *changed,* borrowing a tiny girl she'd seen in the crowd at Shipwrights' Square. The cord became a slack loop around her shoulders.

She shimmied under it, changing back as she shucked off her cloak and draped it over the Stone Sleeper she'd been tied to, arranging the hood to mask their shimmering face. The Sleeper was only a touch taller than her—even if Governor Hettle and her helpers noticed that Ista had escaped her bonds, hopefully the decoy would mean they'd assume she hadn't moved far.

Then she darted across the short gap to Alexo's barrow. The netting didn't make her skin even the slightest bit numb anymore; Alexo must have absorbed its magic-draining wrongness. That explained why she could feel the Tide again. It was more a rush than a flutter now, growing stronger by the second. But Alexo had paid a terrible price for it. He lay stiller than the Stone Sleepers, his eyes closed, his body curled like a leaf around the wooden fish. His skin was changing again, tiny teardrop-shaped marks racing over his nose and forehead.

Guilt skewered Ista's lungs. She'd done this to him.

"Governor!" Moon-Tower Woman was back. "I've got . . . the medicine!"

Ista flung herself behind the nearest Stone Sleeper and peered through the crook of their arm. The woman must have had to go a long way to fetch the lily water. She was doubled over, panting, near the cavern entrance.

"Bring it here!" The governor's reply echoed from somewhere within the forest of statues. She sounded out of breath too—but also pleased, as if she'd just won a race.

In the opposite direction, Ruby burst into view, aimed arrow-straight for the jars of antidote, the man pelting after her. She snatched one of the jars without breaking her stride—but he was gaining on her with every step. He swiped for her arm, and she twisted away.

Ista glanced at her cloak, still draped around the statue. Neither the governor nor the woman seemed to have realized what Ruby was up to—they must have been too preoccupied with the flask and Nat. If *she* could delay the governor forcing Nat to drink the lily water, then Ruby might have time to give at least some of the Stone Sleepers the antidote.

There wasn't a moment to waste. Ista changed, borrowing the bearded man, his feet cramped in her boots as she ran to the woman.

"I'll take it," Ista said, grabbing the flask before the woman could notice the man's suddenly too-short trousers or too-tight shirt. Then she hurried back the way she'd come, toward Alexo and the water—which was climbing in harmony with the magic, waves swelling eagerly over the sand.

Behind her, Governor Hettle's laugh jangled like an out-of-tune piano. "Ah yes, we mustn't forget our audience."

Ista looked round and saw her staggering between the Stone Sleepers in the center of the cavern, Nat clamped to her side, his wrists bound with cord.

"I'll tell you a secret, boy," the governor spat. "This

hasn't been hard work. It's been rather fun—or it was until Alexo started interfering. It's a shame, of course, that some of you won't make it out of here to see my triumphant return. I do hope your brother will cope without you and your mother."

Nat writhed in her grasp, but it was half-hearted writhing, as if the fight had drained out of him.

Ista reached the row of Stone Sleepers near the high-tide line. The waves were crashing now. She looked back again, uncertainty threading down her spine. She needed the governor to follow her this way. She needed to hold her attention so she didn't glance round and see exactly what Ista now could: Ruby, the jar of antidote under one arm, leaping onto a boulder and beginning to scale the craggy cavern wall.

Fortunately, Governor Hettle slowed to a halt as soon as she could see into Alexo's barrow.

"This is far enough. Give me the flask!" She thrust out one gloved hand, still gripping Nat tightly with the other. "Now, you useless man!"

"Yes, Governor!" Ista called, willing Ruby higher. The man was climbing after her, although he was moving more slowly than he had been on the ground.

Every second Ista could delay was crucial. She took two steps forward, then buckled as if her knee had given way, landing with a grunt, the flask still in her hand.

"You clumsy oaf!" the governor snapped.

From across the cavern came a cry and a thud. The man had fallen from the wall. The governor's gaze pendulumed from him to Ista, to the statue wearing Ista's cloak—then back to where Ruby was still climbing.

"Tide's teeth! Someone get that Mallard girl down from there!" Twin comets of fury blazed in her eyes. "As for *you*," she said, rounding on Ista, "I don't know what you think you're playing at."

Ista changed back into herself. She didn't know exactly what she was playing at either. All she knew was that she had to keep the flask away from the governor. And if only there were something she could do to help Alexo. Those strange teardrop-shaped marks now covered every part of his skin that she could see, greeny brown and gleaming.

Like fish scales or something.

Ista froze, possibility chiming like a chord through every bone in her body. *Fish scales*—weren't those what Nat and Ruby had seen covering her hands when she'd tried to borrow Alexo? And there had been that peculiar stretching feeling, as if her cells were being pulled in two directions at once.

She remembered the first night in Shelwich when she'd met Alexo—the huge, sharp teeth that were seared into her brain, but which hadn't been on the grilk puppets they'd found in the cavern. She thought of the picture in the library book, of a person trying to climb back out of the creature's throat, past those sharp teeth. She remembered the enormous eel—the *gelkin*—under the Shrieking Eel Inn when she'd gone to find Alexo. . . .

And she wondered: What if the person and the gelkin were one and the same?

"Ista." The governor's voice turned chillingly reasonable. "It's over. Look."

She pointed. Far across the cavern, Ruby wobbled on the wall, struggling to find her next foothold and cling to the jar. Moon-Tower Woman had set off after her, making far faster progress than the man had, the gap between her and Ruby halving in seconds.

"Give me the flask." The governor held out her free hand again.

"Don't let her have it, Ista!" Nat cried.

Ista shoved the flask under her arm and ran for Alexo's wheelbarrow. She grabbed it by the handles, sending a spray of pebbles flying. Alexo's scales gleamed, as beautiful as the Tide-pearls that led like a trail of burning coals toward the waves.

If she could just get him into the water.

The cold clutched at her, soaking her legs as she sloshed into the shallows, which dropped off steeply into inky darkness. Wrenching the handles upward, she tipped Alexo into the sea—just as a large wave swept up as if it had been waiting for him. It claimed him, barrow and netting and all, and Ista had to leap back to stop it sweeping her away too. She landed with a wet thud on the sand.

The governor's laugh rolled over her, an ice-cold wave of its own. "Well, that's an end to Alexo Rokis." She crunched toward Ista, hauling Nat with her. "I must admit, I'm not completely clear what your plan was, children, but in any event it doesn't seem to have worked."

We'll see about that, Ista thought.

Across the cavern, Ruby wobbled on the wall again, the woman closing in fast, the man watching from below, poised to block any chance of Ruby's escape. But neither of them knew that Ruby Mallard always landed on her feet when the Tide was high. And, oh, it was high now, crackling hot and cold, singing a wild, fierce song in Ista's blood.

Ruby sprang from the wall, arcing over the woman's head—and as she sprang, she yanked the lid off the jar and hurled them both forward, sending a great blue cloud of antidote up into the air. The particles floated like dandelion seeds, showering over the Stone Sleepers as Ruby landed neatly in their midst.

Nothing happened. The Sleepers remained motionless.

Ista looked back at the waves, but there was no sign of Alexo. Whatever she'd hoped for, she'd been wrong or too late, or both.

"Ruby!" Nat shouted. "Waft it under their noses, then—"

"Enough!" Governor Hettle grabbed him by the throat. "That is *enough* from you. You know what? As we've lost our audience, I think we can do this more simply."

She pulled a knife from her pocket. Ista felt as if she'd dropped into a space between heartbeats. The whole world narrowed down to that blade. To Nat's eyes bulging with terror.

There was nothing she could do.

Except maybe one thing.

The governor raised her arm to strike, and Ista changed—into the one person who was in on the plan but notably absent now, as if the governor didn't want him to see the full reality of it.

"Mother?" Ista said in Jarmak Hettle's voice.

It worked. Governor Hettle hesitated, her mouth forming a small O of confusion. Ista leapt forward, yanked the stopper from the flask, and threw the lily water straight at her.

The result was instant. The governor froze, an icy sheen spreading over her face and hands.

For a moment, Nat was as still as she was, and Ista worried that she'd splashed him too. Then he unpeeled the governor's fingers from his throat and took a large, extremely careful step away from her.

Ista, herself once more, looked to where Ruby stood among the Stone Sleepers, grains of antidote swirling like dust motes in the air around them. The bitter scent was strong now.

The bearded man and Moon-Tower Woman looked on, seemingly unsure whether to flee or try to grab Ruby again.

Then one of the Stone Sleepers moaned softly. Another's nose gave a tiny, rabbitlike twitch. And the thaw began to spread, bodies stirring, fingers flexing.

"Where am I?" someone murmured groggily. "What's happening?"

The governor's helpers both turned and raced from the cavern.

We did it, Ista thought numbly. *We won!*

It didn't feel like it should have. And not only because Pa wasn't there—she had a good enough view from where she stood to be sure of that now—but because of Alexo. She glanced back at the gray waves and the stiller, grayer water beyond.

If only he'd trusted her. If only she hadn't lured him into the trap!

But it was too late for *if-only*s. Tears pricked her eyes, and she didn't know if she was crying for Pa or Alexo or just for herself.

"Ista?" Nat was beside her, struggling with the cord around his wrists. "Untie me, would you? I need to help Ravi and— Oh no, the governor! She's waking up again!"

He was right, Ista realized as the antidote's bitterness

caught the back of her throat. The seed particles were spreading, and Governor Hettle looked distinctly less shimmery than she had just seconds before—and the knife was still in her hand.

But behind the governor, the impossible sea had begun to churn.

Another scent filled the air. Salt water. Snuffed birthday candles.

With a shriek, the gelkin's huge, scaled head broke the surface, and from between the great jaws floated a pale green bubble, which drifted on a waft of brackish breath toward Governor Hettle. As it moved, it grew. The size of an egg . . . a fist . . . a head . . . By the time it reached the governor, it was bigger than she was. One moment she was beside it, and the next she was *inside* it, like a beetle caught in amber. The governor's eyes shot wide open, her hand reached out, but it was too late. The bubble reversed, shrinking as it went. The huge jaws opened to receive it, then clamped shut.

Alexo turned to Ista, meeting her eyes with an ancient, dangerous, curious gaze. She nodded her thanks to him, and he plunged away, vanishing into the depths.

27

THE CLARINET

Every meal, Ista thought, should end with gingercrumb
tart and be shared with good people—and the people gathered in the Fletwin's dining room that evening were very
good people indeed. Padley sat to her right, and beyond
Padley was Giddon, then Granny Mallard, Ruby, and Saf,
and then the three Shahs, with Nat on Ista's left.

"A toast." Giddon raised his cup. "To everyone here!"
He glanced at Ista. "And to those who are still much
missed."

Like Pa. Ista had clung on to her hope—as the Stone
Sleepers woke and they all made their way up from the
caverns, as she and Giddon and Padley visited the houses
on Nimble Lane to tell all the people hiding there that they
were finally safe to go home . . . but there had been no
trace of him. There *had* been plenty of very familiar faces,

though, despite Ista never having met their owners before. Her heart had lifted as she'd watched people gingerly step out into the early-morning light after weeks, sometimes even moons, of being away from their families and friends.

She hadn't just been borrowing people; she'd been helping save them. And that was something.

The inn itself had been dark when she'd gone to it, the door firmly shut despite her entreaties. So, as Alexo's confession at the theater had left a *lot* of questions, she'd heaped them all on Giddon as they'd stood side by side at the kitchen counter that afternoon, chopping vegetables for the stew.

"Alexo said I was the decoy, but how did that work?" She'd kept her gaze on the onion she was dicing.

Giddon had put down his knife. "Let me start by saying how sorry I am we didn't tell you what we were doing. I wanted to, but every time I tried . . . well, I just . . . couldn't."

"Yes," Padley had chimed in from his rocking chair— for of course Padley had been in on the scheme, just as he and Giddon shared every other part of their lives. "We are so very, very sorry, young'un. Not only for keeping secrets but for putting you at risk like that. It was on my mind to confess to you hundreds of times, but whenever I tried, it was as if my thoughts slipped sideways."

Which was more than a little suspicious, and Ista had mentally added it to her list of things to ask Alexo about. If she ever saw him again.

"I suppose," Giddon had continued, removing the diced onion from Ista's chopping board and passing her a bunch of carrots, "you'll want to know where we got the names."

"Actually"—Ista reached for the peeler—"I think I know. You dreamed them."

Giddon's eyebrows rose. "So I did. How in the flood did you guess?"

She was actually rather proud of this. "It was the coat. Cauldi said that when you rushed downstairs just after Padley had been taken, you checked the coat hooks. You were looking for the same coat you'd just seen him wearing in your dream as he vanished. I only remembered it this morning, but then I realized your dreams must have been the key."

"That," said Giddon, with something ever, ever so close to a smile, "was very cleverly worked out."

He and Padley told her all of it then. How over the past year, as the Tide's magic had grown stronger, Giddon's dreams had become more vivid. How he'd realized they weren't dreams at all but premonitions. How one night he'd dreamed such specific details of a grilk attack—which did, in fact, occur the next day—that Padley had made him go to the only person they thought might be able to do something about it. Since then, they had both been working with Alexo to save whomever they could.

"Not that we always had enough information—or enough time to prepare—but we did our best," Giddon said. "We'd go to warn people. Not everyone believed us, but most were scared enough of the grilks that they came with us when we told them they were in danger, and asked questions later. The first people we saved, we sent home again, only for some of them to be taken soon after. That's when we realized that each person being taken had been specifically targeted. The attacks couldn't be random—and that meant someone must be controlling the creatures.

"We tried to keep people on Nimble Lane after that— just temporarily, mind—while we worked it out, although some folks we had to sneak home in secret because they had children they couldn't be parted from, or other reasons they couldn't hide. Then . . . you came along." At that, Giddon did smile, just fleetingly, before he glanced away.

"Alexo saw what you could do that very first night," he went on. "We were sure by then that whoever was controlling the grilks must be watching the victims carefully, and—well, what better way to confuse them? Alexo came up with the errand idea on the spot. Each time I had a premonition, we'd send you somewhere public, borrowing the person I'd seen who was about to be snatched. While all eyes were on you, we'd get the real victim to safety. We didn't expect you to start investigating on your own, of course." He gave her a stern look.

"Although if you hadn't," said Padley, "I'm not sure the truth would ever have come out. The governor led us all on a merry dance. I'd certainly never have guessed that those blasted creatures were puppets. Giddon's visions certainly never showed us that."

"It was a clever trick, that's for sure," Giddon added. "Making up something for people to be scared of, then persuading them she was the only person who could rescue them from it. And old Betrik was a con artist as well, it seems. You know, I always felt it was rather convenient that Lightning Lucy had managed to skip around Shelwich so boldly with no one able to trace her, only for Betrik Hettle to catch her so easily."

Ista took all this in silently. Had Lightning Lucy been working with Betrik Hettle before being betrayed by him? Or had she been innocent, set up for a series of crimes she'd never committed, so that Betrik could claim the glory for her capture? And, whoever *had* carried out the actual thefts—how had they done all that skipping around in the first place? The tunnels might have taken the thief around the city, but not into people's houses. And where had the strange netting and the crystals come from?

Some mysteries, she supposed, would never be tied up neatly. There would always be more loose threads to pull.

Priya Shah was determined to pull on some of them, though.

"Mum's launching a full investigation," Nat announced, spooning cream onto his second slice of tart. "Into the Hettles—and into Lightning Lucy. Aren't you, Mum?"

Priya dabbed her mouth with her napkin before she

spoke. "Yes. Lightning Lucy might have relatives alive somewhere. They deserve to know the truth. I think we all do."

"I hope you'll be looking into Brintan Brook as well," said Granny Mallard with a sharp smile. "There's justice to be done with regard to him too."

"Yeah, what a total weasel." Ruby made a jabbing motion with her fork, prompting Saf to snort and dragging a little giggle from Ravi.

One thing *was* for certain: Brintan Brook would *not* be Shelwich's next governor. All day long, people had been gathering in Shipwrights' Square in a way they hadn't gathered for many moons—and, as they'd gathered, they'd talked. Granny Mallard and Giddon were not the only people Brook had tried to pressure into bad business deals after their loved ones were taken. He might not have been behind the disappearances, but he had definitely tried to take advantage of them.

"Giddon would never have sold to Brook, you know, young Ista," said Padley as he and Ista cleared away the plates. I know he told you that at the time, but it's worth saying again. For as long as either of us is here, you'll always have a home at the Fletwin."

Giddon hadn't said that last part before—and although Ista had sort of known it deep down, hearing it out loud made her throat clog and her eyes go so hot and prickly that she had to turn away without answering.

As for the election, it had been postponed. But Kip the

potter had stopped by that afternoon and reported that Wicka Honeyball had been seen at the harbor and already looked almost back to full strength after her ordeal. Apparently, there was a general feeling of tentative hope that she might turn out to be the leader Shelwich had needed for so long.

Yet, as happy as the atmosphere was around the Fletwin's table that night, there was still an undercurrent of something unsettling in the room. It would have been easy to say that the grilks were just a story, and that the story was over now. But the fear had been real, and it had left a lasting mark on everyone. Saf's eyes were anxious as she huddled close to Ruby—their parents were due home any day now, having received word about Saf being taken. Granny Mallard watched both her granddaughters closely. Priya, meanwhile, kept a protective arm around Ravi—and Ravi himself had barely said a word.

"Ista." Nat nudged her. "There's a cat on the windowsill. I think it's looking at you."

Ista turned. Terrible stared at her through the glass. He lifted a paw.

She stood. "I have to go. I'm sorry."

"Now?" Ruby shook her head. "No, not acceptable. We haven't picked which day we're going to the Pearl Fair yet."

The Pearl Fair was due to take place the next week and was, Ista had learned, a highlight of the Shelwich calendar. Every ride and stall would be decorated with

Tide-pearls, and there was one ride, called the Stomach Spinner, that Ruby and Saf had decreed they all had to try. Ista had been protesting—hadn't they had enough stomach spinning? She felt as if she'd like things to stay still for a while.

But now Nat shrugged at her, a dare in the twist of his mouth, and she thought it might not be so very bad if she had people she trusted beside her.

Besides, she was Ista Flit. She was dangerous. She wasn't scared of a ride.

"Any day's fine for me," she said as she strode to the door. "Just send word, and I'll be there."

"Don't forget your coat, young'un," Padley said, chuckling fondly. "It feels like snow."

The entrance hall of the Shrieking Eel was quiet, the elevator cars waiting. Terrible curled up on his porter's chair and immediately began to snore.

"Well," Ista said. "Time to finish this business."

She'd never seen Alexo sitting down before. He was in an armchair by the pink-and-green fire, a mug steaming on a low table in front of him.

"Hello, *Iss*ta Flit." His voice was half hiss. Perhaps he no longer felt the need to hide his true self. He waved his hand. Another chair appeared opposite his.

Ista sat, thinking of teeth and scales, of the bubble disappearing into the gelkin's jaws.

"I didn't eat her," Alexo said as if he'd plucked the thought from her mind.

"Didn't you? Well, that's good, I suppose." Even Betrika Hettle didn't deserve to be eaten. "Um, where is she, then?"

He laughed, the sound wet and gritty, like the river sucking at pebbles, then inclined his head toward a shadowy corner of the room. Ista could just make out the shape of a woman, perfectly frozen, lamplight glancing off her pearlescent skin.

"Alexo!"

He arched an eyebrow. "You think I shouldn't keep her?"

"I don't know what we should do with her," Ista said honestly. It was an extremely thorny problem. "But it shouldn't be up to just you. Or me. I think we have to wake her up and let everyone decide."

"All right. After the election, though, don't you think?" The old Alexo crept through, fox-faced, wolf-eyed. The fire crackled as he searched her face. "You're angry."

She didn't deny it.

"I'm sorry. You are *young*. I thought it best you not know everything."

That only made her anger flare brighter. "If I was old enough to be involved, I was old enough to be told why. And you didn't need to trick me. I'd have helped if you'd asked. Probably. Once I understood how important it was."

Truthfully, a tiny part of Ista wasn't totally sure of that. She wanted to think of herself as good and brave, but you never knew what you'd do in the moment—and she'd been so very, very scared of the grilks.

"I know you did something to Padley and Giddon to stop them telling me," she added. "You can't go around controlling people like that. We're not your Curiosities."

Alexo paused as if he hadn't considered things from that angle before. "I'm sorry," he said again. "Sometimes I forget the rules of being human. I was asleep for so long."

"Asleep?" *For how long?* The second—unspoken— question shivered through her. "Padley told me his ma believed the Tide had always been here—like *always* always. . . ." And that once upon a time all sorts of magical creatures lived in and around the river. "It's true, isn't it?"

Alexo nodded, his gaze slipping to the hearth. She thought he might close the subject there, but after a moment he spoke. "I was born long, long ago, when the world was young and the magic was high. My family roamed all the cold waters, fresh and salt, and sometimes we lived on the land with the people, too. Then the Tide went out until the only magic left was deep down and secret, buried in the ocean floor. So we slept. And when I awoke, the magic was back, but my family was gone."

He stared into the flames, ancient and sad and wild and lost. "I searched the rivers and the oceans, but I couldn't find anyone else like me. Then I remembered that I had sometimes liked to live on the land, with people. And that I'd lived in Shelwich once—although back then it had another name—and that I'd liked the people here."

He glanced up to where the wooden fish and the telescope rested beside each other on the mantel.

"They're yours," Ista said as realization dawned. "From . . ."

"From a very long time ago." Memories danced in Alexo's eyes.

Her throat knotted. *Young,* he'd called her. Yes, she must seem impossibly young to him. All people must. She looked around, seeing with new eyes the Curiosities lining the shelves. Whether shabby or extravagant, what they all had in common was that they had been well used, as if Alexo felt that studying the objects would help him understand the people who'd once owned them.

And in the case of the telescope and the fish, she supposed they'd helped him remember the person he'd been before.

"Are you sure your family isn't out there somewhere?" she asked. It seemed desperately unfair for him to live so long and yet end up so alone.

"It is unlikely." But a flicker of possibility darted across his face. "Though perhaps not impossible. A lot of sailors come here to the inn when they're in port. Some of them do claim to have seen all kinds of extraordinary creatures far out at sea, so perhapssss . . ."

Ista itched to ask more, about the life—the lives—he'd had before, both in the water and on land, but he looked so happy and so sad all at once that she decided not to pry further for now.

"No wonder you risked coming to the theater to get the fish," she said instead.

Alexo's nose wrinkled in puzzlement. "I didn't do it just for that. Your note said you needed me to meet you. I thought . . . you were in trouble."

He'd come to help her. Shame washed over Ista in waves. "I'm so sorry. We didn't know how badly the netting would—"

"It is my fault." Alexo cut her off. "As you said, I should have been honest."

Which was true, Ista thought, but that didn't do much to dilute her guilt. "You don't know where the netting comes from, do you?" she asked. "The governor said her great-grandpa had stored loads of it in the caverns."

"I do not." Alexo curled his lip. She couldn't tell if he was grumpy remembering the pain he'd felt, or grumpy because he'd been as fooled as anyone by the grilks. "Perhaps the whole plan was Betrik's suggestion. The grilks first took people while he was still alive. I should have known they weren't real. I'd never seen creatures like them before, but I thought . . . well, the Tide always washes up new surprises."

"Do you know who the man and woman helping the governor were?" Ista asked.

"No." His expression said he intended to find out.

"And about the wooden fish . . ." Something about that kept nagging at her. "That errand you sent me on . . . why didn't I have to borrow anyone?"

"Ah. Giddon didn't tell you?" Alexo's gaze slid away from hers, then back again. "He had another dream. About the grilks. He couldn't make much sense of it, but he was worried they were coming for him—and, if that was the case, he didn't want you anywhere nearby. He asked me to send you somewhere far from the Fletwin, and so I thought . . . I wanted you to have something nice. A sort of thank-you, for all your help. Well, and I did want the fish."

"It *was* nice," Ista admitted spikily. Evidently she was going to have to have another chat with Giddon and explain to him in no uncertain terms that he was not to keep her in the dark when she might be able to help with things. "Well, apart from your friend Tamlin."

Alexo had the decency to wince. "I'm sorry he scared you. I asked him to look out for you after Padley was taken."

Keep an eye on her. Ista groaned inwardly. "You do realize that if someone were to have accidentally overheard that conversation, it might have sounded slightly threatening."

Alexo fixed her with a look. "I understand that when people are spying, they don't always get a complete picture of a situation."

"No." She fixed him with a look right back, because some people might have been more afraid, knowing who he really was, but she found him less scary now that she understood him better. "He was stalking me. All over the city. And you said . . ."

"What did I say?"

"That if I got suspicious, Tamlin knew what to do."

"And what did he do?"

"He . . ." Ista's eyes widened. "He ran away."

Alexo's smirk was back. "You're a curious person, and you'd get in no end of trouble if you went nosing around after Tamlin. It seemed the only sensible solution."

"And Tamlin really just works for you scavenging treasure from the estuary? You said you went to Glass Island." That explained why Alexo had been in gelkin form the night Padley had vanished. He and Tamlin must have just come back across the river. "Is it really haunted like people say?"

Alexo shook his head. "Not haunted, but strange. I don't recommend going there, even if you could find a boat to take you. And, yes, that's all Tamlin does for me. He wasn't helping us with the grilks and the rest of it."

"Why not?" Surely Tamlin, who seemed able to disappear and reappear at will, would have been the perfect person to help sneak people to safety.

"That boy comes and goes as he pleases." Alexo tutted, in a puzzled way—Tamlin was clearly a knot he was still trying to unpick. "He's not someone you can rely on to be in the right place when you need him." He levered himself up from his chair. "I think that's enough questions for tonight."

"Just one more. Please." They flitted like fireflies in Ista's head—questions about the caverns and the crystals and Tamlin's key and a thousand other things. But all those could wait for another day. She was thinking of the book in the library, and the page about gelkins. "Can you grant wishes?"

Alexo stilled. "It depends on the wish."

"Can you find my pa?"

The beat of silence before he answered was enough.

"No." He placed the word carefully, letting it settle. "I *have* looked." He let that settle too. "But if he is somewhere even I can't reach, perhaps that is a good thing."

Ista couldn't see how. But that was the way of it with eels, she supposed. Their thinking was slippery.

Alexo walked to the cabinet. When he returned, he was carrying two items. The first was the clarinet case. The second was a shell.

"Twenty," he said solemnly, putting them both on the table. "Tide keep you and bless you, Ista Flit. Hang on to the shells. They're worth something."

And then he was gone.

Padley had been right about the weather. As the Tide rose, the snow fell, drifting in fat white petals past Ista's attic window. She'd returned to the Fletwin in time to rejoin the supper party. Now all the guests had gone home, and after helping Giddon and Padley clear up, she'd claimed to be exhausted and said she needed an early night.

She *was* tired, as it happened—bone-tired in the way you can only be when you've won in so many ways but still not found what you were searching for. But what she really wanted was to play the clarinet. Although it wouldn't conjure Pa from wherever he was, she felt it would bring her closer to him somehow.

The clasps on the case were stiff from disuse, but the clarinet pieces had an almost expectant look, the little pot of cork grease and the spare reeds ready beside them. Ista knew she'd never be a fraction of the musician Pa was, but she'd mastered a few simple tunes—so it was a surprise when, though she'd carefully assembled the instrument, a strange, muffled sound was all that emerged when she blew into it.

Frowning, she took the pieces apart again, lifting each one to her eye like a telescope. There seemed to be something stuck in one of the joints. She gave it a shake. A rolled-up piece of paper landed in the cup of her palm.

Ista unrolled it. Pa's writing slanted urgently.

To my clever daughter,
*   When one door closes, another always*
opens, if you have the right key. I will be back
in good time, bringing the key to a door of our
own, but if you need to find me sooner, any door
with a keyhole will do.

                            Pa

Outside, a breeze licked up, sending the snowflakes
swirling. Ista's thoughts swirled too. *To my clever daughter.* That was the kind of greeting Pa would have written,
but the rest of the letter didn't sound like him at all. She
examined each piece of the clarinet again in turn. Then
all the bits and bobs from the case. Then the case itself,
running her fingertips over the velvety lining.

Winking up at her through a tear in the fabric was a
small silver key, engraved with peculiar symbols that
looked almost like musical notes.

"Tide's teeth," Ista breathed.

She remembered exactly where she'd seen a key like
that before.

EPILOGUE

LOW TIDE

Ista was used to putting on bodies like other people put on clothes, but until a few days ago she'd been certain that *who* she was under her skin was fixed in place. That wasn't true, she understood now. Nat and Ruby had reshaped some fundamental part of her being. So had Giddon and Padley—and even Alexo, in his way. She didn't know what was going to happen, but she wouldn't simply vanish and leave them all to wonder.

She took the whole night to plan. Packed supplies, including Pa's photograph and ten of her errand shells, for luck. Wrote a letter—and then made three copies of it, including a meticulously accurate drawing of her key. One she placed in the glass-bug chest; the others she left on the kitchen counter, knowing that Giddon and Padley would deliver Nat's and Ruby's to them.

It was just before dawn, the magic barely a sigh. She fitted the key to the lock of the Fletwin's back door.

Click.

What was beyond the door was impossible.

Ista set the key down on the mat, where it couldn't be missed. She hesitated, just for a heartbeat, before she stepped forward, thinking of the envelopes waiting to be opened. Thinking of the last line of the message she'd written.

If I'm not back in two days, please send help. I may need my friends.

ACKNOWLEDGMENTS

Amber Caravéo, agent extraordinaire, I don't know where I'd be without your support, insight, and guidance.

Natalie Doherty, you understood the heart of the story from the get-go. Editing with you has been an absolute dream.

Karl James Mountford, your illustrations have so perfectly captured the magic, mystery, and peril of *Tidemagic*.

I can't imagine a better home for Ista & Co. than with Puffin. Thanks to Josh Benn, Jan Bielecki, Wendy Shakespeare, Rianna Johnson, Bella Jones, and everyone at PRH who has helped make this the best book it can be. Special thanks to Ben Horslen—very much looking forward to continuing the adventure with you in Book Two.

I'm incredibly fortunate to have found an equally fantastic team in the US. Nancy Siscoe, your enthusiasm and generosity have blown me away. Huge thanks to you and to everyone at Knopf Books for Young Readers.

Like a lot of debut authors, I've had a somewhat epic journey to publication. Thank you to the industry professionals who have taught, mentored, or simply encouraged me—especially Catherine Johnson, Jake Arnott, Anna Davis, and the team at Curtis Brown Creative; Sara Grant and everyone at Undiscovered Voices; Marisa Noelle, Cynthia Murphy, Aisha Bushby, Stuart White, and everyone at WriteMentor; Caroline Ambrose at the Bath Novel Award; and Jo Moult at Skylark.

And to my writer friends . . . well, I am just so lucky to have you. To Alex Atkinson, Amy Feest, Emily Randall-Jones, Gianna Pollero, Gillian Perdue, Katie Dale, Lynn Grace Wong, Ruth Grearson, the class of Undiscovered Voices 2020, the Southbank Writers, all my other lovely SCBWI pals, Team Skylark, Team WriteMentor, the 2024 debut-ers, the MAWFYP-ers, and last but not least, Holly Race and the screenwriters, who had the dubious privilege of being on a retreat with me right before my structural edit deadline for this book. Thank you all, for the cheerleading and commiserating, for the whisper networks and the weekends away, for the last-minute critiques and the peculiar research trips. Publishing often feels like playing roulette, but I have truly great people beside me at the table.

To my family. Thank you for your enthusiasm and unwavering belief. I really hope you all like the book! To my mum, who always said I should be a writer. You were right, Mum. This has been like coming home. To Ed—you *are* my home. Thank you for doing more than your half of things so that I could do this, for never grumbling about my night-owl work habits, and for cheering me on every step of the way.

Finally, dear reader, to you. Thank you for reading *Tidemagic*. It's yours now, as much as mine, and I do hope you've enjoyed it. Until the next time, Tide keep you.